# Eternal
# Mixture

**Words Written, LLC**
www.shevaundelucia.com
Rochester, NY 14616
USA

ISBN: 978-0-615-82803-9

Shevaun DeLucia

# A first kiss...

Our eyes meet and my body is lulled with desire, channeling a craving that's been dormant for so long. His closeness feels so familiar to me, awakening every last inch of my body. My blood rushes through my veins, igniting a fire within me. I burn for him.

He lifts me up and sets me on top of the counter, my legs open and inviting him in. He grips each of my thighs with his hands, digging his fingers into my flesh. His eyes look drunk as they scan the canvas of my body. Without warning, he smashes his lips against mine, thrusting his silky wet tongue into my mouth until we sink into a rhythmic embrace.

My first kiss and all I can think of is what lies next. I'm starved for more, and this is only the beginning. A slight moan escapes my lips. I grab the back of his neck and tangle my fingers through his hair, pulling him closer to me with intense urgency. I can't get enough. I arch my back and wrap my legs around him, bringing him into me. I am in my glory.

Eternal Mixture

# Dedication

To my husband-

May our souls live on for Eternity

Shevaun DeLucia

# Table of Contents

# Chapter 1

It is a Monday morning, late September. I am walking down the hall toward my first period class, listening to murmurs and whispers about "the new kid in school." The girls are in a tizzy over his stifling hotness, and the boys are on guard, ready to mark and protect their territory. Whatever it takes for the girls of this school to remain *their* girls. This sort of behavior seems so animalistic and just downright ridiculous to me. I mean, how hot can this guy really be?

I go through the day hearing more and more gossip. This girl swore he winked at her, and this one had a long, meaningful conversation with him already and so on. Once I finally reach sixth period lunch, I assume I might be able to relax and talk about something different with my friends, but I am wrong. The buzz of this boy swarms around me like a tornado. The girls have war in their eyes, and they are ready to strike in order to knock out any competition that gets in their way. The boys just look downright miserable with pouty faces, as though their shiny new toys have just been stolen from under them.

After grabbing my lunch, I take a seat in the middle of the table with my girlfriends: Jenna, with her snow-white hair in a pixie cut, fire-engine red lipstick and wrist full of colorful friendship bracelets; Bailey, my childhood best friend, with eyes of tourmaline crystal and beautiful long black hair as thick as a horse's mane; and then there's Maddie, my soul sister with natural grace, judgeless brown eyes, and a smile that invites you to tell all. They're so caught up in the buzz that they don't even realize I have sat down.

"Ahem." I clear my throat loud enough for everyone to hear. They all turn with a startled look.

"Oh hey, Raina. We were just talking about that new kid, Brent. Have you seen him yet?" Bailey asks, her blue eyes wide with enthusiasm.

This is unbelievable. My friends, too, have caught on to the "new kid" craze.

"Yeah, he's gorgeous!" Maddie chimes in, her face lit up like a kid in a candy store.

My head snaps back, brows furrowed. "No, not yet, and I really don't care if I do or not." They all give me the same look, implying that I should wait to see the goods before making any assumptions. "Seriously, guys! He's just a boy, for God's sake!" I gripe, trying to snap them back into reality.

"Raina, stop being so cynical all the time, will you?" Jenna begs. "Anyways, we were actually just talking about going to Billiards after school to shoot some pool— you game?"

"Yeah, I'm game," I reply. "Is Jason going to be there?" I only ask her because there's just something about her boyfriend that I don't like. I can't seem to put my finger on it, though, and it's driving me nuts!

Jenna met him at a café in town a couple of months ago. It seemed as though we couldn't escape him, like everywhere we were, there he was. At first I couldn't tell which one of us he was interested in. He seemed to study us, almost as if he were trying to determine who would be the easiest target. Jenna has always been a little standoff-ish when it comes to boys and a little self-conscious when it comes to herself. You would never guess that with the way she portrays herself to others, though. So any attention, good *or* bad, she will accept. That's how Jason entered into her life, *our* lives.

"Of course he's going to be there! Why wouldn't he be?" Jenna asks.

"Jenna, don't you two do anything apart?" Maddie asks.

Maddie's more like me—a strong, independent woman with no need for a man.

"Yeah! Come on, Jenna! Let's just make it a girls' night. Please?" Bailey begs with her blue puppy-dog eyes and folded, pouty lip.

Jenna gives us the evil eye. "Okay, okay. I'll think of something to tell him," she says, finally caving in. Unfortunately, I can see anguish written all over her face, like it actually pains her to be apart from him. How do girls get so wrapped up in someone else that they put themselves last? Is that what love is really about? If so, I *never* want to be in love.

I watch Bailey as her eyes bug out of her head. "*OMG!* There he is!" she whispers loudly, as her eyes fall ahead of me.

I refuse to look. I will not allow myself to become a mindless follower, swooning over some boy who will just pick one of the Janets or Caseys on the volleyball team in the end.

"On that note, girls, I'm out. See ya after school," I shout, throwing up a peace sign. I exit through the back doors of the cafeteria to be sure I don't cross paths with the new kid.

"Oh, *Raina*, come on!" I hear the girls yelling from behind me.

I head over to the library to kill some time before my next class. It's quiet and peaceful in there, and I always feel a wave of calmness when walking through those doors. I think it may have something to do with all these words that have come together, creating stories, written by all these amazing authors who now surround me. I love books. Something about seeing through someone else's eyes and living a mere moment in someone else's life soothes me.

I take a seat at the table in the back, take out Christopher Pike's *Blood Thirst* from my book bag, and dive into the book. The main character, Sita, is so empowering, bold, and immortal, yet carefree and fragile all at once.

The thought of living a thousand years is so intriguing but ultimately depressing, having to outlive everyone and anyone who enters your life. Still, it makes me wonder, what would I give to have all eternity in my hands?

As I contemplate this, I hear a chair skid across the carpet in front of me. I slowly bring my book down, low enough to peek over.

I furrow my brows. "Can I help you?" I ask the boy sitting at the table across from me, feeling a bit perplexed and apprehensive. A smirk spreads across his face as his smoky golden eyes bore into mine.

"No, just taking in the view," the boy answers back with swagger.

Is this kid crazy or something? I know he can't possibly be talking about me, and the library isn't much to look at either.

I glance behind me. "The view, huh? Kinda hard to believe, since we're sitting in a library," I comment sarcastically.

"Very true. But I wasn't talking about the scenery; I was more or less talking about you," he replies. "My name is Brent," he says while extending his hand for me to shake. Immediately, I feel the *thump-thump, thump-thump* of my heart pumping with great intensity. An ice-cold shiver rushes down my arms and throughout my body, and I can't help but stare at his soft, pristinely manicured hand, as though touching it would be the death of me. An end to all means. But most of all, I'm afraid of the burning scar his touch might leave on me.

I continue to stare at him, not sure where this is going. He eventually drops his hand. I'm kind of wondering if maybe this is a joke, like he was put up to this or something. Maybe I'm being punked and everyone is hiding behind the bookcases, waiting for him to make a fool out of me.

But Brent just continues to gawk at me with this indescribable charisma. I feel as though he's drawing me in with the golden blaze of his eyes but making me question his intentions with a devilish grin.

"Ahem." Brent clears his throat, looking amused, and leans his head to the side, waving his hand to get my attention.

"Oh, sorry. I'm Raina," I finally reply after leaving my trance.

"Hi, Raina. It's nice to finally meet you," he says, as though he's been waiting for this moment his entire life.

"*Finally?*" I question, feeling the blood rush to my cheeks. "You say that as though we should already know each other."

I watch as he adjusts his shoulders and reassesses himself before responding. "I saw you in the hallway this morning and then again in the cafeteria. I just felt like you were someone I wanted to meet," he confesses. "The cafeteria felt a little crowded, with all eyes on me, so I left to get some air," Brent finishes, shrugging his shoulders.

"And you followed me here?"

I can't believe that just came out of my mouth. Of course he's not stalking me! Why would anyone want to do that?

"I wasn't stalking you, if that's what you're

thinking. When I passed by, I saw you sitting alone. I felt like this was my chance to introduce myself without any watchers lurking," he admits with a kind of sincerity. At least, I *think* he's being sincere.

Before I can even respond, the bell rings. I stand up and quickly gather my book off the table to place in my book bag. I push in my chair and smile at him as he begins to stand up. I turn to walk away, not knowing what else to say to him.

An intense warmth stings my hand, goose bumps rage through my skin as my hair rises from my body. I pause slowly, turn around, and look down. Brent's hand is now touching mine.

"Raina, when can I see you again?"

The energy from his hand is climbing through my every limb, awakening the parts of me that lay dormant for so long.

"Why would *you* want to see *me* again?" I question, a little dumbfounded, taking my hand back.

He steps closer. "Because I like you." Straight to the point.

I turn slowly around, not sure how to answer this, and I can feel the heat off his body as he walks beside me. I stop when we get to the glass doors. "Listen, you seem nice and all, but I have a boyfriend," I say, leaving him speechless. I'm completely shocked that this lie just came rolling off my tongue so easily. I *hate* lying, but I hate being let down even more so, and I'm sure that's just what he would do eventually.

After gym class, I head to my last period class— History. I head to my seat in the second row. Up until now, the seat behind me has been vacant. Not any longer, though. Now Brent sits directly behind me.

He watches me intently as I place my book bag on the floor. I almost sense a longing in his eyes, but that can't be possible, because he barely even knows me. I feel the heat rising to my cheeks, embarrassed for this thought to even pass through my mind. He could have any girl in this school; why would he want some normal Jane like me?

Brent cracks a smile. I return a quick, sharp one and turn around fast enough to avoid any conversation. I can hear him snicker to himself, but I can't understand what is so funny.

The butterflies in my stomach begin fluttering madly, and that crazy, intense feeling comes swarming through my body again. Just knowing he is close enough for me to reach out and touch sparks my heightened awareness. I do *not* want to feel this way. I *refuse* to feel this way!

Thank goodness our History teacher, Mr. Jones, closes the door to signal the beginning of class. Mr. Jones reminds me a lot of the actor Danny DeVito—short, chubby, and balding. He's been teaching eleventh-grade History for more than thirty years now, and I have to admit that he has the ability to draw me into the past.

Last week, we began the studies of women's rights—the right for women to vote and to join in the workforce. If it weren't for the amazing, strong-willed women from our past paving the way, I wouldn't have my freedom of choice: the choice to be heard, the choice to be seen as my own individual, and the choice to pave my own path in this world, whatever that may be.

"Okay class, please take out your textbook and turn to page thirty-four," Mr. Jones directs, as he picks up the chalk and begins scribbling on the board.

*The life of a woman in the eighteen hundreds.*

Mr. Jones smacks the chalk down on the railing, creating a small puff of chalk dust, and turns around to face the class.

"What comes to mind when you read this?" he asks, walking up and down the aisles and pounding his fists together after snapping his fingers.

Shevaun DeLucia

Brent is the first one to raise his hand, surprisingly. "Ah, the first to step up to the plank," says Mr. Jones. "What comes to your mind when you read this, um...?"

"It's Brent. I see long, tiring days filled with the longing for freedom, forbidden love, hands full of dirt, and eyes full of dreams," Brent responds so poetically.

I look around the quiet classroom. Boys are putting their hands up in defeat while the girls' eyes widen. I just roll my eyes at his pretension, but deep down inside, I'm kind of in awe of the words he chose to use. It was as if he's lived what he spoke about. Strange.

"Well done, Brent," the teacher praises him with a small clap. "I couldn't have said it better myself." Mr. Jones looks around the classroom. "Does anyone have anything to add?"

Before I can tell my hand to stay put, it's waving in the air. Brent looks me over slowly, as though he is wondering what I can possibly add.

"Yes. Raina, is it?" Mr. Jones questions.

I have no idea what on God's earth made me raise my hand. I'm usually never this bold. "Yes," I reply.

"Please, enlighten us." He walks towards me, hands behind his back.

"How about the desire to be equals, the lust to be heard, the option to say 'no,'" I spit out as I squint my eyes in Brent's direction.

"Very good point, Raina," says the teacher, head slowly nodding in approval. He scans the room for any other takers.

Brent has a smirk on his face. I think he's actually getting a kick out of ruffling my feathers. "Why are you looking at me like that?" I question him in an angry whisper.

He leans over his desk, bringing himself a little closer. "You intrigue me," he admits. "And you make me smile."

Eternal Mixture

"*You* find *me* interesting?" I ask with some sarcasm, but also some confusion, at his response. What could he possibly find so interesting about me?

"Ahem," Mr. Jones clears his throat, hinting for us to be quiet.

Brent sits back in his chair, and I turn around. I can still feel the intensity of his gaze burning into my back.

I finish the remainder of the class with tense muscles, a tornado of angry butterflies flying rapidly through my body, and my leg twitching in a nervous spasm. This is such a new and odd feeling for me. I almost feel alien-like. Brent causes all these sensations that I never knew existed—and I barely even know him.

The bell rings for class to let out. Before I can grab my bag and run, Brent is already standing beside my desk.

I slam by books in my bag and look up. "Can you please stop?" I ask, aggravated.

"Stop what?" Brent replies, his hands up and an intentionally shocked look on his face. He can't possibly be serious.

"This. Stop this," I say, flailing my arms about. "What do you want from me?" I throw my book bag over my left shoulder and walk towards the classroom door in a hurry, hoping to lose him. Unfortunately, I don't have a chance.

"I told you. I want to get to know you. Maybe you can show me around. *Please*?" Brent puts on his best puppy-dog face. I have to admit—and I would never admit this aloud to anyone—he's kind of making my heart melt. No one has ever, *ever* made me feel this way, especially in such a short amount of time.

"Okay, okay! I'll show you around sometime," I agree, hoping to keep my distance so I don't fall for him.

As we walk through the hallway in deep conversation, I soon realize we are being closely watched by the rest of the school's population. My stomach drops.

Shevaun DeLucia

I stop in front of my locker to drop off some of my books, hoping he might feel on display and walk away, but he doesn't. Instead, it's almost as though he enjoys having the spotlight on us, which completely baffles me, because he was trying to escape it just a couple of hours ago.

"Good. Come on, let's go. We can take my car," he says, face lit up like it's Christmas. He grabs my book bag from me and begins to walk towards the double doors leading out to the parking lot.

"Wait, I can't go with you now. I have somewhere I have to be," I explain, trying to grab my book bag from his grip. He swings it behind him.

"Well, I'll go with you," he offers.

I try to snatch my bag back again. "You can't. I'm sorry. Where I'm going is for girls only," I state firmly, hoping he gets the point.

"Girls only, huh?" Brent responds with that devilish grin again. "Okay, I get the point. So, tomorrow it is." He hands me my book bag, gives me a wink, and heads off to his car.

I think I must have been holding my breath the whole time, because as he walks away, I let out a chestful of air. I feel a little aggravated, but also a little intrigued.

# Chapter 2

I pull up in front of Billiards and see a couple of kids from school standing in a semicircle near the front door, smoking cigarettes. These are the "emo" kids in school: black eyeliner, black hair, and black clothes with chains hanging from the pants. I give them a quick smile as I walk inside. I've never been one to judge anyone. I try to stay friendly and open-minded to all groups and cliques in my school. To each his own, right? Who am I to say what is socially correct?

My girlfriends are at the third table down from the bar on the right. Maddie and Bailey are shooting some pool one on one, and sitting down on the stool is Jenna, with Jason standing by her side. I had a feeling he would be here, but I was hoping that maybe this one time Jenna could put her foot down and allow it to just be us girls.

"Hi guys. Who's winning?" I ask, pulling a stool up next to Jenna.

"Um, moi, of course!" Bailey responds in an egotistical tone.

"Shut up, Bailey!" Maddie adds, half-joking, half-serious. We all just laugh, except for Jason; he just stands next to Jenna like a bodyguard.

"So Jason, what brings you here?" I question, eyes squinting back and forth between him and Jenna.

"*Raina!*" Jenna gripes, giving me the look of death.

"Yeah, we were thinking the same thing," Bailey chimes in. "This was *supposed* to be girls' time." She lands the three ball in the corner pocket.

"You girls get to see Jenna all throughout the day. I just missed her, can't be without her. What's so bad about that?" he asks.

Jenna becomes completely defensive. "There's absolutely *nothing* wrong with that!" she says, giving us all the evil eye and puckering her lips for a kiss from Jason.

I can't win. Maybe this would be a good time for some interrogating. "Jason, you said you weren't originally from around here. Where are you from?" I ask.

"My parents are from up North," he replies, with no enthusiasm whatsoever.

I'm going to have to drag it out of him. "Up North, huh? Like *where* up North?"

"Canada," Jason snaps. "Babe, I'm gonna get a drink from the bar. You girls want anything?" He purposely squirms his way out of my interrogation.

"No, thanks," Bailey and Maddie respond simultaneously. I just shake my head. As soon as Jason's out of earshot, Jenna starts in.

"OMG, Raina! What *was* that?" she snaps. Bailey comes over to intervene.

"Come on, Jenna. I was just trying to get to know him. What's wrong with that?" I ask, trying to look sincere. But she knows me better than that.

"There's nothing wrong with that. *Right*, Jenna?" Bailey interjects, trying to defuse the situation.

"There *would* be nothing wrong with it if Raina was actually being sincere, but she's not," Jenna says defensively.

I look over at Maddie, and she is completely

oblivious to our conversation. Or maybe she's purposely staying out of the conversation.

"Jenna, I'm sorry but it's been months, and we barely know anything about him," I say quietly, trying to get her to understand where I'm coming from. Jenna just rolls her eyes and Bailey scoots back over to the pool table nonchalantly, warning me of Jason's presence.

He hands a drink to Jenna. "What did I miss?" he asks, obviously feeling the tension between all of us.

I can't pretend to be nice any longer. "Alright girls, I'm gonna head home. I have some homework to do still." I hop off my stool and walk past Jenna and Jason.

"Raina, you just got here," Maddie says, her hands on her hips.

I wave behind me. "Just call me later," I say, heading to the door.

They all wave goodbye. As I look over my shoulder, I can see Jason watching me out of the corner of his eye. Its gives me the chills. I know there's something he's hiding from us, and I am determined to find it out. When Maddie calls me tonight, I am going to recruit her to assist me with this. She's good at research *and* good at keeping secrets.

If Jenna finds out, she'll never talk to me again.

As I pull into my driveway, I receive a text.
"Hey."
"Who is this?" I type back.
"It's Brent."

I am a little dumbfounded at the moment. How in the heck did he get my number already? I never even gave it to him. I feel a little invaded, but also a little giddy inside, knowing he's made this much of an effort already to track my number down.

"How did u get my #?" I text back.

Shevaun DeLucia

"I have my ways," he responds. "R u still hangin with the girlz?"

"No. I'm home now."

I head into my house, and my parents still aren't home yet. This is pretty much the norm for me. Five o'clock and home alone.

My father is a workaholic and my mother follows in his footsteps. I never faulted my parents for not being around much, because I know in my heart that they're working hard for me. My father always tells me that he's investing in my future and that he wants me to take over the family business when the time comes.

My father is a chemist, and my mother is his assistant. He invents, creates, and tests medication for the FDA's approval. He likes to think of himself as one of God's personal missionaries: helping the sick get better. Sometimes he lets me help out by allowing me to donate blood for the use of science. It makes me feel like I'm doing a good deed for others. When I ask him what will happen if I get sick, he tells me I have no need to worry. He says that I am special and that longevity lies ahead for me. Whatever that may mean.

My phone vibrates again.

"Can I come pick u up?" his text reads.

"My parents have dinner ready. I have to go. Sorry." I lie.

I'm really not sure what to think about this. This was only Brent's first day of school, and already he's being way too persistent. First the library, next history class, and now he's texting me when I never gave him my number. I'm not really sure why he has chosen me out of everyone at school, and I'm not too sure I want to give in to it, either.

After working on my homework for a couple of hours, my parents finally come home with some takeout in hand.

"Raina, we're home! We brought some dinner," my

mother yells from downstairs.

I'm starving. I shove my books aside and head down the stairs.

I enter the kitchen. "Hey Mom. Hey Dad," I say as I give them kisses on the cheeks.

"Hey honey. How was school? Did you finish your homework?" my mother asks while getting the plates out of the cupboard.

"Yeah, just got done with it. What's for dinner?" I wonder, smelling something spicy.

"We got some Mexican food," my dad chimes in as he sits down at the kitchen table.

I take my seat next to him. "Oh, yummy. Did you get me a chicken enchilada?" I ask, digging into the chips and salsa.

"Of course we did, honey. So, tell us how your day was. Did you take your vitamin this morning?" my mom asks, putting some rice and beans on her plate and then passing the container to me.

"Of course I did, Mom! Geez," I respond with complete annoyance. I have gotten this question every day of my life like clockwork, and every day I reply with the same answer. I'm sixteen now. At some point, her obsession with me taking my vitamins has got to stop. "My day was little bit strange. This new kid started today, and the whole school was talking about him," I tell them, leaving out the important details.

"Well that's nice, dear. Did you have any classes with him?" my mom asks, sneaking a quick glance at my dad. They must not have thought I caught it, but I did.

"Um, yeah, I have History with him. He seems nice," I respond, eyes glaring at them. "Dad, do you need my help with any of your work this weekend? I can come into the lab with you if you want."

"I'll let you know, honey. Your mother and I have a lot of research to finish this weekend, so we won't be home that much." He takes a big bite of his enchilada.

"Raina, are you going to be okay on your own?" my mother asks, taking a bite of her food. She's always worrying about me. I think deep down inside they feel guilty that they're not here enough, but I really don't mind the time to myself. We don't have a normal parent-teenager relationship. They trust me, and I don't do anything to make them second-guess that trust like most teenagers might.

I roll my eyes. "*Mom*, I will be fine. Don't worry about me, okay?" I respond, trying to soothe her. "I'm tired. I'm gonna hit the sack."

I give them each a kiss on the cheek, place my plate in the sink, and head upstairs. It's time to call Maddie, since she never even bothered to call me like she was supposed to.

I lounge out on my bed and dial Maddie's number.

"Hello?" she answers.

"Um, hello chica! Did you forget about me?"

"No, my mom just made me clean up the house. So, what was up with you leaving so fast today?"

"I can't stand being around Jason. He really gets to me for some reason."

I sit up on my bed.

"I know, it's like Jenna's a different person when she's around him. I don't understand why she can't be away from him for one day. It's like he has some sort of power over her or something."

"Yeah, I know what you mean. *So*, I was thinking maybe we should do a little research on him. Get to know him better, if you know what I mean?" I say with devilish intent.

"Hmm, good idea. I'll start searching the computer tonight, and you do the same. Then we'll see what we both come up with and compare," Maddie instructs.

"Sounds good! Okay, I'll see you at school

tomorrow."

"Okay, bye," she says before hanging up the phone.

I pull out my laptop and Google the name Jason Alexander, but not much comes up. I only find links about the actor from *Seinfeld*. I do a more in-depth search and add in Canada, hoping I can find something on his family.

The only thing that pulls up is the Alexander paintings. These are paintings that date all the way back to the eighteen hundreds. They're detailed; each stroke is carefully placed, the colors dull and faded with reds and browns. But the third painting I scroll down to has a light that spreads across the canvas, so warm and inviting against the walls of a brick castle. The sky is a smoky blue and the lake is a magnificent iridescent turquoise blue, almost dreamlike—a beauty so pure and so perfect the mere thought of disturbing such a place almost stains it with filth.

On the right-hand corner in small script reads *Immortel*. I pause for a moment, staring at the French word. The title of the painting is breathtaking to me. I feel such a strong pull to it. Every inch of my body feels so alive. But why? Why do I feel so connected? This beauty can't possibly have any relation to Jason.

I save the site to my favorites and try scrolling through some of the others, but nothing else pops out to me. I just hope that Maddie had some better luck with her search. I shut down my laptop, turn my light off, and crawl into bed. My phone shines bright as it vibrates against my nightstand. It shows one simple text: "Goodnight." It brings flutters to my stomach and makes goose bumps travel down the length of my body. Brent is the last thing I envision before my mind drifts off into the darkness.

Shevaun DeLucia

# Chapter 3

I hear a distant knock and the door creeks open. My eyelids flutter, squinting from the luminous morning light. My mother peeks in from the doorway to tell me she loves me and to remind me that my vitamin is on the kitchen counter. After she closes my door, I shut my eyes again and my first thought drifts to Brent.

The depth of his smoky hazel eyes that seem to have an eternity of knowledge flowing beneath them. His pearly white teeth and smile of seduction that makes me forget my words dead in their tracks. But mostly, the way my body reacts to just the mere sight of him.

I'm really not comprehending any of this. I've been in the vicinity of many hot guys before, but this is something completely different. I feel as though something deep inside me has been awakened. Every muscle in my body is craving him, and I have no clue why.

It makes me wonder if it's possible for souls to reincarnate and find each other again in a later life. Momentarily, I get the feeling as though I *really* know Brent, not by meeting or by memory, but with my physical body, like our souls may have possibly met in a past life. Every inch of me is screaming this, but I feel foolish when

24

I even consider saying this out loud.

It's only going on his second day of school, and I'm already beginning to feel like every other girl in school: giddy with a schoolgirl crush. But if I'm not mistaken, he seemed to be pretty taken with me as well yesterday.

While I'm still stuck in thought, I can hear my phone ringing in the distance. Muffled by my thoughts and cravings, it takes a moment to snap out of my daydream and bring myself back to reality.

Looking down at my phone, I see Brent's number staring back at me from the screen.

I press the green answer button. "Hello?"

"Hey," he says. I can tell there's a smile behind his incredibly rugged voice. The blood rages through my veins just hearing his voice. I feel my palms begin to moisten with every second, but the last thing I want to do is lead him on to the fact that he makes me utterly unable to function.

"Brent, it's seven in the morning. Why are you calling?" I ask, still warm under my covers.

"I wanted to see if you need a ride. You promised to show me around today. You're not going to break that promise, are you?"

I guess this is Brent playing the guilt card.

"I wasn't planning on breaking it," I tell him honestly. How could I possibly pass up a moment of being near him?

"Good, then I will bring you home after. I'll swing by to pick you up, say thirty-five minutes? Or do you need more time?" I stand up.

"No, that's fine," I say, my heart pounding, knowing in just half an hour I will be close enough to smell his sweet, fresh scent. Goose bumps flow down my body as a chill soars down my spine.

"Okay, see you in a few."

Brent hangs up the phone.

Shevaun DeLucia

I stand there for a moment, phone still up to my ear, stuck on his words circling in my head. But the question that continues to push itself front and center is, why me? Right now he could have any girl in the school, so why me? It's not that I find him to be too good for me or that I'm not good enough for him, but I'm not the most popular or the most pretty, and I'm nowhere close to being athletic. I'm just a normal girl. So what can he see that I can't?

I realize time is escaping me, and I haven't even gotten dressed yet. As I look through my closet, I begin to panic. I search through my hoodies and sweatshirts, push aside my dresses, and finally come across my comfortable gray tee.

Before I know it, Brent is ringing my doorbell.

I jump into my pants, squirming and squatting to stretch them out after the wash, and grab my lip gloss to apply as I run down the stairs. I take a quick pause before I grab the doorknob just to gather myself, and then I take a deep breath and open the door.

There he stands, leaning against the front porch railing, looking almost dream-like. The sun hits the left side of his body, highlighting his sharp features with perfection. His hazel eyes glow like a golden sunset as he looks me up and down. I feel my face engulf with a blaze of heat, coloring my cheeks pink as I watch his eyes caress every inch of my body.

I can't help but feel a little self-conscious of my imperfections, but instead of allowing my mind to wonder into dark, negative thoughts, he grabs my hand and pulls me towards him until I am enveloped in his warm arms.

"Hi beautiful," Brent says softly into my ear. "I feel like I have been waiting a lifetime to just touch you," he whispers into my ear while again making a comment that makes no sense. He's known me a little over twenty-four hours.

Before I question him on this, I close my eyes and

Eternal Mixture

take in his fresh, clean scent to satisfy my craving. Then I push him away to get some distance between us.

I roll my eyes. "Here you go again," I comment as I walk away from him and towards his car.

"Here I go again? What does *that* mean?" Brent asks, eyebrows furrowed.

I turn around to face him. "You keep making these comments as though we've known each other forever."

I stand tall, arms folded across my chest.

Brent steps closer. "I feel as though we have. Is that so bad?" he asks, irritation written all over his face.

"I guess not," I tell him, shaking my head. "Brent, I told you I have a boyfriend," I remind him to put some distance between us.

The light in his eyes fade. "You're right, you did. But there's no reason we can't be friends, right?" Brent says as he opens the car door for me with a smile. At this point, I feel a little embarrassed. Maybe I am reading him totally wrong. Maybe he just truly wants a tour guide and thought unpopular Raina was the best choice, since I obviously have no life.

"Sorry, you're right. Friends," I quickly say as I bite on my bottom lip and look at my feet, sinking into the passenger seat.

I can't bear for him to see the complete embarrassment written all on my face. But Brent gently grabs my chin and turns my face towards his. To my surprise, his face is so close I can feel the heat of his breath against my lips, and if I were to move just two inches forward, my lips would be pressed against his. His eyes bore into mine and he says, "Raina, he's lucky to have you. What I wouldn't give to be in his place for just one moment." He releases my face, turns the ignition on, and pulls out of my driveway.

I'm completely speechless. I have no idea what just happened, and now I'm more confused then ever.

Shevaun DeLucia

We pull into the school parking lot, and it's filled with students. I put my hand against my forehead and slowly slide down the seat. Brent looks over at me while chuckling to himself.

I look up at him. "What?"

He shakes his head. "You just crack me up," he says, pulling into the parking space. The group of girls getting out of the car next to us just stare with looks of disgust. "Raina, you don't really care what other people think, do you?"

"Honestly, I just try to keep a low profile. I'm not interested in being the popular girl or anything. I just would rather get through high school unscathed."

He pauses for a moment and then nods. "I admire that in you. Keeping a low profile is smart," he tells me as he gets out of the car and slams the door shut behind him. Brent comes around to my side of the car, opening the door for me. I climb out of the passenger seat and swing my book bag against my back. "But you do realize being seen with me might cause a stir," he adds.

That's exactly what it does. Walking down the hallway next to him, I can hear the snickers and whispers thrown my way from all of the girls, while the faces of the boys in the hallway turn to confusion as they're probably wondering what Brent could possibly see in me.

I stop at my locker and look around. "Yeah, I think you're right," I finally admit, taking a deep breath.

Brent turns to me. "Will you meet me in the library for lunch?" he asks, waiting for me to finish placing my books into my locker. "*Please?*" he begs again, completely oblivious to all the attention placed on us.

"Okay, I'll be there," I answer quickly before heading towards my class.


**I** have math class with Bailey. Already the rumors

of Brent and I have spread throughout the school. I should have just gone with my first gut feeling to stay away from him.

Bailey sits down in her seat next to mine, staring at me with accusing eyes.

I look over at her. "What?"

"Are you serious? That's all you have to say to me?" she growls, crossing her arms. "What the heck is going on, Raina? I'm your best friend, and I have to hear about you and Brent through everyone else?"

I lean in to her so no one else hears. "There is no me and Brent. We're just friends, nothing else."

"Well, that's not what I hear."

"I don't care what you have heard. We're just friends!" I say, aggravated and not realizing I am being loud enough for the students around us to hear. The teacher makes her entrance just as Bailey's about to snap back, so instead she huffs and leans back into her chair with her arms crossed in defeat.



After class, Bailey waits for me outside the door.

"You are *so* gonna spill it at lunch," she demands.

"I actually have to do some studying at the library on lunch," I reply. If she really knew what I was doing there, she would never leave me alone about it.

I watch as Bailey studies me as though she has just read my mind.

"Okay, have it your way, Raina. I'll call you later tonight then," she smirks and then turns to walk away.

I know Bailey is up to something. She can never just leave things alone, so for her to just accept the fact that she has not gotten any information out of me is definitely not like her.

I make it to the library during my lunch hour, and

Brent is nowhere to be found. My eyes search from one table to the other in hopes of finding him. I find a table near the right-hand corner of the library where we can have the utmost privacy. For some reason, my nerves begin to get the best of me. What if he doesn't show up? I place my book bag on the table and try to keep my mind occupied while pretending to look for something other than him.

As the minutes add up and the seconds begin to feel like eternity, my body must sense something that I can't see. A flood of goose bumps surge through my body, awakening every inch of me. My blood rages through my veins and my heart pounds so intensely that I look around in fear that the whole library can hear it as well. And then I feel them—his warm, manicured hands wrapping around my face, covering my eyes. I feel his hot breath against my ear, which sends icy chills down my spine. As he sits down in the seat in front of me, I am completely in awe.

I finally snap out of it enough to speak.

"So, why did you want me to meet you here?" I ask, beginning to feel the burn from under my cheeks.

"I'm trying to stay clear from that cafeteria; there's too much controversy going on in there for me. I'd rather spend my time here with you," Brent tells me as he breaks out his charismatic smile. "So, tell me about yourself. Something nobody else knows."

"Hmm. Something no one else knows, huh?"

I do my best to stall while I think of something. It's hard to come up with an interesting fact when my life has been so bland up until now. "I enjoy giving blood for the sake of my father's research."

There. Something that even my closest friends don't know.

"Wow. Giving blood, huh?" he asks with a chuckle. "What does your father research?"

"He's a chemist. Basically, he gives the sick a fighting chance when all hope has been lost. A 2013

Eternal Mixture

medicine man," I answer with a smile.

The corner of his mouth lifts up. "I like the way you put that."

"So, tell me something about *you* that nobody knows," I grin.

He takes a moment before speaking. "I'm extremely patient when it comes to love," Brent reveals, offering no more explanation.

"You've been in love before, then?" I feel very odd asking this question, because we're both still so young. The thought of him already knowing what it's like to be in love is shocking and sad at the same time. Every girl would like to think that maybe they could be someone's first love.

"Was, am, and will always be."

It's clear the door is closed on this subject. "So tell me, Raina, what are your friends like?"

My lips form a tight line as I concentrate on one of the bookshelves behind Brent. "Well, Bailey—she's the one with black hair—I've known her ever since I can remember. She lives right down the street from me. Our parents are family friends as well. Bailey's funny," I chuckle. "She comes off a little self-absorbed, you might say, but really behind her tough façade she is kind, forgiving, and a very compassionate person." To my surprise, it seems as though Brent is truly interested in what I am saying, versus these other guys our age who pretend to listen with the intention of getting in a girl's pants.

"Why do you think she puts on a façade?" Brent asks, confusion written on his face as he leans closer.

"She's hurting. Bailey's older brother died in Iraq three years ago, and ever since then, she buries her feelings, pushes them deep down until she is numb. She doesn't want pity or to feel vulnerable. She had to be strong for her parents. They cracked and depended on her to hold the family together when all she really wanted to do was crumble," I finish.

Shevaun DeLucia

Brent's eyebrows lift up. "Oh *wow*, and how did her brother's death affect you? You must have known him well if you've been so close with her." Honestly, no one's ever asked me this before, and I'm not sure why.

"I was close with him in the annoying-little-sister way, although I didn't see him as my brother. I saw him more like a crush. He was my first puppy-dog crush and he knew it, so he took full advantage of it," I admit, chuckling to myself.

Brent smiles. "How so?" he asks, enjoying watching me laugh.

"Oh, he just made me do every and any little thing for him. You know, like get him a drink, clean up his room. 'Raina, do this. Raina, do that,' and so on. *But*, there was this *one* moment when we were alone, and he came inches away from my face. We were both so silent, and he pushed a strand of hair behind my ear so sweetly, looking dead into my eyes. I just remember thinking my first kiss might happen then. Then, Bailey walked into the room *totally* oblivious to what was going on, and that was a month before he was drafted," I confess, saddened by the memory I have locked up for so long. "I never told anyone that. I'm really not sure why I just told you."

Brent looks pained. "I'm sorry, Raina. His death must have been hard on you. You're a good friend for putting her emotions before yours."

We sit quiet for a moment, just gazing at each other. The silence doesn't feel odd or awkward; it feels just right, at the right moment. I find Brent very refreshing and mature for his age. It's as though he has an old soul in a new body.

"It's okay. It's what friends are for, right?" I question.

"Very true. So, what about your other friends? Have you known them as long?" Brent asks curiously.

"No, Maddie moved here from Kansas about two

years ago. She's the one with all the freckles on her face. She was someone I immediately bonded with. I felt as though I'd known her forever. I like to call her my soul sister," I explain, feeling a little dumb for admitting that.

"There's nothing wrong with that," he says, making me feel at ease. Before I can go any further, the bell rings. We both jump as we're slightly knocked out of our deep conversation. Brent laughs as he pushes in his chair and throws his book bag over his shoulder.

"Ready for class?" he asks in a teasing, sarcastic manner.

"As ready as I'll ever be," I joke. "I have gym class next," I tell him, face scrunched.

As we walk down the hall together towards our classes, everything turns into slow motion. The looks, the sly comments behind our backs—it's as though I can hear each and every one of my classmates with their jealous and crude remarks. Brent notices that I suddenly become tense, and instead of cracking a joke about it, he just squeezes my forearm and gives me a quick smile to let me know he's there.

We pass by Jenna's locker. Standing beside her is Bailey and Maddie. I wave as I walk by, and they give me a puzzled look because I don't stop. I'm not ready or comfortable enough to introduce Brent to my friends. I don't want them to get the wrong impression of us, but most of all I don't want to send Brent into a circle of pit bulls. They'll interrogate him until he gives in and tells all. They've been waiting to do just that like the rest of the girls in the school.

My next class flies by. History class isn't as interesting today. The way my body is feeling the intense rhythm of my heart banging against my ribcage and the spasms I feel from my muscles tensing and tightening into little knots is the only thing I can concentrate on. I know his eyes are boring holes into every inch of my back. And how do I know this? It's how my body is reacting to him. Every piece of me is alive, pulsating with the desire and hunger for him. To be honest, it's totally freaking me out! Now I'm wondering if this may be what Jenna feels towards Jason, but I really don't see the feeling being reciprocated by Jason at all. I see it as more of a convenience on his part.

While I am in mid-thought about Brent, my teacher is trying to get my attention.

"Uh, earth to Raina," Mr. Jones says. I can hear my classmates laughing, and Brent kicks my chair to get my attention.

"Yes, Mr. Jones?" I finally come to and answer back, my face burning with embarrassment.

"As I was saying, you and Brent had some good input in yesterday's lecture. Where do you think we would be today if the women of the eighteen hundreds didn't step up?" Mr. Jones questions me, students still giggling and whispering amongst themselves.

Since when did I become the main focus of this topic? I've always kept a low profile, and within the last twenty-four hours, my name has been spewing out of everyone's mouth.

"Women of that time may not have been able to speak up in the beginning, but they were the driving force behind all progressive reforms regarding education, healthcare, and labor movements. I mean, think about it. We've come a long way. It's been a grueling, torturous fight, but without us, the men would still be fighting amongst each other, uncivilized like cowboys and Indians. Behind every man is a strong woman," I finish, wondering if anyone even understood what I just said.

The boys of the classroom whisper "bullshit" under their breath, and the girls seem to all have my back. For once, the girls in this classroom all agree on something.

"Now, now class." Mr. Jones tries to calm the class

down. "Raina has some very good points."

"She's right in all aspects," Brent jumps in loudly, without raising his hand, over the loud humming sound in the classroom. "Men had too much invested in their egos: busy with war, control over land, and business. Women were the ones who controlled the households and taught and raised the next generations of men and women. Ultimately, we wouldn't exist without women *and* vice versa," Brent finishes.

The class is silent.

I turn my head to look at him through my peripheral vision and give him an adoring smile. Another girl sitting in the front row, Casey, holds her hand up. Every time she glances at Brent I can see the lust bursting from her eyes.

"Do you have something else to add?" Mr. Jones asks, acknowledging Casey with her hand up.

Casey is the captain of the girl's volleyball team. She's tall, with slender, toned legs that go on for miles. Her red hair reminds me of the devil, but her green eyes are what the boys in school admire. And of course she is the most athletic, most developed, and most popular girl in school. It's a given that she is going to want Brent, but will Brent eventually want her?

"I do agree with what Brent said. And it's nice to hear a man admit to man's faults, but look at society now. The homes and moral values of the children today are extremely lacking. In many homes, there's no direction or guidance because now both parents are working or involved in some other activities that take away from what's really important: instilling family values," Casey finishes, looking pretty proud of herself while looking Brent up and down like a piece of meat.

I just roll my eyes, wanting to puke. Is she serious? Women have come a long way, and now she wants to imply that because women play an important part in society instead of staying at home, children are now being

Shevaun DeLucia

insubordinate and lacking values? Instead of raising my hand, I just blurt out my thought without warning.

"So, what you are saying is that women should have stayed home and remained barefoot and pregnant? Do you even realize that if women never stood up for their rights that *you* wouldn't be sitting here in class today? You would be learning how to be subordinate to your husband while cooking, cleaning, and raising children, because you would be next in line at this age," I respond with a huff. I can hear Brent chuckling to himself in the background and quiet whispers throughout the room.

"Point taken, Raina," Mr. Jones comments. "And Casey, do you have a response to Raina's debate?"

Casey's face contorts. She's looking at me like I'm scum. "Only that self-righteousness suites her, because reproduction is something that she should avoid at *all* costs," she taunts, with a jab straight to my gut.

The whole class bursts out laughing in unison. Except for Brent. He remains cool and stiff, aggravation obviously swelling.

"Now, now class. Casey, I want to see you after the bell," Mr. Jones states, quickly trying to change the subject. She just rolls her eyes.

Through he remainder of class, I keep my mouth closed and opinions to myself. After the bell rings, Brent waits for me at my desk while I collect my belongings.

"Raina, don't stress about what that chick Casey said. She should apply the comment to her own self," Brent says, trying to boost my ego back up.

"I'm not," I respond coldly. I begin walking in a fast stride out the classroom door to my locker.

"Raina, what's the matter? Are you okay?" he asks while increasing his stride to stay at the same pace as me.

"Brent, I'm fine!" I growl through my teeth. The problem is that before he began attending this school, my life was simple. Besides my close friends, none of the kids

Eternal Mixture

paid any attention to me. I slipped through the cracks unscarred. And now I am the target of all gossip. I just want to go back to being an invisible nobody, finish my junior year, and get the hell out of this school. I already am in dire need of a summer vacation.

"You're obviously upset about something; just talk to me," Brent begs quietly as he keeps up with me through the hallway. He grabs my upper arm gently, pulls me to the side of the hallway, and stops. We're now face to face with each other.

"Listen Brent, I'm fine. We barely know each other, so who are you to say that I'm upset?" I ask him. The truth is he is dead-on with his assumption.

"Okay, you're right. I'm sorry. Just meet me at my car, okay?

"Okay," I answer. I watch him turn and walk away.

Shevaun DeLucia

# Chapter 4

The last bell rings, summoning the kids to depart from the school, and my stomach drops. I'm still feeling a little distant and really not sure about spending the rest of the afternoon with Brent. I just don't want to end up saying anything I'll regret. But I did promise him, so I don't want to back out and leave him standing at his car, waiting.

I wait a little bit so most of the students are cleared out from the parking lot. Less eyes and attention on us means less gossip, I hope.

Walking up towards his car, my stomach begins to do flips. I see him leaning against the back of his white Infinity, chiseled arms, stance of a stallion, and eyes fixed on my every move. The engine of my heart ignites in anticipation with each step I take closer to him.

This feeling is so foreign to me. I do everything possible to build a shield around me before I get to his car.

"Hey," Brent says with that charismatic grin. I watch his eyes as they slowly take in every inch of my canvas. Embarrassed, I look towards the ground.

"Hey."

"Are you ready?" Brent asks, as he opens the car

38

door for me.

"Ready as I'll ever be," I respond, tucking my hair behind my ear.

Brent jumps into the driver's seat and looks over at me with his hazelnut eyes blazing. "Where to?"

"Well, what are you interested in seeing?" I ask him, trying to keep my eyes focused on the scene beyond the window.

"I don't know. How about you show me somewhere you like to spend your time at." He puts the car in reverse and begins pulling out of the parking lot.

"Ok. So, make a left onto Hard Road. It's two lights down from here," I direct, pointing ahead.

Brent slows down for the next turn, using his left hand to steer the wheel while his right hand glides through his thick, glossy hair. He keeps his hair longer than most boys, but not yet long enough to pull back into a ponytail.

"Now just keep going straight until I tell you to turn," I direct again, still not trying to make eye contact with him.

He looks over in my direction like he wants to say something, and then he looks back at the road. I can feel the tension beginning to form between us. He gives me another quick lookover before focusing back towards the road. I'm trying to act as if I'm not noticing his actions, but it's hard to do. I begin to chuckle lightly to myself, a smirk growing across my face as I try my best to hide it. But after the third time, I can't take it anymore!

"Okay, what do you want to say Brent? Just say it already!" I tell him, shifting my body so I'm now leaning against the car door, staring directly at him.

I watch as he squirms a little, trying to decide whether he should say what's on his mind or keep it to himself.

"Well, I was trying to decide whether or not I should ask you about your boyfriend." He looks straight

Shevaun DeLucia

ahead, out the window. It's obvious he has been pondering this for a while, but why does he even care?

"You want to know about my boyfriend, huh?" I answer with a question, trying to stall so I can think up a believable response. "He's a junior in college at Alfred State," I blurt out. "I really don't see him as much as I used to. We're more like pen pals than anything else," I lie again. I want to crawl into a hole and die right about now. Truth is what builds character and separates the good and the bad, and here I am becoming my own worst enemy.

What I won't tell him is that I had a crush on a kid from school last year. He was a senior, accepted into Alfred State, but he had no idea who I was or that I even existed. He might laugh at me or find me pathetic if I share this info with him.

"Wow, a college boy, huh? Tell me one thing you like about him." There's a hint of jealousy behind his voice. He continues to keep his eyes focused on the road.

"He's, um, thoughtful." Oh, that's a good one. "And he never pressures me to do anything that I don't want to do," I blurt out, not even sure where that answer came from.

I watch Brent's knuckles turn white as he is squeezing the steering wheel and taking this information in. I can hear the wheels turning inside his head.

We're in such deep conversation that we almost pass our destination. "Oh shoot! Take a fast left here!" I yell, jumping forward in my seat. He cuts the wheel sharply and just makes the turn into the park entrance. "Nice move!"

"Thanks," he replies without a sweat.

"Okay, after we make it up this hill, take a right into one of the parking lots."

Brent puts the car in park, turns off the engine, and faces my direction, his eyes filled with lust. I can't help but gulp. I'm not sure what to say at this moment. My heart is

Eternal Mixture

booming against my chest and my body is scorching, burning me to the core. It takes everything I have to put out the fire.

"You ready? Let's go," I open my door and jump out, slamming the car door behind me.

"Wait, where are we going?" Brent asks, trying to catch up to me.

He makes his car beep with his keychain and is by my side in an instant. I don't answer back; instead, I continue walking without a word.

I find the trail that's hidden behind the tall grass. Slowly, I descend down and pray that I don't lose my balance and fall. The trail comes to an abrupt stop as we're greeted by a wooden bridge that crosses over a stream. The stream flows freely, no more than a foot deep. I don't look back to see if Brent's following me, because I can *feel* him behind me.

Brent obviously cannot take the silence any longer. "Raina, what's with the no talking?"

I stop and turn around without a warning and almost run smack-dab into him. Taking a step back, I say, "Why must you always feel the need to fill the void with talking? Can't you just enjoy the moment?" I turn around and continue to walk into the valley of grass.

He grins with pleasure.

No one's here; the park has this eerie silence to it. I walk over to the right where the swings are located and sit in one of them.

"So, this is where you like to come?" Brent asks as he sits down on the swing next to mine.

"Yeah, one of the places," I answer, beginning to pump. I stretch my feet and bow forward then back until the wind begins to blow through my hair.

Brent starts to swing too, but it looks like he is pumping faster and harder, hoping to get above me. I concentrate real hard, my lips pressed together and eyebrows furrowed, to make sure that doesn't happen. I look over, and he's watching me intently with an impressed smirk on his face. I can't help it. Instead of continuing, I begin laughing and he immediately does the same.

We slow our swings to a stop. "Tell me why you like it here?"

"Well, in the summers this place is loud and vibrant with kids and families, and I like coming here with my friends. But during this time of year, it's quiet and calming. I can come here alone and think. I like both atmospheres," I finish, shrugging my shoulders.

"You have a kind of sadness to you, Raina."

I immediately get defensive. I mean, who does he think he is? Or maybe the real question is, how can he get me without even really knowing me? The last thing I want to be is an open book.

"I'm not sad!" I huff and get off the swing. I begin walking towards the picnic tables on top of the hill, and Brent quickly follows behind. "I wish you would stop analyzing me. When you've known me for longer than a week, then maybe you'll be entitled to."

"Raina, I just want to be your friend. Why are you making it so difficult? Isn't that what a friend is supposed to do: say what's on their mind?"

We both sit on top of the picnic table. "I guess I don't like people seeing weakness in me. I'm not sad, though. I guess you can say I'm still trying to find my way." I lean my elbow on my knee and put my hand on my chin. "I feel like there's a whole world out there that I don't know about, and after next year's over, I'm not quite sure where I'm gonna fit in," I admit, gazing out into the openness.

"Believe me, I don't think you have anything to worry about. You have eternity to figure that one out," Brent says, shaking his head.

There he goes, speaking in his cryptic weirdness

Eternal Mixture

again. "Eternity? You act like I have found the fountain of youth or something," I reply with a snicker, shaking my head.

I see Brent tense up for a split second out of the corner of my eye, and then he relaxes.

"It was a figure of speech. You're young; you're not expected to figure that out yet." When he looks in my direction, I look towards my feet. I wonder what caused him to get tense. I don't even know if he realizes I noticed it or not.

"I know, you're right. I just get ahead of myself sometimes."

Brent changes the subject pretty quickly. "So, I think you finished with Maddie and left off with … Jenna, is it?"

I just keep thinking that there's got to be something wrong with this kid. There's no way he's this perfect. He has the listening skills of an owl, memory storage like an iPod, looks that any man would kill for, *and* he wants to spend all of his time with me? He has to have some type of ulterior motive behind all of this.

"Jenna, where should I even start with her?" I smile, squint, and tap my finger on my cheek.

"How about what is up with her hair?" Brent laughs.

Jenna decided one day that she didn't want to be seen as "normal," so she did the complete opposite of normal by chopping her hair and bleaching the shit out of it and applying the brightest colors possible to her face as a total facade.

"Her hair?" I chuckle. "Jenna is actually the complete opposite of what you see. She uses her craziness to throw people off. Deep down, she's insecure and emotionally vulnerable. She has a lot of family issues, which have been the driving force behind her insecurities. It kills me to see her like that, and now I feel she is getting taken advantage of by her boyfriend because of it. He's just all wrong for her."

"Why? What does he do to make you think that?" Brent looks at me, forehead creased.

I pick at my nail polish. "It's not really what he does, per se. It's the feeling I get in my gut. There's just something about him that rubs me the wrong way." I get the sense Jason's like a chameleon, and I'm going to find out what his true color is.

"Maybe you just need to give him a chance."

Yeah, right! Is he crazy? "No, I don't think so. He creeps me out," I say with a shiver.

"When someone feels comfortable around a person, they eventually let their guard down and then information will flow. What I'm trying to say, Raina, is make him feel comfortable and you may not have to snoop around. He may just lead you to the information you need by dropping his guard," Brent gives me a quick wink.

My heart flutters.

"Hmm, you might be on to something," I admit, giving him a quick wink back.

"I'm a guy. I know these sort of things," he says with a confident smile.

I stand up and stretch, arms over my head and back arching, ready to move on from here. I look back at Brent, and his eyes are exploring my body until he realizes he is caught red-handed. He shifts his eyes quickly to the ground.

My face begins to heat up.

After an hour or so of being here, it's beginning to get chilly. I wrap my arms together around my chest.

"Come on, let's go," I tell him, waiting for him to stand up from the picnic table before I start walking.

"Where are you taking me now?" Brent wonders, walking by my side.

"Well, I actually have to do some studying. Do you

Eternal Mixture

mind dropping me home?"

I see the disappointment in his eyes, but then he smiles and unlocks the car door, opening it for me to get in.

"Sure, no problem."

Brent starts the ignition and reverses out of the parking space.

"Now it's your turn," I say to Brent.

He turns to look at me. "My turn for what?" he asks, looking back at the road and then back to me.

"I don't know anything about you. You could be a crazed serial killer for all I know," I smirk. Brent just shakes his head with amusement.

"You should have thought about that before you got in the car with me," he jokes.

"So, tell me about where you just moved from." I watch as his eyes squint while trudging through his memories.

"I lived near Buffalo."

"With your parents?" I watch his face turn hard.

"No, with my aunt, Lillian. My parents are dead," he says so matter-of-factly. He sees my face drop. "It's okay, you don't have to feel bad for me. I've had a long time to accept it."

A big lump forms in my throat. I try to say something, but I can't seem to get it out.

"They died in a boating accident. Aunt Lillian is my mother's sister. She's been real good to me."

"Brent, I don't know what to s-say," I stutter. "That's terrible. I couldn't imagine life without my parents," I tell him, looking down, fiddling with my fingers.

He places his hand over mine, and when I look up, his eyes meet mine and I can tell he's found peace with what happened.

"Tell me about your aunt," I beg softly.

He takes a deep breath. "She was only a couple of

years older than us when my parents died. We've kind of grown up together. Don't get me wrong—she can be the authoritative figure when she needs to be—but most of the time, she allows me to make my own decisions and my own mistakes."

We pull into my driveway. It's obvious no one is home. Brent parks off to the side of the driveway.

"My parents are kind of like that, too. They don't hover over me like most parents do. They guide me but don't make decisions for me."

I look out my window to my house. "Do you want to come in?" Brent doesn't even answer. He turns the car off, takes the key out of the ignition, and walks over to the passenger's side to open the door.

The first thing I do before getting my homework out is head to the kitchen for something to eat. "Are you hungry?" I ask Brent, placing my book bag on the floor.

He sits down at the kitchen table, moving his chair to face me. "Whatcha got?" he asks.

I open the freezer door. "Um, you like pizza?" I ask with my head in the freezer.

"Sure, sounds good."

I feel Brent's eyes on me as I maneuver through the kitchen, turning on the stove and setting the heat for the oven. I open the fridge door to see what we have to drink.

"I have pop, milk, or Crystal Light iced tea. What would you like?"

"Iced tea's fine."

I pour us two glasses and set them down on the table. "So, what do you have to study for today?" Brent asks.

I immediately take a sip of my tea to avoid his eyes.

"Psychology. This class is so hard; I have to study twice as hard in this class than the others," I admit, running my hands through my hair and banging my forehead against the table.

Eternal Mixture

"Well, I guess it's a good thing that I'm pretty good on this subject," Brent winks.

"Really?" I sigh in relief, get up, and grab my book bag.

The oven shrieks, letting us know it's been preheated. I unwrap the pizza and slide it into the oven.

"What chapter are you working on?" Brent questions, sliding his chair closer to mine so he can lean over my shoulder to look at my book.

I feel his warm body heat radiating off him. My breathing halts and my body goes stiff. He must notice the change in my body. "Are you okay?" he asks, smirking, eyes drifting down to my lips.

My heartbeat picks up. "Um, yeah. I'm fine. Why?" I ask, trying to play it off. I open my textbook and fumble through the pages.

He shakes his head and chuckles. "Nothing, you just tensed up."

I can't look him in the eyes or I'll give myself away. Instead I just blurt out the chapter like an idiot. "Chapter five!"

"Okay, so you're doing the chapter on memory?" Brent questions, clearly noticing my nervousness.

"Yes."

The timer beeps loudly. I quickly jump out of my seat, happy for the distraction, and take the pizza from the oven.

"Think of your brain like a library. There's your memory, which gives you the ability to store and retrieve the information just like bookshelves store books. And then there's the other part: cognition, the process of acquiring that knowledge and using it, like using the information inside of a book."

I listen to Brent as he goes over the chapter with me, teaching me anomalies for the things I couldn't quite get while we eat our pizza. After a couple of hours of studying, my parents end up coming home.

"Oh shit! I didn't realize that it was this late!"

"Are your parents going to be okay with me being here?" Brent asks, helping me clean up the table.

"I'm not sure. I've never brought a boy home." Brent grins with satisfaction.

My mom walks into the kitchen followed by my father. "Oh, Raina, I didn't know you had company," my mom says, putting her purse on the counter.

Brent stands up, immediately walking towards my mother and father with his hand out. "My name's Brent, Brent Jewels," he says, shaking my mother's hand and then my father's with a charming smile. My mother eyes my father sneakily just like last night at dinner.

"Nice to meet you, Brent," my father replies, leaning against the kitchen counter with his ankles crossed and arms folded across his chest.

"Yes, Brent, very nice to meet you," Mom agrees as she begins to clean up some of my mess. I can't get that look that my mom gave my father out of my mind. There's some sort of meaning or reasoning behind that, and I am going to find out!

"Raina and I were just studying together," Brent explains, surprisingly not looking a bit nervous.

"Oh, that's nice, dear. What were you guys studying?" Mom questions, looking between the both of us.

My father, I think, is actually enjoying seeing me squirm. He remains quiet with a smirk, looking back and forth between the three of us.

"He was just helping me with Psychology. This chapter was extremely hard!"

I put my schoolbooks and papers in my book bag and swing it over my shoulder.

"You don't have to leave on our account, dear," Mom tell us.

"No Mom, we're done. I can't store any more

information in my brain tonight. Sorry about the mess," I tell her. I give them both kisses on the cheeks, and Brent gives them a quick nod as we walk past them, towards my bedroom.

As I cross the threshold to my room, Brent pauses, looks behind him, and asks me if I'm sure this is okay with my parents.

"Brent, my parents trust me. Besides, it's not like we're going to be making out or anything," I almost regret saying this statement as soon as the words leave my mouth. I clear my throat and take a seat on my bed.

I watch as Brent slowly walks around my room, hands behind his back and curiosity overflowing. He stops to look at my collage, full of pictures, and chuckles at the one of my father and I with goofy faces. His fingers rub against the plaque from my dance recital that sits on my desk. And then Brent makes it over to my nightstand, sitting next to me on my bed. He picks up the picture of my parents and I from my younger years.

"How old were you in this picture?" he asks, still staring at it.

"I think I was about eight."

He puts the picture down and turns to look at me, face stern and serious, eyes full of hunger. I swallow, chest heaving, unable to break his gaze. "Why do you look at me like this?" I whisper, eyes still locked on his.

"I just feel this amazing, erotic connection to you. I've never felt it before. I've met a million women throughout my years, and none of them have come close to touching me the way you do."

"Brent..." My voice drifts off as he slowly comes closer. His face is only inches from mine and our breathing is now in sync. Just as our lips are about to touch, my bedroom door slams open.

"Hey, Rain—" Bailey turns towards the hall and then comes back in the room, obviously flabbergasted with

Shevaun DeLucia

what she almost just witnessed. "Whoa!"

"Shit!" I say, jumping up from my bed and rushing over to close my door.

"*So* you two, what is going on?" Bailey's eyes glare between Brent and I, mouth grinning from ear to ear. This is the moment she was hoping for—to catch us in the act. She couldn't stand the fact that I was keeping Brent from her, and now she's standing here gleaming with satisfaction.

"Bailey, this is Brent. Brent, this is my friend Bailey," I introduce them, taking a seat back on my bed, leaning my head against my headboard.

Brent already moved to the chair at my desk. "Hey, nice to meet you."

"And *very* nice to meet you, Brent," Bailey responds, still glowing.

Brent stands up, seeming uncomfortable, and says goodbye to both of us. As soon as we hear the front door close, Bailey immediately turns and faces me with accusing eyes.

"*What?*"

"What do you mean, 'What?' Raina, you're my best friend, and you couldn't even tell me?" Bailey asks angrily as she gets off my bed and paces across my floor.

"Bailey, there's nothing to tell!" I screech quietly.

I grab my nightclothes out of my dresser drawers and rip off my pants and shirt, strewing them on my floor.

"Bullshit, Raina! Were you not just here a minute ago when I walked in on you two?" Bailey shrieks in a whisper, throwing her hands in the air.

"Fine. Yes, you walked in on us *almost* kissing. But that's it! We are just friends. You probably just saved me from making a huge mistake," I admit. "By tomorrow, he'll probably realize it too."

Bailey takes a seat next to me on my bed. "Raina, why can't you see how beautiful you are? And I don't just mean physically. You're a beautiful person inside *and* out. I wish you could just see what the rest of us see. It's obvious Brent sees it too."

She wipes a tear that has escaped from my eye, and the moment we look at each other, we burst out laughing at the situation.

After Bailey leaves, I nestle up in my bed to read some of my book. I hear a quiet knock on my door. My father peeks his head in.

"Hey, Daddy."

"I just came in to say goodnight," my dad says, giving me a kiss on the forehead. "Your friend seems nice."

"He is, Daddy. Where's Mom?"

"She turned in early. Sleep tight," he says, closing the door behind him.

I bury myself deep down in my warm sheets and open my book again, but before I can read a sentence, my phone rings.

The number on my cell phone screen is Maddie's.

"Hey, Raina. Did you forget to call me?"

"Honestly, I totally did! I'm sorry!" I feel terrible.

I sit up to grab my laptop from the cubby hole in my nightstand. I power it on, go to my favorites, and pull up the page I saved.

"So, did you find anything?" I eagerly ask her.

"Wait! Before we talk about Jason, what in the heck in going on between you and that new kid?"

I knew this was coming, but I was hoping I could stall her just a little while until I could come up with something convincing. I asked Bailey not to say anything, but keeping this from Maddie is almost impossible.

"He's just a friend, Maddie, nothing else," I say so matter-of-factly.

"Raina, it doesn't look like he just wants to be your friend. The way he looks at you says everything *but* friends."

Shevaun DeLucia

They must be seeing something that I'm not.

"I don't want to talk about Brent anymore, okay?" I pick at the string on my comforter, waiting for her answer.

"Okay. So, what did you find out about Jason?" Maddie asks, changing the subject.

I scroll down the site on my laptop to the pictures of the Alexander paintings. "Not much. I just came across these paintings, but they're from the eighteen hundreds," I tell her, hoping she may have found something better.

"*Well*, I ended up getting Jason's middle name out of Jenna, and I did a couple of searches using his full name, Jason Edmund Alexander," Maddie explains with excitement.

"*And?*" I am dying to know what she came up with. My heart starts pumping like crazy with anticipation.

"When I first entered his name, I couldn't come up with anything but that Seinfeld dude. And then, I thought if someone wanted to blend in or be incognito, they might give out incorrect information. *So*, I played around with his name. I put in Jason Alex Edmund, and got no result. Then I switched it around some more until I actually came up with something," Maddie pauses.

"Oh my God, Maddie, you're making me nervous! What did you find?" I sit straight up in my bed, anticipating something crazy. Maybe he's been arrested for selling drugs, or I wonder if she found a picture of him on Facebook with a girlfriend!

"I came across this site, and it talks about some of the powerful families in Canadian history and the Alexanders are one of them. The thing is, I tried to research the history of the family and the lineage, and I found absolutely nothing, except the son of this family goes by the name of Edmund Jason Alexander."

I can't help but interrupt. "So what does that have to do with Jason?" I ask, aggravated.

"At first, I didn't think anything of it, but then I

came across a painting of this family and there he was: Edmund Jason Alexander," Maddie finishes, leaving me even more confused.

I stand up, pacing back and forth across my floor. "I still don't understand."

"Raina, when I looked at the picture, it was him!" Maddie screeches, voice in a high whisper.

"Him who?" I snap back, forehead creased with confusion, my hands flaring in the air.

"Jason!"

I sit for a moment, trying to comprehend what she is saying. This doesn't make any sense. Is she really trying to tell me that Jason has been alive for over a hundred years? No way! There has got to be something that she is missing. "Maddie, give me the website!" I demand, sitting Indian style on my bed, pulling my computer on my lap.

As I am typing in the site, I hear my doorknob turn and my door flings open.

"Raina, what's all this screaming about?" my father questions, seeming a little worried and annoyed.

"Oh shoot, Raina! Is that your dad?" Maddie asks. I ignore her for a moment.

"Oh sorry, Daddy. Maddie was just telling me some gossip," I lie, batting my eyes.

My father huffs with exasperation. "Try to be a little more quiet; your mother is sleeping."

"Sorry, Daddy. I will," I say in a sweet voice. My father closes my door after he finishes reprimanding me.

I quickly pull up the website and scroll to the picture she directs me to. "*Oh my God,* Maddie!" My mouth is hung open, eyes bulging. I slowly cover my mouth with my hand, utterly speechless.

Maddie senses my uneasiness. "Do you see it too?" She asks, still not believing it herself.

"I do, but this *has* to be one of his relatives," I say, running my hand through my hair, trying to convince

Shevaun DeLucia

myself as well as her.

The boy standing in the picture has the same hazel eyes and creamy skin. Stone-cold face and sun-streaked hair, just like Jason. But that's not possible; this would go against everything I was taught and everything I believe in. Similarities happen all the time from generation to generation. This is the only logical explanation. The man staring back at me is some distant relative.

"I don't know, Raina; they look identical! It's pretty creepy, if you ask me," Maddie says.

I switch back to the site I found with the Alexander paintings. "Do you think that these paintings were part of Jason's heritage, too?" I wonder, looking back through all of them.

"I don't know, Raina, but I just have an eerie feeling about all of this," she admits.

I close my laptop and push it aside. "I know, me too," I agree. "Let's just keep it between us for now, okay?"

"Okay, but don't you think we should at least show Jenna?"

"No, Maddie! I don't want her to say anything to Jason to tip him off. You know she tells him everything!" I remind her.

I get a beep announcing a text message. I take a quick peek at the name across the top of my phone, and it's from Brent.

"Maddie, I have to go. I'll see you at school tomorrow. Just remember, keep this between us." I reinforce what I just said so there's no confusion.

"Don't worry, Raina. I will. I promise," she pledges before she hangs up.

I immediately scroll through my text messages. The muscle in my chest is pumping a tad louder as I view my screen. Brent wishes me goodnight, and I reply the same to him. I throw my head back on my pillow, phone to my chest, eyes dazed with a goofy smile on my face. I'm not sure how after only two days my whole demeanor towards this boy has changed, but it has, and I'm scared shitless.

Shevaun DeLucia

# Chapter 5

The dew is now showing itself on blades of grass, while the morning air is turning thick and crisp, inching closer every day to winter. Leaves color the trees and speckle the streets, squirrels scurry across the ground, their mouths bulging with nuts in preparation for the long, cold winter ahead.

The heat has yet to be turned on in my house, and I recognize a cold chill running along my hardwood floor when I step out of bed in the morning. After I finish in the bathroom, I throw on a warm, snug hoodie before heading downstairs. My cell phone on my nightstand vibrates across the surface. My stomach twinges with a sinking feeling that Brent might be waiting outside. I glance out of my window, and there in my driveway is Brent's white Infinity. I take a deep breath before picking up my phone.

I press the answer button. Before I can speak, Brent is already talking.

"Before you say no, I was hoping maybe you would come with me after school," Brent says with excitement.

My eyebrows crease together, unsure. "*And* where would we be going?" I question, putting on my sneakers and grabbing my book bag to head downstairs.

"I want to show you a place that I like to spend time

at," he answers, quietly waiting for my response.

  Phone still to my ear, I head into the kitchen to take my vitamin. "Okay, why wait? Why not show me now?" I taunt, planting the idea of skipping school to see if he will take the bait.

  "You want to skip school?" I can hear the surprised tone in his voice. "I'm not sure that's such a good idea, Raina. I don't want to be the cause of you getting in trouble."

  Before I can respond, the doorbell rings. "Why didn't you just knock, silly?"

  I hang up the phone, open the door without greeting him, and walk back towards the kitchen. As I drink some orange juice to swallow my vitamin, Brent walks around the island I am standing behind. He stands behind me, placing his hands on the counter on either side of me.

  My back stiffens, immediately feeling the energy trapped between us. I can feel him chuckle behind me, obviously getting a kick out of my reaction.

  "What is so funny?" I question, aggravation boiling to the surface. I push his hand aside forcefully and turn to face him.

  "I like seeing you squirm," he admits, smiling from ear to ear, obviously pretty proud of himself. I cross my arms tightly across my chest, completely unamused with what he just said, still staring him down.

  "Listen Brent, we are keeping this completely platonic, okay?"

  Slowly he steps towards me, eyes never leaving mine. "What if I want to be more than platonic?" Brent asks, face stern and serious.

  I try to break his gaze but he softly grabs my chin, forcing me to look his way. "I told you—"

  "I don't care about your boyfriend, Raina. He's not even living in the same town as you. I'm here. Why don't you worry about what is in front of you?"

Shevaun DeLucia

I shift my weight from one foot to the other, trying my hardest to avoid his gaze. I place both hands on my hips. "How about you tell me about this girl you are still in love with first?" I know this will cause him to change the subject, just from his reaction to the topic yesterday. Also, a little part of me is interested in knowing about this girl who holds his heart.

"Well, um, let's just put it this way: I have feelings for a girl who doesn't have feelings for me. Can we now leave this subject alone? *Please?*"

Brent walks away, pain spread across his face, and goes out to the front porch. I stand in the kitchen alone, feeling guilty for pushing the subject. But there is something deep inside of me that needs to know about this girl—maybe for nothing other than peace of mind, or because a small part of me wants to know what I am up against. I follow him out to the porch to apologize for prying.

I stand behind him quietly, trying to find the words to use. "Brent, I'm sorr—" Before I can finish my sentence, he turns around and cuts me off.

"Shh. Please let me speak, Raina," he says, eyes looking to the ground before meeting mine. "Raina, when I'm with you, I'm not thinking of anyone else. And I promise someday I will tell you my story about this girl, okay?" He slumps down to look me straight in the eyes.

I gulp deeply and take a long breath in. "Agreed."

"Good. Now let's get in my car," Brent says, turning and walking towards the driveway.

I lock the door and head off for our adventure.


**W**e have been driving along the lake for about thirty minutes now. The music is playing in the background quietly, and Brent doesn't seem like he is interested in talking. I watch outside my passenger-side window, trees quickly flashing by with the colors of fall. Geese appear in the gray-blue sky, triangular in formation. Finally, the car turns onto a small side road.

I sit up and look out the windshield in front of me. Brent notices my interest and tells me that the road leads to a private beach.

"How did you find this place?" I ask, wide-eyed.

He parks the car on the dirt at the end of the road. "I was exploring when I first got into town. I love the water, so I followed the main road next to the lake out here, and something just told me to turn down this road. When I did, this is what I found. I spent a couple weekends here, expecting someone to find me and throw me off their property, but no one did."

"Where's the beach?" I ask, looking at the tree-covered surroundings.

Brent points to a tiny split in between the grass and trees. "See that opening?"

"Uh-huh," I say, nodding my head.

"We have to go through there."

He shuts off the engine, looks in my direction with a brief smile, and gets out of the car. I watch as he walks towards the trail, turns to look at me, still sitting in the car, and motions for me to join him.

I'm enjoying the view. The light filtering through the leaves hits his body just right, accentuating his cheekbones and masculine jawline. The corners of my mouth turn upwards with the quick thought of my lips pressed against his. As quickly as I picture this, I just as quickly shake my head, erasing the thought.

I shut the car door and follow him down the path. He holds his hand out for support, but I refuse it. I can't touch him. I won't give myself away. The more I spend time alone with him, the more I feel vulnerable and susceptible to his charm.

After five minutes of descending down the trail, we

Shevaun DeLucia

walk out to a beautiful view of the sun glistening across the water. Waves gently splash the surface of the beach. Mesmerized, I take a step beyond the trail and hear the stones crunching beneath my feet. Brent takes a seat on a piece of dried driftwood, patting the space beside him for me to sit.

"Wow, Brent, this is beautiful." I take a seat on the driftwood next to him.

We sit for a moment in silence. "When I first came here, the boat engines hummed across the water, causing the waves to smash against the rocks. But each weekend I came, the boats decreased in number and it became quieter, more composed," he adds, looking far into the distance.

"You said you came here for a couple of weeks— why didn't you start school earlier, then?"

A breeze picks up, causing me to shiver. Brent notices and wraps his arm around my shoulders. I freeze for a moment, unsure how to react.

He laughs but doesn't question my reaction to his touch. "I just needed to mentally prepare for what I was about to encounter," he responds, leaving me clueless as to what he means. It's obvious he sees the confusion on my face.

A small strand of hair comes loose across my face, and he gently tucks it behind my ear. "High school can be intense, especially being the focus of everyone's attention. So I asked my aunt for some 'me' time, to get a handle on myself. Lillian's very understanding when it comes down to it. She knew I wouldn't have asked if I didn't need it," he finishes, rubbing my arm to warm it.

"You're definitely right about that one. Being the focus is what I've always tried to avoid. I think it's better to remain a question rather than an obvious answer like Casey."

Brent shakes his head and laughs again. "Raina, you always seem to surprise me." I lean in a bit more, feeling

Eternal Mixture

the heat emanating off of him.

"Well, I'm happy to do something other than bore you," I joke.

"Bore me? I don't think that is possible." He pulls me in, his chin now resting on top of my head. "You fascinate me."

"Well, I think that's a first," I chuckle. "You know what fascinates me?"

"What's that?" Brent wonders while taking in the scent of my hair.

"The possibility of past lives. Sometimes I feel a strong sense of déjà vu, like something or someone feels so familiar to me."

I feel Brent's muscles immediately tense up. I can tell I've said something he was not expecting, and he looks a little shocked. Before I can even question him about it, he appears more at ease.

"So, you believe you may have had a past life?"

I take a long deep breath, getting lost in his scent. Brent's smell is so invigorating and familiar to me, yet so distant. Our bodies are tangled together and the energy flowing between the two of us is igniting some sort of far-away memory that I can't see but I can feel.

"Yes, I feel like it could definitely be a possibility."

Brent squeezes me then removes his arm from around me. "Are you ready to get going?" he asks, stretching his arms out in front of him.

"Did I say something to offend you?" I ask, feeling the energy between us shift.

"No, of course not! I just thought maybe you wanted to go somewhere a little warmer," Brent says with a mischievous smile.

"Oh, okay." I smile, standing up to follow him to the path. "Where do you want to go?"

"I was thinking maybe my house? My aunt is working and won't be home until later tonight," Brent states as we head up the trail. The trail is filled with roots from the trees; my foot slips and my palm catches my fall.

"Ouch!" I yell as I push myself off of my hands. I look at my right palm, which now bears a small scrape with blood. I snap my head up towards Brent, praying he didn't just see that.

"Raina, are you okay?" Brent asks as he rushes to my side. "Did you hurt yourself?" he questions, worried. He grabs for my hand, but I yank it away and place it behind my back. I can't let him see my hand just yet.

I have a small gift. It's something I've never quite fully understood and something that I'm slightly afraid to question. For as long as I can remember, my wounds have always healed within a matter of seconds. I've never had any serious injuries other than a scratch or two, so I really don't know how to explain it. I'm afraid if he sees this, he might run in the other direction.

"I'm fine!" I huff, rolling my eyes.

He stands in front of me, looking towards the hand I am holding behind my back. "You're not fine, I just saw blood on your palm," Brent insists, again grabbing for my hand.

"Brent, *please*! I'm fine. See, no blood," I try to convince him, holding up my palm, lips spread in a half-hearted smile.

He continues to stare at my palm, rubbing his thumb over my soft, unscathed skin. "You were bleeding. I saw it with my own eyes, Raina." He looks up from my palm with inquiring eyes.

Aww shit! He saw! I take a deep breath and rip my hand from his grip, walking past him to head up the trail. "I told you I was fine, and I was *not* bleeding, obviously," I lie, turning around before I get to the car door. I face Brent, holding both my palms up in the air.

He smiles, amused, and unlocks the car from the button on his keychain. Brent hops in the car, causing the air surrounding him to swirl. I close my eyes to take in his sweet aroma. It calms me. I open my eyes, half-expecting Brent to continue questioning me about my hurt palm, but instead he is staring at me, mystified. He shakes his head softly, smiling to himself, and starts the car.

Shevaun DeLucia

# Chapter 6

After a quiet ride to Brent's house, we pull into his driveway. His house is pushed back from the road, trees and bushes camouflaging the exterior. Inside is small and bare, reeking with the fact that they have just moved in.

"Are you hungry?" Brent asks, walking in towards the kitchen.

The kitchen is U-shaped with maple wood cabinets, blue countertops and white appliances. Pretty basic. "Um, not yet," I say, standing with my back against the counter.

Brent throws his keys on the counter, grabs an apple from the fruit bowl, and heads out of the kitchen, nudging his head for me to follow. "We're not going in the living room?" I ask, following him down the hall while looking back at the couches as they appear farther and farther away.

"No, we're going to my room; there's a nice, comfy bed in here," Brent says, looking back at me with a grin on his face, waiting for my reaction.

I stand outside his bedroom door for a moment, looking in. "Uh, I don't know what kind of girls you have dealt with in the past, but I am not one of *those* girls," I warn him, making sure we are crystal clear.

Brent laughs, grabbing the remote. "Raina, I was just messing with you. But, we do have to sit on my bed to

Eternal Mixture

watch a movie. We don't have a TV in the living room yet," he explains, spreading himself out. He places his hand behind his head and turns on the TV with the remote.

I step into his room—still feeling as though he might have another agenda—and take a seat on the *very* edge of his bed. The TV on the opposite wall is enormous—fit for a king.

"You can get comfortable; I promise I won't bite," Brent jokes. "What kind of movies do you like watching?" he asks, flipping through the new releases on On Demand.

I usually watch the gushy romance movies, but there is no way I am telling him that. "I like action movies," I lie.

"Okaaay," Brent says, dragging the word out. "Action it is, then."

The next hour and a half is uncomfortably intense. The energy surging between our bodies is indescribable, and each time Brent looks my way, my muscles tense up. It is taking everything I have not to turn towards him right now. If I follow through, he may end up being my first kiss, and I'm not ready to share that with him just yet. It's not that a first kiss has ever been important to me, but the longer I have waited, the more I feel it should be with someone worth sharing it with *and* someone who won't laugh if I'm actually a horrible kisser.

The movie finally comes to an end. "Wow, that was an intense movie," Brent says, sitting up and stretching out his arms.

"Intense is right," I comment under my breath.

Brent snickers. "What did you just say?" He obviously heard.

"Nothing!" I reply quickly. "Denzel Washington is always good in his movies."

"He is definitely a good actor," Brent agrees. "I'm starving. You hungry yet?" he asks, scooting himself off the bed.

I get off the bed and follow him down the hall. "I could definitely eat something. What are you gonna make?"

"I've got some sandwich meat," Brent looks into the refrigerator. "Ham or turkey?"

"I'll take ham."

I wonder how many other girls he has brought to his house and played the respectful 'I want to be just friends' role. In fact, I wonder how many girlfriends he's had altogether.

"How many girlfriends have you had?" I blurt out without warning.

Brent's eyes widen in shock. "Whoa! That question's a little out of left field," he responds, shaking his head. "We went from ham to *this*?"

He taps his finger on his chin while looking up, as if in deep thought. "So that many, huh?" It's obvious he is stalling and doesn't want to scare me away.

"I've had to keep myself occupied," Brent says, bringing both our sandwiches and chips to the table.

"Occupied? Occupied from what, school?" I say, laughing. I fill my mouth with sandwich.

"That, and to make the time and the years go by faster," Brent answers, then takes a huge bite of his sandwich.

To make the years go by faster? He's only eighteen. He acts as though he's fifty years old. I let that answer sink in a bit as I work on the sandwich. We both glance up at each other periodically as though we each want to say something, but we don't.

"Okay, so I've dated some girls. What about you? Other than the boyfriend you have now?" Brent questions, scrutinizing my face.

I finish chewing my sandwich. "There was no one before Josh," I tell him. He seems relieved as he cracks a small smile.

Eternal Mixture

"So, only one boyfriend?"

I roll my eyes. "Yes, only one. Is that so hard to believe? I've never been a hormone-crazed teen." The truth is that no one was ever interested.

"Have your parents met your boyfriend?"

"No, actually you're the first boy I have brought home, remember?" I remind him.

He just looks up at me, eyes twinkling, and gets up from the table and cleans off our plates. I finally receive a text from Bailey, wondering where I am. I can either lie and get caught because I am a horrible liar, or I can tell the truth and deal with her line of questioning for the next hour.

I take the truth route and text her back.

"Hey, I'm at Brent's house. We skipped," I write, waiting for the interrogation to begin. Brent looks at me, curiously.

I hold my phone up. "It's Bailey. She's wondering where I am," I tell him, without him having to ask.

The light on my phone blinks, indicating a new text. And I was right; Bailey sent me a million questions in one text. "You skipped school with Brent? What are you guys doing? OMG, it's just you and Brent there alone? Did you kiss him?" And so on.

"What are you going to tell her?" Brent asks, taking a seat next to me at the table.

I finish texting her back. "I just told her we're hanging—no big deal. And to keep it to herself and that I will call her tonight."

"You think she is going to tell anyone else?"

"No! When I tell Bailey not to say anything, she won't say anything. *But,* if I don't say those magic words, she knows its fair game," I say with a laugh.

"Well, at least she knows her boundaries as a friend," Brent says. "But, what I want to know is, what are our boundaries as friends?"

I was not expecting to have to answer this. And as

Shevaun DeLucia

the seconds go by, a million different answers fly through my head.

I mimic him, tapping my finger on my chin while looking up. "Um, I don't know. What do you think our boundaries should entail?" I ask, trying to put the question back on him.

"Oh, no! I asked you the question first. Nice try, though," he snickers, shaking his finger at me.

I take a deep breath and exhale, forcefully. "Okay, I don't really want to make any lines between us yet, other than we are friends. And we should act and do as friends do."

He sits back down. "You know there are such things as friends with benefits," Brent comments. I automatically smack him on the shoulder, and he laughs loudly. "Okay, okay, I was just joking!"

I decide to joke back with him and slowly lean into him, entwining my legs with his, my knees rubbing against the seam in between his pants. I move in extremely close, my face only inches from his, our breath is jagged and his eyes are wild. I reach up and slide my fingers lazily down his cheekbone, staring him dead in the eyes. He gulps harshly but continues to gaze back, slowly inching closer to me until I smile and begin to giggle. He abruptly backs up, steaming with anger, face stern, refusing to laugh along with me.

"Aww, come on! I was just messing with you. You deserved it, admit it!" I tell him, still laughing.

Brent gets up and picks his car keys up from the counter. "Are you ready to go home?" he asks, his face still harsh and jaw clenched.

My heart drops. The tension and animosity I feel spewing out of him is catching me off-guard. He's joking with me one second, but when I joke with him, this is what I get in response? It makes no sense to me.

"Are you serious? You're really this upset with

Eternal Mixture

me?"

I get up and follow him out towards the living room. He can't even seem to look me in the face. Before he grabs the front door, he stops and turns around to me abruptly.

"Raina, you just don't understand how long I have been waiting for this, *for you*, and I may joke at times, but what you did just put me over the edge. It was no longer a joke to me, it felt real. And then when you laughed, it tore me apart," Brent says, letting me in just a little more.

"Brent, I'm sorry. Really, I was just getting you back for joking with me. Please don't be upset with me," I beg.

He stands there, looking broken-hearted, and it crushes me. I do the only other thing I can think of and embrace him in my arms. I wrap myself around his body tightly, and his arms embrace me back. I feel his fingers running through my hair as his arms squeeze me tight.

"Do you forgive me then?" I question, lifting my head up from his warm chest to look at his face. I desperately need his forgiveness.

"Yes, I forgive you," he says, light-heartedly. "I didn't mean to turn things so dark and intense on our third day of getting to know each other. I just got you back," he tells me, whispering the last part under his breath.

I heard him; every word is sinking down to my very core. There's something here that is so familiar, yet I don't know if it is his words, his touch, or his scent that is awakening it. I know my body knows something that I don't or that I can't remember, and it's scaring the hell out of me.

"I'm ready to go home now," I say to him quietly.

He gives me one last squeeze and we walk out the door. Brent has the music blasting on the way home, leaving no need for talking. I'm guessing this was done on purpose.

Shevaun DeLucia

We pull into my driveway. It's still early and I would normally just be ending my last period class. I'm really not in the mood to sit in my house alone today, but I feel Brent's energy is depleted and he needs a break from me. I give Brent a quick wave goodbye as he does the same, and I watch him drive off before I enter my house. I close the door behind me and stand there for a moment, looking around, taking in the stillness. I decide I am *not* staying here. So I turn around and head back out the door.

I pull up to Maddie's house and ring the doorbell. Her parents won't be home for another hour or so.

Maddie opens the door. "OMG, Raina! Where have you been?" she screeches, hugging me tightly. "I thought maybe you were home sick, so I didn't want to bother you," she tells me, moving to the side to let me in.

I follow her up the stairs to her bedroom. We both plop down and sprawl out on top of her queen-size bed. Maddie's room is very girlie; pink and black polka dots cover her walls and comforter. Tons of pictures of all of us girls are hung up in pink sparkly frames, and candles in every corner give off a sweet fragrance.

"I actually spent the day with Brent," I tell her, waiting for her to spaz out.

Her eyes grow wide. "Are you serious? I can't believe you spent the day with him! *But* more than anything, I can't believe he got you to skip school!"

"That ... was actually my idea," I admit, squeezing my eyes closed, afraid to look at her.

"Who *are* you?" Maddie says, giggling. "And what has he done with my Raina?"

For some odd reason, I feel a little protective over the details of my day. Almost like our time together won't mean as much or I'll be betraying Brent if I share it with an outsider. But it's *so* hard to keep things from Maddie. She

Eternal Mixture

understands me more than anyone. Bailey and I have been friends the longest and have a very strong bond, but with Maddie, it's different. I don't have to say a word, she just knows what I'm thinking or feeling, and right now my emotions are everywhere.

I look up at her, and she must see the conflict on my face. "Raina, it's okay. You can tell me how your day went when you're ready. All I want to know is how you feel about him," she questions, obviously sensing my dilemma.

"I actually like him a lot, Maddie. And it scares the shit out of me, because I barely know him," I tell her. I just don't mention the part about something deep inside that feels like I should know him or I *already* do know him.

"Then go with it, Raina. You deserve to be happy, *and* he's really hot!"

We both giggle while we reminisce about our many school-girl crushes. All the boys I've come across have been so plain compared to Brent. He just has this presence about him that's different, and my body is drawn to him like a magnet. Resisting him is unbelievably hard. It feels unnatural, and I don't want to fight it any longer. Maybe Maddie is right, I *should* just go with it.

"You know what, Maddie? I think you're right. I'm going all in with him," I decide, smiling with excitement for what tomorrow might bring.

Maddie gives me the biggest hug and we screech together like little girls.

"Hey, have you talked to Jenna at all?"

"No, why?" she answers, grabbing her book bag to remove her homework. Aww crap! Now I'm going to have double the homework tomorrow, I totally forgot!

"We haven't talked since Billards. She used to call me every day."

"Have you tried calling her, though?"

I know exactly where she is going with this. "No, and I already know what you're gonna say. Since she's gotten closer to Jason, I feel her and I have gotten farther apart," I say.

"Then just call her and talk to her. Tell her how you feel. I know she will understand."

"I'll talk to her tomorrow at school. So what's the new gossip around school?" I question, knowing since both Brent and I were missing, someone had to have said something.

"Well, I hear Casey has a thing for Brent."

I stand up from the bed. My heart sinks. I walk over to her window, feeling agitated and a little worried. Casey always gets what she wants, and now she wants the one person I feel belongs to me and I belong to him. A part of me keeps saying to give up while I'm ahead, but the other part wants to fight—go to all lengths to keep him from her.

"Of course she does. I could see it written all over her face in history class yesterday," I confess, biting on my nail.

"Raina, I wouldn't worry about her. From what I can see, Brent only has eyes for you," she tries to convince me. But I know better. Last year, Casey went after my crush, Josh, almost like she knew I had a thing for him, and of course she came out the winner. There's never been any competition when it comes to her and I.

"Yeah, well, I guess we'll see."

"Just don't think about it right now, Raina. She's only ever about one thing anyway, and most guys just run right through her, if you know what I mean," Maddie says, trying to make me feel better.

"Um, that *so* does not help me!" I gripe, throwing my arms in the air.

Maddie covers her mouth, realizing what she just said. "Oops, you're right. I'm sorry!" she apologizes, face distorted, knowing my heart aches from her comment.

"It's okay," I tell her. "So, what's Bailey up to?" I try to change the subject to wipe Brent and Casey from my mind, but no such luck.

"I'm not sure. I think she had to go to dinner with her parents tonight."

I finally sit back down on her bed to help her with some of her homework. A couple hours go by and it's now past dinner time. I leave her house and head home.

My house is pitch black as I pull up my driveway. It's seven and my parents are still not home from work yet. I enter the house, turning all the lights on as I go. I feel like a dark house takes on a personality of its own: floors creaking, windows settling and trees rustling against the exterior make it feel alive. Most kids my age would love the fact that their parents were still not home, but I enjoy my parents company and I miss them. I've spent way too many nights alone and have had too many frozen dinners in a week's time to enjoy the house by myself. With the lights on, I feel a little more at ease.

Tonight, I am turning in early. I undress, placing my clothes on a chair, and throw on my sweats. I take out my laptop, click to my favorites page and pull up the painting of the blue lake. I feel so connected to this place. The energy lulls me to sleep, and this is the last thing I remember before my dreams take over.

Shevaun DeLucia

# Chapter 7

This morning, I wake up energized and excited. Today is the day I plan on telling Brent that I want to try being more than just friends with him. I need as much confidence as I can scrape up today, so it's crucial I look my best.

I take my time, spending each minute meticulously painting my face and curling my hair. I choose my outfit carefully, wanting to put out sex-kitten-meets-controlled-virgin vibes in hopes he might see me as girlfriend material.

I check my phone periodically to see if Brent has texted me like he has been every morning, but I find nothing. Weird. He said he forgave me for joking with him, but now I wonder if he may have been just trying to appease me.

I make sure to take my vitamin before I leave, and by the time I get to school, the first bell has already rung. I run down the hall and make it to class just as the teacher is about to close the door.

I reach my seat—out of breath—and set my book bag down. When I look over to Bailey, I see she is grinning from ear to ear. I never called her last night, and I know she is absolutely dying to hear about what happened between Brent and I yesterday. I shake my head, face the front of the room, and wait for the inevitable.

A tiny piece of paper ricochets off my head. And there it is. I look over at Bailey. "What are you doing?" I whisper.

"You never even called me last night," she mouths.

I look up towards the teacher to make sure her attention is not on us. Mrs. Liberty is busy adding math examples to the board. I turn back to Bailey. "I'm sorry. I was at Maddie's, then went home and went to bed."

Bailey rolls her eyes at me. "You had the most important day in pretty much your whole life, and you're too tired to *call me*?" Bailey whispers, extremely loud.

"Girls, is there something you want to share with the class?" Mrs. Liberty asks, walking down the aisle towards us.

My face burns red. "No," I tell her. Bailey also shakes her head. Behind me to the left, I can hear Janet blabbing something to her friend Elisa about us. "Yeah, they want to share that they are losers," she says, loud enough for me to hear.

Mrs. Liberty turns back around, spewing math equations out as if she never stopped. I grab my notebook and quickly begin scribbling my notes down. I see Bailey in my peripheral view, trying to get my attention again.

I slightly turn my head just enough to look at her. "What?" I mouth again, annoyed this time.

"Did you kiss him?" I can see the anticipation is killing her.

I shake my head, and the excitement that was just on her face a moment ago has now turned to disappointment. She leans her body against her desk lazily, places her head against her hand, and pretends to *suddenly* be interested in Mrs. Liberty's math lecture. I know she thinks I'm lying, but I believe she will be able to tell the difference in my presence when I do kiss someone for the first time. It will be written all over my face, and she won't have to ask; she'll just know.

After class ends, we walk through the hall together. I tell her bits and pieces from yesterday, but leave out the parts that I feel are most intimate. The hall is packed, continuous noise passing by from one conversation to another, and as I pass by Brent's locker, my mouth drops and my heart slams to the ground.

I see Brent hovering over Casey at his locker. Their faces are only inches apart. They look like lovers in deep conversation, as if the rest of the world doesn't exist. She bats her eyes, and he grins mischievously at her. Time and everything around me slows, and my heartbeat bangs like thunder in my ears as everyone disappears except the three of us. My worst fear has come true. I feel broken, betrayed, and empty. He's so deep in thought with her that he can't even feel me behind him. I thought we had this special bond, a connection only shared between us. I was obviously wrong and should have stuck with my initial gut feeling: people like Brent don't end up with people like me. If so, the world would be thrown out of alignment.

The noise of life comes rushing back to me in full speed, engulfing me like a tsunami. I look over at Bailey, and I see pain and anger stamped across her face as she watches them and then looks back at me. A small tear falls down my left cheek, and before Brent or anyone else can witness my pathetic display of heartbreak, I turn and dash to the first bathroom I can find.

I snap around and lock the door without a second thought. Lucky for me, no one is inside. I stand in disbelief for a moment, numb and in excruciating, debilitating agony. The pain slashes through my heart like a sword, twisting and puncturing every part of my body, penetrating me to the core. I finally let out a breath—not realizing I was holding it in this entire time—and collapse to my knees

Eternal Mixture

in body spasms. I want to crawl into the darkest hole I can find and die. There's a faint pounding on the door behind me and Bailey's calling my name, but I can't catch my breath enough to answer her. Sobs come crashing over me in waves.

I saw this coming. I knew he would end up going for her; I just had a glimmer of hope that maybe he would be different. I can't understand why this happened to me the second I decided to let him in. I felt as though he was trying for days to get me to open up, but for what? To crush me into a million pieces? I gather enough strength to stand up and let Bailey in. I don't know how long I have been locked in here, but it feels like days have passed.

She pushes the door open, then locks it. "Oh, Raina!" She embraces me tightly. "He is such an asshole!" she screeches.

I must look like a fool. I've spent the last couple of days denying him to myself as well as my friends, and here I am, having a complete breakdown from the sight of him and Casey together. I am weak for allowing him to touch me in this way. I won't allow it to happen again. From this moment on, I will close myself to him. I will lock my heart up and throw away the key.

"I'm sorry. I don't know what got into to me," I tell her, wiping the tears from my face.

Bailey unhinges herself from me and gets me a paper towel. "Don't apologize. He was obviously leading you on, being a complete douchebag!" she says angrily.

I shake my head. "I was going to tell him how I feel about him," I sniffle. "I guess it's a good thing I didn't, huh?" I ask, laughing a bit.

Bailey wipes the tears from my cheeks. "He doesn't deserve you, Raina."

I look into the mirror, and I see a complete mess looking back. "How am I supposed to go to class now?" I turn towards her and point at my face.

Bailey wets another paper towel with cold water. "Here, put this over your face to help the swelling in your eyes," she says in a motherly manner.

We wait in the bathroom until the next bell rings.

By the time lunch comes, I am conflicted about where I should go. The library is most likely the first place Brent will come to look for me, so I decide to take my chances and head into the lunchroom.

I enter through the back doors, scan the room before entering, and head to my table.

Maddie and Jenna look as if they have seen a ghost. "Raina!" Maddie screeches. "I feel like I haven't seen you in ages!"

I shake my head. "Maddie, I was just at your house last night," I respond, laughing. I look over at Jenna. "Hey, Jenna."

"Hi," she says coldly, turning back towards Maddie to finish their conversation. Bailey snaps a quick glance at me and then shrugs her shoulders.

"Jenna, what's going on? Are you still upset with me about questioning Jason?" I ask, leaving no way for her to ignore me.

She gives me the evil eye. "You've changed, Raina. I don't know who you are lately," she says, purposely trying to get a reaction from me. I decide to play it cool today. The last thing I need to do is make a scene; I don't want to welcome the attention.

"I'm not sure how it's possible to change in only a couple of days. You're not making any sense, Jenna."

"Jenna, don't you think you're going overboard with this?" Maddie asks in my defense.

Jenna looks at Maddie as if she is the enemy. "No, Maddie. I don't! I love Jason, and Raina is going to drive him away from me if she keeps acting like a psycho!"

I have no idea where this is coming from, and I know for a fact it is not coming from my friend. I feel like

Jason is filling her head with things, coercing her to act like this out of fear of losing him. Maybe he's scared I can see right through him and thinks I might try to dig up his past, which makes me *more* intrigued than anything.

"Uh, sorry to break it to you, but you're the one acting like a psycho!" Maddie jabs back. "Jenna, you and Raina have been friends for a long time now. Why are you letting a man come between that? She was only trying to get to know him."

"Jenna, I don't want to fight with you," I admit.

Before Jenna can respond, Bailey's eyes nearly pop out of her head.

"What's the matter with you?" I ask her, about to follow her gaze. "No, Raina! Don't you dare turn your head!" she orders.

"Um, why?" I ask, confused.

Jenna gets up, pushing her chair in with a huff. "I'm outta here," she says.

I watch her walk away and my heart twinges with pain. No matter what, I love Jenna and I hate her being upset at me. I am going to fix this somehow, even if it kills me.

"I can't believe him!" Maddie chimes in under her breath.

"Okay, what the hell is going on?" I question them both, hands in the air. I decide to ignore Bailey's attempt to keep me in the dark and turn around.

Here it is, right in front of me again: the sight I was trying to avoid. Brent is sitting at Casey's lunch table, laughing with her and her friends. The boys at the table seem to enjoy Brent's company, while the girls are hanging on his every word. Casey, sitting right by his side and twirling her hair in an attempt to look cute, is making me nauseous.

My heart aches. Before I turn away, his eyes meet mine. It's strange. For a split moment, I can almost see remorse in his eyes. But in the next moment, they fall cold. His attention goes back to his table of new friends as though I don't exist.

"Raina, I'm sorry. I didn't want you to see that again," Bailey says, shaking her head grimly.

Maddie just holds my hand, not saying a word. "I'm okay," I say with a small smile. "It just wasn't meant to be. I thought I knew him, but I was wrong. I mean, what was I thinking? I've only known him a couple of days. I can't really blame him. It's not like he actually came out and said he wanted to be with me."

"Raina, don't you make excuses for him! You have every right to be mad at him!" Bailey expresses boldly.

Thank God the bell rings and everyone in the cafeteria jumps up and heads out the doors. Through my peripheral vision, I see Brent walk out the main doors, so I take the back.

Bailey heads off to her class, but Maddie stops me and pulls me to the side.

She looks around before speaking. "Raina, did you notice anything different about Jenna today?" Maddie asks, face full of worry.

"Other than her wacko mood swing?" I joke.

"No, under her eyes look dark, kind of bruised, and her cheekbones are more protruded," Maddie explains. Now that I think of it, she's right. I didn't notice it because I was so caught up in the ruthless comments spouting from her mouth.

"Yeah, I guess you're right. Do you think she's been fighting with Jason? She looks as though she hasn't slept in days."

As a matter of fact, as long as I've known Jenna, her face has always been flawless. And she and I have never once gotten in any sort of altercation, until now.

"I don't know, Raina, but I just have a gut feeling something isn't right," she admits.

Eternal Mixture

The next bell rings. We both look around, realizing the halls are empty and it is just her and I standing alone. "I guess we still have some research to do then," I reply. "We're gonna be late though. Call me when you get home!" I yell to her as I run in the other direction.

**I** run into the locker room to change for gym. The last of the girls are running out toward the gymnasium. I open my lock and slam my book bag and clothes into the locker, jumping into my shorts and yanking my T-shirt over my head as I rush towards the door.

Gym class is definitely the last on my list of favorites. Today is a wild card day and dodgeball won the most votes. A fast ball thrown at my body is not my idea of fun. Our gym teacher, Mrs. Taff, splits the boys and girls up into even teams. One blow of the whistle gives us permission to turn animalistic. In the next moment, balls coming flying at me from all directions. I get struck in the leg, and I'm immediately called out. I hurry to the sideline with my hands over my head, trying not to be pelted again.

I look up at the big clock on the cement wall and realize I am only minutes away from coming face to face with Brent. Suddenly, I would rather place myself in the line of fire with a million balls rather than go into my next class.

The bell rings and I trudge into the locker room, change, and head out into the crowded hall. My chest is pounding through my shirt, and my palms are shaky and clammy. I feel acid churn and burn in my stomach with each step closer to my next class. I walk through the threshold, and I still feel this magnetic pull towards him. He is the negative, and I am the positive. We're made perfectly to fit, but why did he all of a sudden change his mind? What did I do that was so bad yesterday to deserve this type of punishment from him?

Shevaun DeLucia

I make sure to look past him as I walk down the aisle to my seat. I continually repeat "He doesn't exist" in my head to keep me from looking at him directly. Unfortunately, I can't fool my body. I can feel his energy radiating off of him, my body trying to compel me to him. I close my eyes, take a deep breath in, and slowly exhale, trying to compose myself and force his energy away from me.

Class is dragging. If I have to sit here for one minute longer, watching Casey twirl her hair and bat her eyes at Brent, I'm going to projectile vomit all over her. As soon as Mr. Jones scribbles our homework on the board, the final bell rings. I jump up from my seat and storm towards the door, leaving no trace of me behind.

I feel like my legs are betraying me because they won't move fast enough. I just want to get into my car and drive—leave this place behind and never come back.

Eternal Mixture

# Chapter 8

I pull up my driveway and see my mother's car. I wonder if something may be wrong, because she is never home at this time. Usually, she will call me to give me a heads up if she is coming home early, but today I received no call. I have to admit, this makes me a little worried.

I walk in the door, feeling anxious, and immediately I get hit with the delicious smell of warm cookies with melted chocolate chips, my favorite since I was a little girl. Confusion sets in.

"Mom?" I yell, walking down the hall into the kitchen.

"Oh hey, honey," she replies, getting the cookies out of the oven. "How was your day at school?"

I watch her set down the sheet pan. "Mom, is everything okay? You usually call me when you're coming home early," I say, grabbing a hot, gooey cookie as she places it on the plate.

"I just wanted to surprise you. I thought maybe we could cook some dinner and watch a movie together before Dad gets home," she says, watching me inhale one cookie after another.

My eyes brighten up and my smile reaches ear to

ear with excitement. This is rare; there are very few evenings that I get to spend alone with my mother.

"So, what should we cook?"

She opens the fridge and pulls out some chicken and lettuce. "I was thinking we can season this chicken and make a nice, big salad. How about you make the salad, and I'll stir fry the chicken?"

"Sounds good!"

I get up from the barstool and dig into the fridge, grabbing the tomatoes, cucumber, and feta cheese. "Hey, Mom?"

"Yes?"

"Is everything okay?" I ask her, feeling like there's an ulterior motive behind all of this.

She looks up at me, eyes a little sad and tired, while she cuts up the chicken. "You can always read right through me," she admits, shaking her head. "Your Dad and I are working real hard on this special project. We're so close to a breakthrough, but yet so far away. It's just putting a lot of stress on us, because this particular project is very dear and important to us," she tells me.

I can now see the dark circles under her eyes, but the rest of her face still remains flawless as always. I see other mothers, most wearing the wrinkles that the stresses of life leave, but my mother does not. She reminds me of a porcelain doll. Occasionally, I'll ask her how she manages to stay so young and vibrant looking, and see tells me it's all in the skincare. Yet she owns no products.

I continue to rip apart the lettuce. "Is there anything I can help with?" I offer while filling the salad bowl.

"Oh dear, you've helped more than you know," she says, placing the chicken into the skillet. "Just your understanding of the time and energy that Dad and I have to put into work is more than enough," she says, adoringly. "Did you take your vitamin this morning, honey?"

I look up at her, cutting the tomatoes and

Eternal Mixture

cucumbers, "*Yes!*" I answer, agitated. I still feel there is
something far deeper than what she is telling me. I finish
the salad, Mom dumps the chicken on top, and we sit down
at the table to eat.

"Dad's still at the lab?" I ask, taking a big forkful of
salad.

"Yeah, he'll be there for a couple more hours.
Maybe this weekend we can go to dinner. I'll see if Dad
can take a couple hours off," Mom states before taking a
bite of chicken.

I finish chewing. "That sounds good. There's a new
Italian place that just opened up, Bailey and her parents
went there yesterday. She said it was really good."

"That sounds delicious! I could go for some
Italian," she agrees as she takes the last bite off of her plate.

"Mom, can you tell me the story of how you and
Dad met again?" I ask her. It's been a while since I heard
the story. "*Please?*"

She grabs the plates as she gets up and places them
in the sink. I grab the rest while Mom puts the dirty dishes
in the dishwasher. She remains quiet for what seems like an
eternity before she responds to me.

"It seems like a million lifetimes ago when your
father and I met. Maybe another time, dear. I'm tired. We
should get started on that movie," she replies, brushing me
off. It's not like my mother to refuse a story. Ever since I
was little, she's found great joy in storytelling. Every night
before bed, I would beg her to tell me a tale. She would
think real hard, then ramble out the most beautiful
fairytales, sinking me into a deep sleep.

I decide tonight that I'm not going to argue with
her. "Okay, Mom," I answer with a smile. "I was thinking
maybe we can watch an old favorite: *Dirty Dancing*?"

My mother smiles brightly. "That sounds perfect!"
she says with delight.

I put the movie in and sit down on the couch with

Shevaun DeLucia

her, grabbing a blanket to keep us warm. I look over to her, wanting to tell her about my feelings for Brent. I'm not quite sure how she will react, though, since I've never really talked to her about boys.

I take a small breath in and just blurt out my question. "How did you know that Dad was the one for you?"

My mother's eyebrows lift up immediately with surprise. She clears her throat. "Well, it took him a little while to get my heart. Back when we were younger, it was called 'courting.' First, he had to gain the trust of my parents, then he had to get their approval, and last he had to steal my heart. Which, between you and I, wasn't that hard to do. Your father was very easy on the eyes," she says. "What's this all about, Raina?"

I begin nibbling on my lips with nervousness. I'm still on the fence about whether I should tell my mother, but I am going to go with my gut feeling and just spit it out. "I have feelings for someone, and I came so close to telling him until I saw him talking to this girl I can't stand. Now I don't know what to think," I confess, waiting anxiously for her response.

"What makes you think he likes this girl? Maybe there was a good reason for their conversation. Did you ask him?"

"No, but it was the *way* they were talking. The closeness. *And* the fact that he told me he couldn't stand her. Then the next thing I know, they're sitting with each other at lunch!" I blurt out, exasperated.

My mom takes a moment to choose her words. She often does this when she wants to make sure to get her point across. "Raina, there must be some reason why you have fallen for this boy. I know you, and you don't just give your heart away. My advice to you is to give it some time. Don't jump to any conclusions without talking to him, and believe. If it is meant to be, it will be. You are an

Eternal Mixture

*amazing* girl with a remarkable soul, and only a boy worthy enough will realize that," she finishes. She gives me a kiss on the forehead and then presses play on the remote.

My mother *always* provides words of wisdom that allow me to see clearer. She's right; if it is meant to be, it will be. I'm going to keep my distance from him, though. If he doesn't have the same feelings towards me that I do for him, then the last thing I want to be is a nuisance.

I look at the clock as the credits roll, and it is now seven. My dad's still not home yet. I feel like it has been days since I've seen him, and my mother must see the anguish all over my face.

"He misses you too, you know. He hates working these hours, but, honey, I promise he is doing this all for you," she says.

"I know, Mom. I just miss him," I reply, giving her a hug as a tear falls down my cheek. I may miss my parents, but I know I'm grateful to still have parents, unlike Brent. I would take my situation over his any day. "I'm going to do some homework in my room," I tell her, giving her a kiss on the cheek.

"Okay, dear. Let me know if you need anything. I'm going to turn in early."

I run up the stairs, skipping every other step, and close my door quietly. I can't concentrate on my homework at the moment, because there is just too much going through my head. Spending time with my mom almost made me forget about my run-in with Jenna at lunch today, which makes me think of Jason.

There has got to be some books on this Alexander family, and it's still early enough to go to the library, which gives me an idea. I get my cell phone out of my book bag and dial Maddie's number.

Her ringtone plays. "Hello?" she answers.

"Maddie, meet me at the library!" I demand.

"Now?" she asks, confused.

Shevaun DeLucia

"Yes, now! We need to start digging deeper."

"I'm on my way," she hangs up, with no other explanation needed.


**I** pull up to the library, and Maddie is already waiting. She comes running up to my car, waiting for me to open the door.

"Oh my God! Such a good call, Raina!" she praises me, jumping up and down. When Maddie gets excited, she regresses back to a little kid.

"I know there *has* to be some sort of books on this Alexander family. They were important enough to have photos taken, so there has to be a story behind them," I explain as we walk into the library.

"No, you're definitely right! I was thinking the same thing. I mean, I think we need to figure out what he is doing here. If his ancestors were as well-off as they looked and as powerful as the site said, then why wouldn't he want to stay where he would be known?" she says, expressing her concerns.

I didn't really think of it that way, either. "Wow, that's a real good question! Did Jenna ever mention if he lives with his parents or not?"

"Um, no, and I never really asked," she answers, still in thought.

We walk up and down the aisles until we reach the history section. Here is where we have to begin the digging: centuries of logged time.

"Where do you think we should start?" Maddie asks, completely bug-eyed.

I run my hand through my hair and exhale, completely overwhelmed. "I have no idea," I admit. Which is an understatement. How am *I* supposed to uncover centuries of secrets, which have probably been smothered by lies, only now showing bits and pieces of the truth?

"The paintings were from the eighteen hundreds, and the pictures you saw were from the same time, right?"

"Right."

I slowly look across each long shelf, skimming the titles. "The only feasible thing to do would be to start there, then. Take out anything that has to do with the eighteen hundreds or powerful icons from that era," I direct. We walk in opposite directions to cover as much surface as possible. The library is a place I love, but with this mission and hundreds of books ahead of us, I can only feel apprehensive, unsure if what we're looking for is even here.

I come across a worn, dingy book with gold scripture on the binding, titled *Le folklore des Immortels*. I pull it out slowly, being extremely gentle, my blood pumping fast as I stroke my fingers over the engraved writing. Out of all these books, this one called my name. I felt compelled to pick it up. I look over at Maddie with her handful of books, and we head to the table in the very back for the utmost privacy.

The first book she puts down is titled *American History*. I shake my head and look up at her like she's crazy. "What?" she asks defensively.

"*American History*?" I repeat, pointing at the title.

"Oh, whoops," she says, laughing. I look at the other two she found and they look promising. "I'm going to go ask the librarian if there are any books on just Canadian history."

I pull out a chair and take a seat. "Good idea! I'm going to start skimming through these. We only have an hour and a half left," I remind her.

I place the fragile book I found in front of me, thinking back to the title of that painting. I get a flutter in my stomach, open the cover carefully, and read through the table of contents. This book is filled with legends and myths of the immortals, but isn't an immortal a vampire?

What can this book possibly provide that I haven't already heard?

I begin flipping through the pages, hoping something will catch my eye. I stop at a page that states, "Immortality is attained through the eternal soul." The legend of Hindu princess Rukmini is the story of a girl who fell in love with a man her father did not approve of. She was already promised to marry another, and on the night of her wedding, her lover, Lord Krishna, came to rescue her.

They married that night under the stars. Bound each other's souls together for all eternity. Rukmini soon became ill, cursed for betraying and leaving her intended behind. On her deathbed, Krishna swore he would avenge her soul, but she told him there was no need. She would come back to him in another life.

Rukmini believed that each soul was intended for only one other: a rare magical phenomenon, like finding two identical stars in the night sky. One who walks this earth and finds their other half will truly become immortal. Life after life, death after death, those two souls will always find each other, moving from one physical form to another for all eternity.

I sit for a moment completely in awe. It never crossed my mind that souls could be immortal. How do you know when you have truly met your soul mate? I'm sure lightning doesn't strike the ground and chimes don't ring through the wind, so how will one truly know?

I'm so deep in thought, I don't even realize Maddie is talking to me. "Raina? Um, earth to Raina?" she repeats, waving her hands in my face.

I look up, eyes clouded over. "Oh, sorry. I was just reading. Did you find anything on Canadian history?"

"Yeah, I actually found one book," she says opening it up. "Did you find anything so far?"

"I found this book mixed up in the history section. It's about folklore," I tell her. She just looks at me, lost and

Eternal Mixture

unsure what to think about it.

"Why would that be stuck in the history section? Shouldn't that be in the fiction section or something?" she wonders, forehead wrinkled.

I pass the book to her and tell her about the legend of Rukmini. Maddie is amazed and dumbfounded all in one. "This book looks ancient, Raina. Do you think any of this could possibly be real?"

"I have no idea, but it's got to have some sort of connection to the Alexander paintings. They named the one painting, *Immortel*, and this book is the folklore of immortals. I just feel the connection lies in here somewhere," I explain.

Maddie turns the book back to me. "Well, I hope you're right. I'm not too sure about all that mumbo-jumbo stuff."

We both get back to business and dig into our books. I flip through about another fifty pages and find the legend of *The Fountain of Youth*. This is a legend that has been around for centuries; the one who drinks the water from the fountain finds eternal beauty. The legend is of the Louise Family who traveled across the seas to gain control of the northern land. Raynella Vancouver married Victor Louise, an ancestor of Queen Elizabeth's, at the age of fourteen. She traveled many miles, leaving her family and everything she had ever known behind.

He promised her and her family days filled with pampering by many handmaidens and nights filled with extravagant balls. Gowns made from exquisite silks and jewels that only little girls dreamt of would be hers. Instead, she got a locked chamber with a window to dream from; a hay-stacked cot; bland, tattered cotton dresses; days full of work and nights filled with pleasing her husband to bare him a child.

Victor was a ruthless savage, only interested in money and power, only wanting a wife for an heir to his land and riches. Raynella tried for years to have a child but had miscarriages, one after another, and soon Victor realized she was useless. He divorced her, beat her nearly to death, and threw her to the wolves before bringing in a new wife.

Raynella was discovered by a couple who worked the land. They dipped her lifeless body in the small, crystal-blue lake and her wounds sealed magically, healing her and bringing her back to life. She soon learned the secret of the lake: drink the water and all time will halt, beauty will be eternal, and forever will be promised.

This family, now forever frozen, created a small army to retaliate against Victor Louise in order to keep the Fountain of Youth hidden. Immortality conquered over humanity, and a new name became the ruler of the land.

I finish with the story, close the book, and just sit in thought. Maddie looks up at me with concern. "Raina, are you okay?" she asks, worried. "Your face is pale," she tells me, looking between me and the book.

"I don't know," I answer, shaking my head. I feel as though everything is spinning around me. Like the world around me is about to collapse. My senses are heightened and awake, yet I can't make any sense of what I just read. The crystal-blue lake this legend talks about seems so familiar, and immediately the Alexander painting flashes through my mind as though it's calling to me.

Before I can answer Maddie, the librarian comes by to tell us we have ten minutes left until the library closes. I almost feel as though the librarian was meant to come at this exact moment. I was just about to spill everything to Maddie, and at the last moment, I decide to keep the story to myself.

"Did you come across anything?" I ask Maddie, trying to get the attention off of me.

"There are a couple of families that this book mentions. It talks about the first prime minister in the late eighteen hundreds, and then about this very powerful family that just vanished: Victor and Gwyneth Louise. It was said that Victor was in the same bloodline as the Queen. After the year 1873, there is no record of the Louise family existing," Maddie finishes.

My eyes grow wide with shock. "What? Are you serious?" I screech and grab the book from her.

"What's the matter?" Maddie questions, obviously a little caught of guard by my reaction.

I quickly read through the facts, but there is nothing here that can validate the Fountain of Youth legend. I *can* validate, though, that this legend's roots have come from someplace in Canada, where Jason is from.

"Nothing, I just thought for a second that sounded like something I just read, but it's not."

Maddie continues to look at me, unsure. "You are acting very weird," she tells me. We look around us and realize it is time to go. We gather the books and put back what we don't need. I decide to check mine out. There are still some things that I feel are untouched, and I need some time with this book so I can uncover whatever it is.

"So, what do you think's gonna happen tomorrow?" Maddie asks me.

We stop in the parking lot next to our cars. "With Brent?"

"Yeah."

"I don't know, but I *do* know I'm going to do my best to just avoid him."

The longer I avoid him, the easier it might be for me to forget him. Eventually, I'll get used to the idea of him and Casey together and time will move forward as normal.

"I just have this feeling that he's doing this on purpose, like he's trying to get your attention or something," Maddie explains.

I have to admit that has crossed my mind because of how we left things the other day. "Regardless, Maddie, if that's what he is attempting to do, he's going about it all wrong. I'm not about to sit back and allow him to hurt me. I'm going to do what I do best: pretend he doesn't exist."

"So what are you going to do about Jenna?"

I take a deep breath in, "I think I might just show up at her house tomorrow. Then she will have no choice but to talk it out with me."

Maddie shakes her head. "I don't know about that, Raina. You think that's a good idea? What if Jason's there?" she asks, expressing her concern. "I think you need to talk to her in a place where you know Jason won't be around. If he has some sort of influence over her, then him being there will only make things worse."

She is completely right, if Jason is there, there will be no way she will be open to fixing things between us. "Yeah, I didn't think about that. You always give good advice!" I joke with her, hip-checking her. "Okay girlie, I'll see you tomorrow," I say, waving as I get into my car.

On the way home, I begin to replay all the moments that Brent and I had together in our short amount of time together, and I still can't figure out why he did such an instant one-eighty. I think about the little comments he made that would throw me off-guard, like when we were in the library the first day we met and he said, "It's nice to finally meet you." And at his house he made the comment, "He just got me back." I still am not sure what he meant by those comments, but I know I felt something and so did he.

I've learned some good information tonight, and I can't help but feel I'm on the right track to figuring Jason out. I'm just not sure what I am going to do with the information once I find out the truth.

I reach my house and notice my father is home. Before I can even get the front door open, he is waiting for me.

"Hi, Daddy!" I am so happy to see him. I feel like a little girl again.

Eternal Mixture

He gives me a big hug and a kiss on the forehead. "Hi, sweetie. Where did you just come from at this time of night?"

I place my book on the third step of the stairwell. "Maddie and I went to the library to get some studying done. Mom was already in bed, so I didn't want to bother her," I explain. "Did you eat?"

Dad has a seat in the recliner while I grab a drink from the refrigerator. "Yeah, I grabbed something on the way home."

"Daddy, you know fast food isn't good for you. I would have whipped you up something," I scold him. I take a seat on the couch, place my drink on the end table, and ask him how his day was. Just like my mother, my father looks worn down.

"Mom told me you are working on a special project."

He rubs his eyes with his fingers before he answers. "She did, did she?" he chuckles. "Yes, I'm on a time limit on cracking this formula. We've come so close; I just can't figure what the last ingredient is," he says with frustration.

I've never seen my father so defeated. He is an amazingly brilliant chemist who always has hope in believing he will crack the "code" on whatever medication he is inventing, but tonight his energy feels different.

I stand up and give him a kiss on the cheek. "Daddy, you are a brilliant man. I believe in you and so does everyone that surrounds you."

He squeezes my hand before letting me go. "I love you, honey. Sleep tight."

I change into my night clothes and hop into bed. I lie here, wondering what tomorrow holds, praying some light shines on my situation and hoping for the strength to move on from Brent.

# Chapter 9

A couple of weeks have passed, and nothing has changed at school. Jenna is still not speaking to me. I've tried numerous times to talk to her when I've caught her alone, but she still insists that I've changed—for the worse—whatever that may mean. Brent no longer initiates conversation with me or begs me to spend time with him, because his time is now occupied by Casey.

I watch her prance around him during lunch, doing anything possible to catch his eye. My heart twinges with pain every time I see this. Still, he seems distant towards her; there's no twinkle in his eye when speaking to her and no sign of lust when looking at her. This gives me hope for a mere moment, until I knock myself back into reality: he doesn't want me either.

After gym class, I meet up with Bailey and she walks me to class. Ever since the last episode of having my heart stomped into a million pieces, Bailey feels protective over me. She has made it very clear to Brent, every chance she gets, just how upset she really is. She's the queen of snide remarks.

We stop to talk in front of my classroom door before the bell rings, and students steadily walk by. Bailey puts her hands on my shoulders and looks me dead in the

96

eyes. "Okay, Raina. You are strong and beautiful, and he is no longer worth your time. Just keep repeating that," she says.

I close my eyes, take a deep breath, and repeat those same words in my head, trying to will myself to believe them. "Okay, I think I got it," I lie, hoping she might believe me this time.

"Whoa! Did you see how Jaime just looked at you?" Bailey screeches quietly.

Jaime is the class president and the captain of the boy's lacrosse team. He's very well- rounded and extremely popular when it comes to the girl population. It must be his dark complexion, shiny black hair, olive skin tone, sculpted muscles, and washboard abs that drive the girls crazy.

"Bailey, relax. He just smiled at me. That doesn't mean he's head over heels for me! Geez!" I respond, laughing.

I take a step into the classroom, and repeat Bailey's pep talk in my head, over and over again, until I reach my destination. I figure it can't hurt to repeat her silly words, right? I make it to my seat safe and sound, except for the fact that I can feel Brent's energy probing at me with its little fingers. I can't help but still feel this amazing magnetic pull to him; just sitting this close to him is torture. I only wonder if he may feel the same thing. I close my eyes to catch my breath and to halt the room from spinning around me. If I can just gain control over my emotions, I will be fine.

I open my eyes, and Jaime is standing at my desk, dressed in sexy fitted blue jeans and a cream button-down shirt showing just the right contours of his body. I'm completely caught off guard and jump back slightly. "Oh sorry, Raina, I didn't mean to scare you," Jaime says sweetly. He takes a seat in the empty desk next to mine.

I continue to stare at him, unsure of what to say.

Shevaun DeLucia

"So, I was wondering if you want to go grab something to eat after school?" he asks with a genuine smile. I look around the class, waiting for someone to laugh at this practical joke, but no one does.

I feel the heat flare up from under my cheeks and my palms begin to shake with nerves. "Um, you're asking *me*?" I question, feeling a little skeptical. I've never once been asked out on anything until Brent came along.

Jaime chuckles. "Yeah, I'm asking *you*," he says. In the next moment, he must realize there is a possibility I may turn him down, and his face turns from amused to concerned. "Un-less you don't want to," he adds, eyeing me carefully.

I'm finding it very hard to focus. I feel Brent's eyes burning a hole through me, and the tension swarms the air as he watches the conversation unfold between Jaime and I. Jaime must notice the uncomfortable feeling too, because his eyes occasionally glance back in Brent's direction and then back to me. In a moment, Brent will know I intentionally lied to him about having a boyfriend, but I am so mad at him at this point, I don't even care

"No. I-I mean, yes! I would like that very much!" I blurt out. We both laugh together for a moment. My nerves begin to calm.

"Okay, I'll meet you in the parking lot, and then I'll follow you home so you can drop off your car."

"Okay," I answer in disbelief. Is this even possible? Jaime's never even once looked in my direction and now he wants to take me out? The stars must be out of whack today.

Jaime gets up from the seat and walks past Brent with a stern, hard face. "Brent," he dips his head in acknowledgement.

"Jaime," Brent replies back in an annoyed, angered voice.

It's no secret that Casey and Brent are dating—at

Eternal Mixture

least that's what Casey has led everyone to believe. But I still can't help but feel something is very off with their situation. Maybe if I just speak to him, he will tell me the truth about what happened between us. Maybe then he can actually clarify there is no "us" and never was. I think if I heard it from his mouth, then I might be able to stop fantasizing about him wanting to be with me, and I'd be able to finally move on once and for all.

I actually think Jaime might have come my way at the perfect moment. I wished for a distraction last night; maybe the one above answered my prayer.

This whole class has been extremely uncomfortable. I feel as though I'm in the Twilight Zone. Jaime has been glancing in my direction the entire class, hoping to steal a smile. I see Brent out of my peripheral vision, glaring at Jaime. Casey is watching Brent watch Jaime watching me! I don't know what is going on, but as soon as the bell rings, I fly out of my seat to get as far away from this classroom as possible.

I pull up my driveway, Jaime following behind, and park my car. My stomach is doing flips and twirls as I walk towards his car. Before I even get to the passenger door, Jaime hops out and opens the door for me. A perfect gentlemen so far.

"Hey." He greets me with a beautiful smile.

I push my hair behind my ear. "Hey," I reply shyly as I take a seat in his car. He drives a black Audi R8 5.2—a loud and clear sign of his family's wealth. My parents are *extremely* well off, but they like to be more discreet about their riches. They feel that giving me a "normal" life will allow me to be seen through non-judgmental eyes. Money doesn't buy love and happiness; it draws attention and invites haters.

"So, where are we going?" I ask, doing my best to start up a conversation.

He backs the car up and goes full throttle out of my

driveway. I grab ahold of the seat as my head is forced back against the headrest.

"Don't worry; I'm a safe driver," he comments with a wink.

I release my grip from the seat. "Yeah, I can see that," I reply sarcastically. Normally, this kind of crazed, reckless driving freaks me out, but it sort of fits his look and actually kind of turns me on.

He chuckles. "I thought maybe we'd go grab a burger over at Charlie's, unless you only eat salads like the rest of the girl population."

I look at him like he is a two-headed monster. "Um, no! Burgers are fine for me. I have the rest of my life to eat salads. For now, I'll enjoy the fat and grease while I can."

Jaime laughs out loud this time. "That's the kind of girl I like!"

We pull up to the burger place and order our food. We take a seat in a back booth where it's private. I watch him take a huge bite of his big bacon burger without any hesitation. He must go on these outings a lot. He doesn't seem nervous or self-conscious one bit. I, on the other hand, feel a little giddy and shy.

"So, Raina, tell me what you like to do in your spare time?" Jaime starts the questioning.

I finish chewing my fries. "I like to discover new places, secluded places. But you didn't ask me here to talk about my hobbies, did you?" I hit him hard, getting straight to the point.

"No. I guess you're right. I asked you here because I've liked you for a while now, but wasn't sure how to approach someone like you," he explains.

"Someone like *me*?" I ask, not quite understanding what he means.

"Yeah, you're not like the other girls. You're quiet. You carry yourself with dignity and don't jump from one boy to the next. I watched you with Brent, and I saw what he did to you. You didn't deserve that, Raina."

I feel a slight stab in my heart, as though a wound has just been re-opened. Was it that obvious for everyone to see?

I look down at my fingers. "He didn't do anything that I didn't allow him to do. I'm fine, always was, so you don't have to feel bad for me," I snap back, immediately feeling guilty. "I'm sorry! I didn't mean to snap at you." God, what is my problem?

He still looks at me softly. "It's okay. I stepped out of line. So, tell me, what are your plans after we finish high school?" he asks, taking another big bite of his burger. I follow and do the same before answering.

"Hmm, after high school? I really am not sure. I was thinking about traveling for a little while instead of going straight to college, but my parents really want me to start college as soon as I get out so I can follow in my father's footsteps."

"I think that's what most parents want—for us to follow in their footsteps. But sometimes you have to make your own destiny, follow your own callings," Jaime replies, making unbelievable sense in a Dr. Phil sort of way.

I sit silently, staring at the definition of a perfect man. He knows all the right things to say, he's easy on the eyes, and he has money. But I can't help drifting off to thoughts of Brent. He may not always say the perfect things, but he knows how to get my blood boiling. He drives me completely crazy in every sort of sense: emotionally and, most importantly, physically. With Brent, my body's been awakened with tingles and wet warmth in places I've only read about in adult romance novels.

"What about you? Where are you planning to end up after high school?" I ask. The thing is, Jaime seems safe and predictable versus Brent who is a complete wild card. I can deal with safe, and since I haven't really dated, maybe that's what I need for now.

Shevaun DeLucia

"I got a scholarship to Duke University for lacrosse. So, I'll be in North Carolina this time next year. I'm doubling up on classes so I can graduate a year early," he tells me with a proud smile. I feel a sense of pride and happiness for him, but that means if we somehow become more than friends, I get stuck with a long-distance relationship.

"Wow, you must be really excited! Good for you! What are you planning on studying?"

A couple of girls from our school fill up the booths near us. They look over in our direction and begin gawking with jealous eyes. Jaime gives them a quick smile and brushes them off. They immediately pout and turn around, beginning their own conversations.

"I'm gonna study political science. Hoping to become the president one day."

My eyebrows lift up in shock, waiting for him to start laughing and tell me he's joking, but there is no laugh. He is completely serious. "That's a very high goal to shoot for, but if you believe in it, then why not?" I shrug.

I pop another fry in my mouth as I watch the corner of his mouth curl up. "Do you want to see a movie or maybe go out to dinner with me on Friday?" Jaime asks with a little more confidence this time.

"Yes," I agree, smiling back. He grabs my hand and entwines his fingers with mine. His hand feels warm and soft, strong and masculine, but ultimately, he's not Brent.

He drives me back to my house, and I see both my parents' cars in the driveway. There's also a third car in the driveway, which never happens at this time of day. We sit for a moment in quietness. I look over, and he leans in towards me. For a moment, I think he is going to try to kiss me, but instead he gives me a tight squeeze, then kisses me gently on the cheek.

I turn to open the car door and freeze. I see Brent standing on my porch, arms crossed over his chest,

Eternal Mixture

watching us intently.

"What is *he* doing here?"

I look at Jaime and can see the anger burning in his eyes as he stares at Brent and vice versa. My heart is beating so hard, I feel it might explode out of my chest. "I don't know," I answer truthfully. "I'll see you tomorrow at school."

I step out of the car and close the door.

I turn and watch him speed out of the driveway, then I turn back towards Brent. What the hell is this kid doing here? My blood is beginning to boil, and my hands ball up into fists full of anger. I can't believe he has the nerve to show up at *my* house after how he has made me feel!

I storm up to him, get right in his face, and look him straight in the eyes. "What are you doing here?" I demand to know, fuming with hurt and anger. We stand here in silence, just staring each other down with accusing eyes.

"What are you doing with him, Raina?" he interrogates, obviously aggravated.

Is he out of his mind questioning *me*! I am no longer fuming with anger—I am *enraged*! The only thing I see when looking at him is the color red!

My mother opens the front door. "Oh, honey. You're home, finally," she says ecstatically. As soon as my eyes turn in her direction, she takes a step forward. "Raina, what's going on? You look upset."

I walk towards her, eyes blurred, tears filled to the brim, confused about why Brent is even here. "Mom, what is going on? *And* what is *he* doing here?" I inquire through my teeth, completely fired up.

Mom looks over at Brent who still has his back towards her, obviously trying to control his own anger. "Why don't you both come in? Raina, Dad and I need to talk with you," she tells me, holding the door open for me to walk ahead of her.

Shevaun DeLucia

I take a step in and see two suitcases lying near the stairs. I look back at my mother puzzled. "Are you and Dad going somewhere?" I question, becoming a little worried. If they leave, who will I stay with?

My mother follows me into the kitchen where my father and a young lady are sitting. He sees me and immediately introduces me to his newest lab assistant, Lillian. This name instantly rings a bell, and I put two and two together.

"You're Brent's aunt?" I ask her. I hear a cupboard door slam and look back towards my mother, who is making coffee.

Lillian has a light and warmth about her. She smiles at me, and I feel a sense of love, compassion, and pureness that I haven't really felt from anyone before. She makes me feel calm to the point that my blood is no longer boiling, and I can now think clearly. That is, until I hear Brent walk in behind me.

Lillian comes my way with arms out, ready to embrace me. I feel a little standoffish, but I do the right thing and welcome her embrace. The last thing I want to do is be is disrespectful to the woman who's taken care of Brent.

"Yes, Raina, I am Brent's aunt. It is really such a pleasure to meet you. Brent's told me so much about you!" she gloats with happiness.

I look back at Brent, who is now leaning against my kitchen counter, and roll my eyes. My mother catches me and shakes her head with a grin.

"Yes, same to you. But I'm confused. Can someone please tell me what this is all about?" I beg, looking for answers in each face in front of me.

My father, still sitting at the kitchen table, rubs his eyes and then spills it.

"Raina, your mother and Lillian have to go out of town for a while on business. It might only take a couple of weeks, or it could take longer, depending on how the conferences go," he explains. And then he lays the big one on me. "Brent will be staying with us," he breaks the news, putting the last nail in the coffin.

My mouth falls to the ground, and when I look back towards Brent, all I see is that smirk of pleasure. He is getting a kick out of my reaction, and the worst part about it is he has probably known this for days. I glare at him, infuriated.

"Um, do *I* even get a say in any of this?" I look back to my mother and then to my father. They both glance at each other as though they're talking with their eyes. "Hello?" I yell, waving my hands around.

"Johanna, maybe this isn't such a good idea," Lillian comments to my mother.

"Don't be silly, Lillian. Raina will adjust just fine. Right, Raina?" my mother turns to me, purposely putting me on the spot so I will feel guilty.

I exhale forcefully, moving my strands of hair. "Fine!" I agree with defeat. "When are you two leaving?"

My mom brings over cups of coffee for Lillian and my father. "Tonight, dear. Sorry for the short notice."

She turns in my direction, places her hands on my shoulders, and looks into my face with guilt. "I'll do my best to make this a fast trip. Meanwhile, why don't you show Brent around town? He's still new around here, and it will give you something to do while Dad's at work," she insists, giving me a kiss on the cheek.

I glare back in Brent's direction. "He has Casey for that," I snap, trying my best to hit him below the belt, but it backfires. All he does is laugh under his breath. "I have some homework to do. So if you don't mind, I'm going to head upstairs."

I turn around on my heels and rush up the stairs with a desperate need to get away from this kitchen. I feel betrayed. My house has been invaded by the enemy, and I have no safe place to hide.

I shut my door and begin pacing my room. This really cannot be happening to me! What if he brings Casey here? Am I just supposed to be okay with that? Oh no, it is definitely time to set some rules and boundaries for the house. There is no way he will be flaunting any relationship in front of me in *my* own house!

I hear footsteps coming up the stairs. I stop pacing and put my ear to the door and listen as my mother shows Brent to his room, which, by the way, is right across the hall from mine. She talks to him like a long-lost son who's just came home from college rather than a stranger.

I hear the hardwood floor creak beneath me, and I immediately freeze, afraid of being caught spying. I slowly back up as I hear footsteps headed in my direction and quickly jump on top of my bed, grab a book from my nightstand, and pretending to be reading.

My mother knocks softly on my door before opening it. "Come in," I yell.

She enters my room and sits on the edge of my bed. "We're gonna be leaving in a few minutes. Are you sure you're going to be okay?"

Now my mother asks me this? First, she practically shoves this idea down my throat, no questions asked, and now she's asking me if I'm okay? I nod my head lightly and decide to simplify things by not making her worry.

"I'll be fine. Don't worry, Mom."

"Just make sure you take your vitamin every day." She gives me a big squeeze, kisses me on the forehead, and then slides out my door, quietly leaving it open a crack. I lay down on my back, staring at the speckled ceiling. Maybe I'm just dreaming. If I pinch myself, I will awake and this will all have been just a nightmare.

I hear another soft knock on my door and immediately I think it is my mother again. "Mom, did you—" I stop mid-sentence as I sit up and realize it is Brent standing in my doorway. My blood begins to bubble again as my heartbeat jolts into strong rhythmic pumps. "What do *you* want?" I growl, wishing I was a lion so I could rip his head off.

He ignores my attempt to sound scary and sits down on my bed anyway. I just continue to glare at him, eyes squinting, and mouth pressed in a tight line. I bring my knees up to my chin and wrap my arms around my legs, wanting to ball myself up so I won't feel vulnerable.

"I wanted to say 'hi' since we're gonna be roomies," he teases, acting as though nothing has changed between us.

"Hi. Are you happy now?" I ask sarcastically. He just continues to smirk at me, on the brink of laughter. "Listen, I have some homework to do, *alone*. So, if you don't mind?" I stand up and walk over to my door, waiting for him to get the hint and leave.

He continues to sit on my bed, not budging a bit. I can't help but glance down at his bulging arm muscles, sliding my eyes across the mountains and valleys of his chest, directly down to his washboard stomach that lies clearly beneath his T-shirt. He must have followed my eyes because he begins laughing.

My face is on fire and my armpits are beginning to sweat. "*What?*" I ask defensively, hoping he doesn't call me out on my shit.

"What am I going to do with you?"

"More like, what are you going to do with Casey? We need to go over some house rules."

I cross my arms over my chest.

I watch him turn from arrogant to suspicious in two seconds. "Ah, house rules? Okay, shoot."

I tap my finger on my lips and pretend to think. "Number one, no girls in *or* outside the house. Number two, I don't want to hear the name Casey in my presence," I instruct, shifting to a pace. I watch as his suspicion turns

Shevaun DeLucia

to amusement. "Number three, keep the toilet seat down."

He interrupts me by raising his hand, making a complete mockery of me. "So, these rules apply to you as well, right?"

I stop dead in my tracks and put my hands on my hips with seriousness. "Um, no! I live here. I don't have any rules other than what my parents have given me."

Brent immediately shakes his head. "You're out of your mind," he voices loudly. "Don't be a hypocrite. If I have rules, so do you."

I know he's not going to back down on this, so I have no choice but to compromise.

"Fine. One rule: none of your girlfriends in the house. There, happy now?" I flare my arms, aggravated that I had to bow down. "Oh, and the toilet seat rule stays too!"

"Okay, fine. The toilet rule stays," he agrees. I swear, just for a moment when I looked at him, he had that twinkle in his eye.

I walk over, holding my hand out to shake on it. I believe he'll be a man and keep his word. At least I hope he will. Brent stands up, eyes never wavering from mine, and walks slowly towards me, until he is inches away. Toes to toes, body to body, and face to face. He leaves no room for me to escape as he backs me up, pinning me against the door.

I am speechless, unable to breathe, and my mind is full of dread, knowing if he comes any closer I may just give in. Everything in my body is screaming for him to just kiss me, but my heart is afraid and my mind is telling me not to do it.

Seconds feel like minutes and minutes feel like hours as he continues to stand here without saying a word. The silence is killing me and is causing the tension in my body to build up. If he touches me, I'm afraid I am going to explode.

His hand finally reaches mine. He shakes on our

Eternal Mixture

108

deal and leans down to place his velvety lips against my hand. There is no way he can deny feeling the vibrations of this electric current flowing between us. He *has* to feel it. I still remain frozen, afraid to take a breath of air. If I breathe in his scent, my knees just might buckle and I will lose all control.

In this next moment, Brent leans in close to my ear, his breath tickling the hair against my neck, and tells me, "I see you, Raina. I see right through you."

Before the words can even sink into my head, he is gone, and I am left standing here alone. My thoughts are stuck in a muddy haze. I try to tunnel through the muck to see clearly, but I can't. His words echo through my head, and I become defeated. How am I supposed to stay in control when I continue to open myself up to him? I allow him to crawl deep inside me without permission.

I want to chase after him to confront him about stealing my heart, but my feet won't budge. Maybe this is a good thing, because if I confront him, I will be admitting my feelings to him. Brent gets off on watching me squirm, and he knows just the right buttons to press. I have to find a way to keep him at arm's length, which may be nearly impossible since he is now living directly across the hall from me.

I shut my bedroom door and head over to my window, watching my mother drive off. My father has already returned to work, which means Brent and I are now alone.

The hours pass by, unveiling the dark sky. My curiosity begins to get the best of me after hours of homework. I haven't heard a sound from Brent's room, and I'm wondering if he is even still here. Did I miss him leave? I walk over to my bedroom window, and Brent's Infinity still sits in the driveway. So why is he so quiet?

Shevaun DeLucia

I crack my door open, and a fragrance so mouth-watering and delicious tickles my nose. I close my eyes and inhale the heavenly aroma, and my stomach immediately growls with hunger. I can't help but follow it down my stairs and into the kitchen.

Brent has my mother's apron around his waist while he is busily chopping onions, peppers, and cilantro. I clear my throat to announce my presence.

He continues to chop, not looking up in my direction, and smiles. "Are you hungry?" he asks, placing the ingredients in the pan of searing oil.

I take a seat on the barstool, carefully watching him. He throws the dish towel over his shoulder and turns in my direction.

I take another whiff. My stomach rumbles. "Smells good. What are you cooking?"

"My specialty: chicken fajitas," he announces proudly.

"Where did you learn to cook?"

He stirs the veggies, then places the chicken in. "Just years of practice."

"So you taught yourself?" I ask, swaying back and forth on the stool.

"Yup."

Brent's gaze intrigues me, like he is holding a secret that he cannot share. "What are you thinking about?"

"You."

I squint my eyes, wondering if he's going to tell me, or if I'm going to have to drag it out of him.

"Elaborate, please?"

He continues to stare at me as he racks his brain about whether he is going to elaborate or not. Once his decision is made, he drops the bomb.

"I'm trying to figure out why you lied to me about having a boyfriend," he reveals.

I knew this topic would come front and center

Eternal Mixture

sooner or later, but I wasn't ready for it at this moment. I look down at my fingers, picking at my nail polish, trying to stall long enough to come up with an answer.

Brent turns off the stove and scoops the food onto our plates. I grab the tortillas, and we lay it all out on the kitchen table. His gaze is intense as he waits for my response.

"First, I want to say I'm sorry for lying," I apologize, hoping he accepts. "I don't have a boyfriend. I was unsure of what your intentions were when you wanted to hang out. I got nervous and was trying to keep you at a far distance," I admit.

Brent sits very still as he allows my words to sink in. "Raina, my intentions were to get to know you, that's all. There was no reason to push me away."

My face turns to stone. "There is no point in getting to know each other. We obviously have *nothing* in common. I see the type of people you like to surround yourself with," I sting him, and then take a bite of my fajita.

He leans back in his chair. "Is this about Casey?"

A chill flows down my back after hearing him say her name. "Honestly, I don't give a damn what you do or *who* you do. You're not my business," I tell him, trying to hurt him like he hurt me. I can't even eat the rest of my food. I feel sick to my stomach.

"I see."

I get up and place my plate in the sink. When I turn around, Brent is standing directly in front of me. He bores holes into me, drinking me in with hunger-filled eyes. I try to disconnect from his gaze, but he won't allow me to.

"Raina, look at me," he begs.

Our eyes meet and my body is lulled with desire, channeling a craving that's been dormant for so long. His closeness feels so familiar to me, awakening every last inch of my body. My blood rushes through my veins, igniting a fire within me. I burn for him.

He lifts me up and sets me on top of the counter, my legs open and inviting him in. He grips each of my thighs with his hands, digging his fingers into my flesh. His eyes look drunk as they scan the canvas of my body. Without warning, he smashes his lips against mine, thrusting his silky wet tongue into my mouth until we sink into a rhythmic embrace.

My first kiss and all I can think of is what lies next. I'm starved for more, and this is only the beginning. A slight moan escapes my lips. I grab the back of his neck and tangle my fingers through his hair, pulling him closer to me with intense urgency. I can't get enough. I arch my back and wrap my legs around him, bringing him into me. I am in my glory.

Brent's phone shrieks with importunacy, cutting through our hazy fog. Still kissing me, he answers the phone. I can hear the high-pitched voice of a girl, of Casey. Without another thought, I push him away. He tells her he will call her back and hangs up.

I jump off the counter, eyes stinging, and remember the true reality: he is not with me. He is with her.

I turn my back to him, not wanting him to see me cry. "Raina, I'm sorry. I didn't realize who it was when I answered. Please, come here," he asks, reaching for my arm.

I snatch my arm from his reach, wipe my tears, and turn to face him.

"We made a mistake. This should never have happened," I inform him, heart closed and eyes ice-cold.

He searches my eyes for any hint of emotion but finds none. "She doesn't mean a thing to me, Raina. I just used her to get to you. I needed you to realize that you have feelings for me!" he confesses.

Is he kidding me? He did this all on purpose to make me jealous? Couldn't he have just tried to court me

Eternal Mixture

like a real man is supposed to do? Some girls would be flattered at his attempt to put on a show for attention, but not I. I find it pathetic, immature, and a complete turn-off.

I walk up to him, disgust smeared across my face. "You could have just tried honesty," I say before I walk away.

I can't seem to make it to my room fast enough. I run up the stairs, reach my room, and slam the door shut. Tears stray from my eyes as I slide to the floor against my door. How could I be so stupid? To give away my first kiss to someone so undeserving of it.

I can never get it back; I can never get that *moment* back. The worst part is that the kiss solidified my feelings for him. There's no question in my mind—and it doesn't matter how much I try to deny it—I am crazy about him.

Shevaun DeLucia

# Chapter 10

Morning comes and the sensation of trepidation flows over my body in waves. I can't face him. He weakens me with the piercing stare of his hazel eyes. If I give him any more control, I will become a slave to him.

Now the issue that lies ahead is what he's going to do about Casey. There is obviously no need to pretend anymore, since he let the cat out of the bag last night. Since Casey has never been denied or dumped before, she is surely going to retaliate in any way possible. He should be afraid, *very* afraid.

I feel a little guilty, though. I don't really know where Jaime and I are headed, but I know that beginning any relationship with lies is not a good thing. If I make the choice to just withhold some information from him, is that still lying? I know he is going to question me about Brent being at my house yesterday, and once I break it to him, he may not want to see me again. I have to be prepared for the inevitable: a break-up before the relationship has even begun.

I look at the time, jump out of bed, and rip my door open in a rush to the bathroom. My hand reaches for the doorknob, but instead, the door snaps open and I lose by balance and fall into Brent's naked chest.

114

"*Really?* Did you just have to just open the door like that?"

Droplets of water trickle down the ripples of his body, meeting at the triangle below his bellybutton and leaving a trail of shiny wetness behind. The only thing between his naked body and me is the fuzzy green towel his hand is holding together very loosely. I try my damnedest not to gawk at the impeccable beauty that stands before me, but I have to admit, I am failing miserably at it.

"Are you seriously going to blame me for opening a door?" he chuckles, looking at me like I have lost my mind.

I watch his eyes glide over my body, making me suddenly feel self-conscious as he takes in the view of my pajamas. My white tank top—extremely thin—reveals the coldness I feel with the absence of my bra. The sweatpants I have on are baggy, with holes from extreme wear and use, but they are my most comfortable pair. I cross my arms, trying to block his view while trying my best to remain mad.

"I think we need to come up with a schedule for the shower," I blurt out.

He continues to smirk, then laughs out loud. "Now I *know* you have lost your mind. It must have been the kiss." He rubs it right in.

My mouth drops in shock. I can't believe he just brought that up.

"You are disgusting!" I shriek, pushing him out of the way and slamming the bathroom door in his face.

I stand for a moment with my ear against the door. He doesn't move for another minute or so; he must be letting the conversation set in. Finally, I hear the floor creek as he walks away. I close my eyes and exhale. My energy is drained.

By the time I get out of the shower, Brent is already gone. Even though I wanted to be away from him, my heart still aches knowing he left without saying "goodbye."

Shevaun DeLucia

There's a small part of me that enjoys arguing with him. The way he makes my blood boil—I've never felt so alive. We have such an intense amount of raw emotion when we are around each other. Pure passion pours out from deep within. I just wonder what it is about him that makes me so crazy. Maybe we're just too much alike.

I take another look at my clock and realize if I don't leave now, I'm going to be late for first period class. I grab my book bag and run down the stairs to the kitchen. I have to take my vitamin or continue to hear my mother's nagging voice in my head. I often wonder what would happen if I didn't take it for one day. Would my mother even notice? Probably not, but I'll take it just in case.

By the time I reach school, the first bell has rung. I run down the hall and make it to my classroom just as Mrs. Liberty is about to shut the door. I see Bailey's face light up with excitement as I take my seat.

"What took you so long?" she whispers.

"I had a late start getting in the shower."

Bailey shakes her head. "I swear, if the world depended on you being on time, we'd all be dead!"

"Real funny," I say sarcastically.

Mrs. Liberty decides she wants us to work in pairs on our calculus packet. This gives me the perfect opportunity to tell Bailey about everything that happened yesterday.

"So, Jaime asked me to grab something to eat with him after school yesterday," I inform her. I wait calmly for the shriek.

She starts jumping up and down in her seat. "I told you! So, what happened?" she asks, ecstatic.

"Okay, okay. Relax," I say with a laugh. "We went to that burger place on Empire Boulevard. He was nice, very sweet. I'm just not sure if he's right for me."

"Let me guess, this is about Brent? Raina, *he's* not right for you. You need someone who will treat you like

Eternal Mixture

you deserve to be treated, and Jaime is the all-around perfect guy."

I roll my eyes. "You're right; he is the perfect guy. I just don't know if he is the perfect one for me."

Mrs. Liberty walks by, checking our work. "Girls, a little less talking, please."

"Okay, Mrs. Liberty," Bailey agrees. As soon as she walks away, Bailey starts in again. "You haven't even given him a chance yet!"

I lean in close, so we can't be heard. "Well, there's more," I admit to her.

"More what?"

I know she is going to freak when I tell her the news about Brent staying with me.

"You promise not to freak?"

She just nods. "Brent's aunt works for my parents. She went out of town with my mother, and Brent is staying at my house."

Bailey doesn't even pause long enough to soak the information in. "Are you serious, Raina? Did you talk to him? What did he say? Did he apologize?"

"Whoa! Okay. He basically told me he is only with Casey to make me jealous, and then he kissed me."

I wait for my words to sink in. For once, I made her speechless. "OMG, Raina. He kissed you?" she shrieks, quietly.

"Yeah, it was the most perfect kiss, that is, until Casey called his phone right in the middle of it," I admit. Just thinking back to that moment makes me sick to my stomach, and I'm going to have to face all three of them at once pretty soon. Maybe I should just skip the class. I'm not ready to confess the truth to Jaime, and I'm sure not ready to see Casey paw all over Brent.

"Aww, Raina. I'm sorry."

"It's okay. I just don't know where to go from here," I confess, feeling completely exhausted with overthinking everything. It's so hard not to run every single second of our kiss through my head over and over. It was such a monumental moment in my life that it's now been burned into my mind.

"Raina, just don't make any fast decisions. You have time, and with time comes answers."

"You're right, B. I'm just going to live in the moment. I have all the time in the world to make decisions."

Math class ends, and Bailey walks with me to my next class. I pass by Brent's locker, but I see no sign of him or Casey. Bailey taps me on the arm and nods forward. When I follow her direction I see Jaime walking towards me. Butterflies begin to flutter in my stomach.

"I'll leave you two alone." Bailey excuses herself quickly.

"No, Bai—"

I try to grab ahold of her shirt, but she's too fast and Jaime is already in front of me.

"Hey, Raina."

"Hey," I reply back, subtly looking around to make sure Brent is not in view.

"I'll walk you to class," Jaime offers with a huge smile.

The way he looks at me is as if I am the only girl in the world. Normally this would be every girl's dream, but I have too much guilt to enjoy this.

"You don't have to."

"I want to," he says with a smile. "So, what did Brent want yesterday?"

His smile turns to concern as he quietly waits for my answer.

"Um, it's kind of complicated," I admit, trying to ease into this conversation.

He now looks stressed. "Oh no, you're not going to give me that line, 'it's not you, it's me,' are you?"

"No! Not at all!" I reply immediately. The truth is I actually like Jaime. I may like Brent a little more, but Jaime is sweet and just the type of boy I *should* go for. Bailey's right, I should give him a chance. "I'm sorry, it's just that Brent will be staying at my house for an unsaid amount of time." I watch his face waver between suspicion and uncertainty.

He takes a deep breath, still allowing the information to sink in. "Sooo, you two are now sleeping under the same roof?"

I don't know where he's headed with this line of questioning, but I stop him dead in his tracks. "Listen, *yes* we are under the same roof and *no*, not by choice. He is staying with me, and that's as far as it goes. You don't have anything to worry about, okay?"

He now looks a little relieved but skeptical at the same time. "I believe you," he tells me. I'm not so sure I believe him.

The bells rings, and he gives me a kiss on the cheek. Before I turn in to my class, I see Brent out of the corner of my eye, just watching. My gut sinks and guilt swarms over me. He turns and walks away.

I have the urge to run after him and tell him it's not what he thinks, but for what? We're not together, and who knows if he even told Casey to buzz off or not. After what he just saw, he might want to keep her around now.

My morning classes fly by, and I'm now headed to lunch. The closer I walk to the cafeteria, the more anxiety I get. By the time I reach the doors, my whole body is trembling, and I just can't gain control of myself.

I decide to go to the library, since I'm not at all ready to face Brent with Casey. Even though I know his reasoning behind being around her, it still doesn't make seeing it any easier.

I take a seat on one of the couches in the back of the library and take out my book. It's been a while since I've sat down and read. I've been neglecting my reading, and I think its time to get back to the basics. It's the simple things that make me happy.

I'm less than five pages in when someone taps me on the shoulder. I turn around and see Brent leaning against the back of the couch, smiling.

"Hey," I greet him with suspicion. I hope he is not here to argue, because I am already mentally exhausted from this morning. The fragrance flowing off of his body is mouthwatering; it makes me want to devour him in one bite.

"Can I sit down?" Brent asks.

"Sure."

I can see the hurt in his eyes with just one glance.

He doesn't even take a moment to ease into a conversation; he just jumps right in. "So, Jaime looks like he's really into you."

"Does he? We're just getting to know each other," I tell him honestly.

Brent's eyes don't leave mine. "Believe me, Raina. I'm a guy; I know these things."

"Why aren't you in the cafeteria with Casey?" I ask, trying to turn the tables.

"Because I'd rather be right here with you," he tells me, making my face begin to prickle with heat.

"Really? Even after this morning?" I snicker. Now that I look back at my actions, I can't believe I overreacted like I did.

He tucks a piece of my hair behind my ear. "Even after this morning."

The energy between us shifts and evolves into this amazingly intense thirst. I can't help but feel compelled to him. He draws me in with his magnetic golden eyes, and I almost feel doomed. I've lost all control, once again.

"Raina, I don't want you seeing Jaime."

Oh, boy. Here we go.

"Brent, that's too bad. I like hanging out with him. He's nice."

I can almost see the steam rising off of him. "He's not for you," Brent stresses.

"How do you know who is for me and who is not? You stopped talking to me for weeks, and now, because someone else wants to hang out with me, you have a problem?" I hiss. "I'm sorry, Brent, but you don't get a say in who I hang out with."

"Okay, fair enough. Can you do me a favor then?"

"What?"

"Give me the same chance you're giving him. Let me take you out, get to know you, and who knows? You might actually like me," he says.

I think it over for a minute before answering. Just trying to keep him on his toes. "Okay, I can do that."

"Good! How about I take you out this Friday?" His eyes gleam with excitement, and I feel horrible because I already have to shoot him down.

"I can't Friday. Jaime already asked me."

His face drops, but it comes right back. "What about Saturday?"

I pick at my book for a second before answering. Then I look back at him and smile. "Saturday sounds good."

"You know, since we are living together, we might as well be environmentally friendly and take just one car to school and back," he suggests with an obvious agenda.

"So, now you're worried about the environment?"

"Actually, yeah. I'm a nature person."

I open my book to see what page I left off on. "Do you recycle?" I ask with a smirk, still flipping through the pages.

"I do, and I always use paper products. You know, a hundred years from now this world might be filled with garbage if we don't take ownership of our lack of respect for this earth. Don't you remember the world last century? It was beautiful. We never used anything that we couldn't put back into the earth," he rambles on, looking distant.

My head snaps up. "Um, did you just hear what you said?" I shake my head, wondering if he has totally lost it.

He snaps out of his daze. "What?"

"You just asked me if I remember what the world was like one hundred years ago."

He sits real still, as though he's trying to contemplate his answer very carefully. "Yeah, I meant from seeing the pictures in history books, and with everything being made out of natural materials back then. What did you think I meant?"

"I don't know, you just … I don't know. Never mind," I shake the thought from my head and realize I must be overreacting. To even think for a moment that he really meant "a hundred years ago" is just ridiculous. I think I need a nap.

"So, you never answered my question."

"You never asked one," I tease.

"Okay, okay, you're right," he admits, chuckling. "So, what do you say? Do you want to carpool together?"

"I would love to. As long as you don't piss me off in the mornings."

"I promise," he agrees, holding one hand against his heart and the other up in the air.

The bell interrupts, and it's time for next period class. Brent walks out into the hallway with me, and I watch as his eyes search across the hall, probably looking for any sign of Jaime.

"Don't worry, he has Science this period. He's over in the west wing," I tell him, trying to ease his mind.

Brent snaps back. "I wasn't looking for him," he lies. "I'll meet you here after class."

He is so full of shit. If I didn't have class in less than five seconds, I would *so* call him out on it.

Eternal Mixture

"Okay."

He almost looked as though he wanted to kiss me and then thought twice about it. But, now that I think of it, maybe he wasn't looking for Jaime—maybe he was looking for Casey. My gut drops with this thought.

Today is my off day and it's Art instead of Gym this period, which I welcome any day. I continue to look at the clock, watching the little hand tick slowly around. I feel uneasy when thinking about what's to come in my next class, but a small part of me is ready to see how the relationship between Casey and Brent will play out.

Will he just ignore her or has he already told her the deal? I'm feeling bolder these days, like I don't mind taking some risks. If it weren't for Jaime's feelings getting hurt, I would probably walk up to Brent and lay a kiss right on him in front of Casey. But, I'll take the more conservative high road.

Brent doesn't miss a beat. He is already outside the classroom door waiting for me. He seems docile and extremely focused on whatever emotion is passing through his head.

"What's the matter with you?"

"Nothing, why?" he asks.

We maneuver through the thick hallway, Brent cutting through, leading the way to History. "You look tense, what's on your mind?"

He stops by the threshold of the door. "Raina, there's just so many things I need to tell you. You're on my mind. It's always you."

Brent's making me nervous. What could he possibly need to tell me, and why is he holding back? Whatever it is, I trust him. I have complete faith in him, and I honestly have no idea why. There is something deep inside of me that just knows these things. Whatever it is, I know he will tell me in time, but the problem is that patience is something I lack.

Before I can even respond, Jaime is standing in front of us. Brent scowls at him, grabs my hand, and pulls me through the classroom to our seats. I look back at Jaime with pleading eyes; the last thing I want is for him to be upset with me.

I turn in my seat to face Brent. "What is your problem?"

"He's not good enough for you."

"Then who is Brent? *You?*" I ask with a scowl.

Brent looks a little defeated but still answers with certainty, "Yes, Raina, we belong together more than you know."

I can see Jaime in my peripheral vision, watching our every move. But at this moment, I don't care. I just want to hear what Brent has to say. He keeps beating around the bush, and I wish he'd just say it already. I want to understand what he is hinting at or what he knows. I feel as though there is a part of him that is trying to protect me, but I can't fathom what he's trying to protect me from.

Mr. Jones begins his class lecture and this halts our conversation. I can't even concentrate on the task at hand, because I am still stuck on Brent's response. His words of us belonging together are flashing across my mind in bright neon letters, and then I look ahead of me. Casey has been watching Brent and I, just as Jaime has. Her face is contorted with anger and at this point, I know I have been listed as her number one target.

The uncomfortable energy that is surging through this room is insane, and it's obvious that Brent has let Casey in on the fact that they are no longer an item. I'm just not sure she will be able to except it so easily.

I look up at the clock. With only five minutes left, I am dying to get out of this heavy atmosphere and be able to actually catch my breath for a moment. I hear a low "psst" from behind, and when I turn around, Jaime is leaning over his desk, trying to get my attention. It's clear Brent is extremely annoyed, not working hard at all to hide the irritation while Jaime asks me to meet him outside the hall after class.

I agree with a smile and glance back at Brent before I turn around. I catch his attention with my eyes, and even though I can sense a disapproval from him, he still looks at me with soft, gentle eyes. This gives me the reassurance that he won't hate me if I give some of my attention to Jaime.

The bell rings. Brent stays in his seat, purposely waiting for Casey to leave before he gets up. I take this as my chance to have a moment alone with Jaime.

"So, what's up?" I ask him, standing outside the classroom door.

He looks sad and unsure of himself. "Are we still on for Friday?"

"Of course! Did you think I was going to blow you off?"

It is clear that this line of questioning has to do with Brent. Jaime's insecurities must be getting the best of him.

"I wasn't sure if maybe you had changed your mind. I have something really nice planned. I won't be in school tomorrow; I have to visit my grandmother with my parents. But I wanted to tell you I will pick you up around seven on Friday."

"Okay, that sounds perfect. So, what is the dress attire?"

He looks so cute when he's worried. I am just grateful he's still willing to talk to me, even with my weird situation at hand.

Jaime gives me a once-over with his eyes and then smiles. "Anything you want to wear will be fine. I'll see you soon," he tells me and then gives me a long, sweet kiss on the cheek before he walks away.

Brent walks up behind me and grabs my fingers with his, locking them together. It doesn't matter how many times we touch—every time is like the first. My insides react to him like no other, and when I feel this tornado of wild energy, I almost know why he says we belong together. I can feel it, too.

We walk to my locker in silence. I am more aware of him than I have ever been. I can hear his breathing fluctuate and his heart beat forcefully against his insides, and when I stop at my locker and turn to face him, he looks torn.

"Brent, can you feel this?" I ask, still holding on tightly to his fingers, my heart running at full speed.

"I've felt this way ever since I laid eyes on you," he says. "The first moment our eyes connected, I knew I was prisoner to your love."

My mouth hangs open, and I'm unable to get my words out.

"Meet me at home? I mean at your house," he corrects himself. But the word "home" felt so right. I just nod in agreement and watch him walk away.

# Chapter 11

I reach my house and see Brent's car already parked in the driveway. My palms feel clammy, and my body is trembling deep down to its core. I slowly walk up towards my porch, one foot in front of the other, staring at the front door as though it's going to morph into some sort of vortex. I'm almost afraid to walk through the threshold. I know what lies ahead, and it's not Brent I am worried about—it's something else that I can't seem to explain.

I stand outside of the door, waiting a moment to calm myself down, but the door swings open and Brent stands in front of me. His eyes gleam with something I do not recognize, and he moves aside without a word spoken.

An eerie sort of energy flows fiercely through every inch of the house. I feel alive, I feel crazed with profound emotions that have been lying deep within me. When I look at Brent, I feel as though I know him. I mean, *really* know him. The cloudy fog is beginning to clear as I see him standing before me.

"Brent, what's happening?" I ask, feeling strange and panicked.

He walks up to me and takes my hand, never removing his eyes from mine. He touches my skin with his lips and a soft moan escapes my throat as I take him in.

Shevaun DeLucia

"This is how we've always been, Raina," he whispers to me.

"How we've always been?"

He rubs my hand against his cheek. "You and I have spent lifetimes together. You always come back to me."

I search his eyes for the answer, "Lifetimes? I don't understand what you're saying. Brent, you're freaking me out!"

For a second, I'm not sure I want to know the answer to my question. Ignorance may be the better option.

"Raina, I think you should sit down for what I'm about to tell you," he says, bringing me over to the barstool. "It doesn't matter how many times I have had to do this, each time is still as hard as the first."

"Bre…," my voice trails off as he puts his finger to my lips.

"Shh. Please, let me speak," he asks. "You and I are not like everyone else. We have a very long history together. Raina, *we* are immortal. We are not like other human beings. *You,* yourself, are like no other," he confesses, carefully watching my every move.

I am speechless. This can't possibly be true.

"Our souls are bonded together for eternity. You are my eternal soul mate and I am yours. This is why we have such a magnetic connection, this is why your body reacts to me in the way it does, and *this* is why we always find each other."

"Brent, you sound crazy," I tell him, taking my hand back from his.

Does he even hear himself? I mean, he sounds like a complete nut. Why is he trying to fill my head with these incomprehensible stories? Even though I want to believe he is out of his mind, something deep inside me is telling me he is not.

"I want to show you something," he says, going

Eternal Mixture

over to the refrigerator and grabbing my parent's water bottle out.

He takes a knife from the wooden holder and slices a cut deep across his palm. I suck in my breath watching his skin split and the red blood ooze from his deep cut.

"Brent, are you crazy? You just cut yourself! Let me take you to the hospital; you're going to need stitches!" I screech, jumping forward to his rescue.

"No, Raina, just watch."

I stand before him as he removes the top from a water bottle and drips it over his cut. He begins to heal immediately. His skin seals together and his cut disappears. I back up, shaking my head in confusion. I must be hallucinating. This isn't possible.

"Raina, I am no different from you, except for the fact that water heals me and your blood heals you," he explains, walking closer to me.

I shake my head vigorously, only because what he said is actually true. How does he even know this? No one else knows this but my parents. I never showed him or even told him, and yet, *he knows*.

I swallow. "Brent, if you knew, why didn't you say anything at the beach?"

He grabs my hand and entwines his fingers with mine. His other hand is against my cheek. I slowly lift my hand and place it over his and feel the uncontrollable blast of electricity flowing between us. He is right; what I have been feeling is *very* real.

"Because I knew you weren't ready for all of this yet."

"I'm sorry, this is just a lot to take in," I admit. I close my eyes to take a rest for a moment and let my mind drift.

If everything he is saying to me is true, then this goes against all I've ever known. Anything and everything I have been taught not to believe in is now a possibility. If

Shevaun DeLucia

I, Raina Richmond, am truly immortal, does that mean that vampires and the Loch Ness monster could exist as well?

"Raina, are you okay?" Brent asks, looking me over, concerned.

I nod my head as I continue to think and make sense of all this. "So, *if* what you are telling me could possibly be true, then where does that leave my parents? Do they know?"

He hesitates for a moment. "Yes, they know, but the only reason they haven't told you is because they want you to live a normal life. They want you to experience as much as you can as a mortal human being *and* they want to protect you. In the past, you haven't taken it so well, either."

"Are my parents immortal also?"

Please say yes.

"Yes."

Phew. I let a big breath out.

"And you said in the past? I don't understand. How many times have you had to tell me these very words?"

He runs his hand through his hair and exhales forcefully. "I'm sorry. I just want to say this the best way possible."

I watch him as he concentrates very hard, face serious and still as stone.

"Do you believe in reincarnation, Raina?"

"Yes, I do."

"All things good and pure will be reborn. You *were* and *are* beautiful and pure, our love is beautiful and pure, and because of that, we have been given the gift of eternity to love one another."

"You mean like in that Hindu legend?" I ask, intrigued.

His eyes glow with excitement. "Precisely, the one who was cursed for following her heart but gifted eternity for finding her one true soul mate."

Eternal Mixture

I am confused. "So, are you telling me that any human can be immortal?"

"Just their soul, and only if they beat all the odds stacked against them. Finding your other half is not an easy task in a world this big. It is actually very rare."

I think for a moment before I spit out my next question. "How does somebody know, though?"

"Do you feel what happens to us when we are near each other?"

"Yes."

"That is how they will know. The only difference is they will never know about their next life or the life they just came from. Each life gives them a fresh start to fall in love all over again."

"So why are we different?"

Brent chuckles and rubs his eyes. "We have sort of cheated, Raina. We found a hole in the divine plan. Unfortunately, I feel as though you and I have been cursed because of it," he says with immense sadness.

"How so?" I wonder, almost knowing the answer already.

"You always seem to be taken from me as soon as we fall in love again. I have spent years trying to figure out how to stop it from happening. I can't figure out for the life of me why we are so cursed. The only thing I can think of is because we have gone against the natural cycle of life."

"So, this means I am going to die?" I ask, my eyes getting watery.

I've just begun to live since Brent came into my life. I feel more alive than I ever have. I have always been scared of what the future holds, but now I'm scared of losing my future, losing my parents, losing Brent.

"Some things have changed, Raina. *You* have changed. You no longer need what the rest of us need. We need this mixture," he says holding up the bottle from the fridge. "If we go too long without this, we die."

"And me?"

"Your blood is immortal. That is why you can heal yourself." Brent grabs my waist and looks me straight in the eyes. "You're special. You have a gift, Raina. Our type would kill for your blood. I promise you this, though, I will protect you for all eternity."

"You sound like someone could be coming after me."

"We all need to keep a low profile. If someone finds out about you, we are going to have some problems."

I bury my face in my palms, then look back into his eyes. "How many are there like us?"

I'm getting the impression that there are a lot of immortals in the world, like it might be something common or contagious.

"Not very many, but there has recently been a disruption in the hierarchy—in the way things are supposed to flow. Please, let's not worry about this today. You are safe when you're with me, and I will never let anything happen to you," he tells me with such raw emotion. I believe him. I believe his every word.

"Brent, how old are you?" I ask with trepidation.

"I am 157 years old. I was born June 15, 1856. My family discovered the Fountain of Youth that allows us to be immortal when I was seventeen years old, in my mortal life."

My mouth drops in astonishment. "Hold on, hold on," I say, putting my hand up for him to pause for a moment. "You mean these legends are based on *your* family?"

"Most of the legends and myths told and written have some sort of truth behind them; they've just been distorted a bit. There are the stories of Alexander the Great and, of course, Ponce de Leon, both trying to find the water that gives eternal beauty, which I am sure have some truth to them, but they never actually found what they were looking for."

"Wait, you told me your parents weren't alive."

"Yes, they were murdered."

I see the anguish flood across his face. My heart aches for him. I hate seeing him this way, and knowing that he will never see his parents again saddens me. But what he is saying still doesn't make sense to me.

"I thought you said they were in a boating accident?"

"More like a boat explosion. We were in a battle over our mixture, and they were kidnapped. My parents got away and fled across the water by boat. Their captors chased them and killed them," he explains, looking in the distance, surely replaying it in his mind. "I never got to say goodbye."

I can't hold back any longer, I grab him in my arms and wrap myself around his body, bringing him close into me. He squeezes me tight, gripping my back with his fingers. I feel his love, finally, and I can feel his desperate need for me to love him back.

"Raina, I love you. I have *always* loved you, and I *will* always love you. You were the one I was talking about weeks ago. There is no other in my life, just you for all eternity," Brent spills.

I have so many emotions running through my body, and I want so badly to scream that I love him to the whole world, but I can't. I don't even know if I love myself right now. I have no idea who I am anymore, who Raina Richmond is. The rollercoaster I have been riding is now stuck in the air upside down, and I have no way of getting off. There are still so many questions left unanswered, but I don't even know where to begin.

"It's okay, mon amour; I am not looking for a response right now. I have thrown so much at you in the last couple of hours. How about we go for a drive?"

"Can we go to that little beach you took me to

before?"

I need air and openness. Everything is starting to close in around me, and being near the open water will calm me.

"Let's go!" Brent says with exuberance.


We take the long drive to the remote beach. I look out the window, seeing the world through different eyes. I am no longer the same, and the universe is now a place where fairytales and legends are possibilities. But what does that mean, exactly?

We finally reach our destination and travel down the little path, the same as before. This time I take his hand willingly, and I follow him down towards the driftwood.

We sit quietly, my head snuggled into his chest and sunset on the brink of closing. The sky is smeared with tropical colors of oranges melted with pinks, and the sun illuminates a golden bronze against our skin. I stretch my arm out, watching the glow saturate my pores. The skin that covers my body felt so delicate and soft just hours ago, and now feels durable and mighty.

"Brent, what was it like for you to find out you were immortal?"

He looks out at the water while he thinks. He has to trudge through decades of memories. "I felt exhilarated and powerful like the world was in my hands. Not really a good combination for an egotistical teenage boy, but I was untouchable. The thought of forever charged through me, giving me an arrogant attitude towards life," he finishes, showing a spark of light in his eyes, which quickly dims.

"I envy you for feeling that way."

"Raina, give it time. It hasn't even been twenty-four hours yet."

Give it time? The issue is that I now have all the time I could ever wish for, so what do I do with it? It is

134

good to know I won't ever have to leave my parents behind
or watch them die. And come to think of it, I now
understand why my mother has such beauty and the skin of
a porcelain doll. Some things are beginning to make sense
now. But how does one become immortal?

"Brent, how did it happen?"

"How did what happen?"

I turn my body to face him. "How did I become
immortal in the first place?"

He pauses for a moment, looking a little conflicted,
almost making me wonder why or what he has to hide. "I
remember the day like it was yesterday. The air nipped at
my skin, chilling me to the bone, and the snow hadn't stuck
to the ground quite yet. The sky was a dull gray and the
forest looked dead and brittle with winter creeping near.

"My mother was humming while sweeping the
floor, and I was playing chess with my older brother next to
the fireplace. Sunset was about to come upon us, and my
father was on his way home from his daily hunt for dinner.
He came across a girl lying in the brush. Her body was
frozen, and her blood was already dried across her ice-blue
skin. She must have been there for a while.

"I heard my father screaming as he got closer to the
house—blood-curdling screams. My mother ran out the
front door in hysterics, and when my father appeared inside
the doorway, he was carrying a corpse-like figure.

"He wiped our table clean of the ivory chessmen
and laid her across it. She was so cold, almost translucent.
The blood that stained her ripped nightgown—from the
beatings and whips she endured—was a deep maroon. With
every moment that went by, she was dying right in front of
me. I remember feeling scared and confused. I almost
turned away, but when she opened her eyes for a split
second, our worlds collided together with this amazing
energy that tied us together. In that moment, I was bound to
her, and my life was no longer worthy unless she was in it.

Shevaun DeLucia

I begged my father to help her, to help *you*," he says, as he looks deep into my soul.

"You were so close to death, and if my father didn't turn you, you would have died—*I* would have died."

I watch a tear drip from his eye, glide down his soft cheek, and fall down to his lap. My near-demise must haunt him every moment of his life. He's had to endure many of my deaths, and it is clear to me that reliving them rips opens a scarred wound.

There are still so many questions. "Who would want to hurt me and leave me for dead like that?"

"Your husband," he answers so matter-of-factly.

Did he really just say *my husband*? "My husband? I was married?"

The thought of reincarnation definitely boggles my mind, and then adding the reality of being married already in a past life—that just *completely* strikes me speechless.

"Not by choice; it was arranged. You were many miles from your family and alone, afraid, naïve, and extremely young. He was a cruel and selfish man who only wanted a wife to create an heir to his land. You didn't love him; you actually despised him. He kept you locked away, and when he realized you weren't able to carry his child, he got rid of you. The guards beat you, nearly killed you, and left you in the freezing cold woods to die. My guess is they were hoping the animals would finish you off."

God, this seems so familiar. I just can't place my finger on it.

A tear escapes from me as well. It's hard to hear what was and what my former self had to face. "How old was I?"

"By the time he had released you, you were sixteen."

"And how old was he?"

He takes a deep breath. "In his early thirties."

Holy crap! That's child molestation! These days, he

would be sentenced to years in jail and then placed on the sex offender's list.

"How old was I when we married?"

"Fourteen."

I feel sick and violated. I wrap my arms around my stomach, feeling the gut-wrenching pain deep within. "How could my parents do this? I was just a baby."

"Raina, things were different during that era. It was normal. They married you off in hopes you would have a full, rich life. And the dowry given to your family helped them survive," Brent explains.

"Yes, I remember learning about this in my history class, but I would have never thought I would be a *part* of history."

Brent chuckles. "Yes, we are a huge part of history. If only you could remember your past lives, you would be opened up to so much knowledge."

"So, tell me Brent, how did your father turn me?"

He takes my hand and locks it into his. "We lived next to a small lake. The water was different there, and it had this iridescent glow that was just so magnificent. My mother was into herbs and home remedies for everything, and she learned those things from her mother.

"I was just about to turn seventeen when I became sick with fever. There had already been stories going around for years about the yellow fever. My mother was in complete distress as mine lasted for weeks, nothing was helping, and I only became weaker by the day. My father had brought back a root, Astragalus, from one of his hunting trips. He said it was known as the healing root.

"My mother, reaching for anything possible, made up a mixture using the water from the lake. I took the first sip, and I can still remember the exhilarating warmth it caused from within my veins. It spread through me like fire, licking every last molecule of my insides. I felt strong and rejuvenated. My parents were amazed with the amount of time it took to heal me, and after a couple of weeks, things began to change. *I* began to change.

"My agility was unbelievable. With only a quick thought, my muscles would flex and bound effortlessly. My hearing and eyesight were explicit, and the first time I cut myself, I healed instantly with just a drop of the mixture. After months of trial and error, we knew what we held in our hands was a mixture for longevity," Brent finishes.

"So, that is what your father gave me? The mixture?"

"Yes. He wouldn't have done it if it weren't for me. I loved you the moment I set eyes on you. I couldn't bare living another minute in the world without you," he confesses.

"And, what happens if you no longer drink the mixture?" I wonder.

Brent sighs, and then looks down at the sand. "You die."

My head snaps up from his feet to his eyes. "What? Is that how I died over and over?"

"Raina, I don't *know*. You never stopped drinking the mixture *until this life, where you didn't need it.* But, somehow you always became weak, frail, and then your remains would turn into ash," he tells me, completely distraught. "Believe me, I have tried for years to figure it out, but I just had no luck. I am so thankful for your father, though. I feel as though the one above has chosen him just for you."

The time has passed and the sun is ready to descend from the horizon. We look around, realizing dark is now coming upon us, and head up the trail to the car. The air is bitter cold and his black leather seats are freezing. Brent forces the heat out of the vents on high and pulls onto the main road.

The last words spoken sting my head. My father, has he been my father throughout my lives or just this one?

Eternal Mixture

I am almost afraid to know the truth. I don't want to know about any other fathers. I *love* mine.

"Brent, how many families have I had? Have I had brothers and sisters before?"

He continues to stare at the road. "No, Raina. Johanna and Alonzo have always been your parents. You have never had any others. And yes, you had siblings," he says.

I thought when you reincarnate you begin a whole new life as someone else.

"So, you're telling me for the last 150 years I have been reincarnated to the exact same parents?"

He pulls the car over and we sit in complete darkness. I look for him and can see a flicker of fire in his eyes. I feel the lust ignite us both, but I have to push it aside for the moment. There is just too much I need to process, and his kiss will not help.

"Please, don't look at me like that. I just need some time to process this all still," I plea, knowing my body is presenting a different offer.

"Okay, you're right. But I really think your parents should be the ones to explain that."

Is he freaking serious? He throws this all on me and now he refuses to answer something I have a right to know about my past? I am livid!

"Are you serious right now, Brent? You owe me this much! You changed me without even asking my permission, and now you refuse to answer my question?" I scream in complete anger.

"Raina, it's not that I don't *want* to answer it, I just feel this is something that your parents are entitled to tell you and talk to you about, that's all," he responds, defensively.

"Just take me home!" I demand, turning my body to face the windshield.

"But, Rain—" he tries to clarify, but I stop him dead

Shevaun DeLucia

in his tracks with my palm in his face.

"I don't want to talk anymore. I just want you to drop me home!"

He snickers under his breath, shaking his head. "Okay, I'll drop *us* home," he teases, obviously trying to make a mockery of me.

"Whatever! Just don't follow me to my room!" I huff.

I know I may be acting a little childish, but I can't help it. I am on complete overload and keep thinking about the fact that I was never given a chance to decide if I wanted immortality. I never chose my destiny, and now the thought of living forever is beginning to freak me out. What the hell am I supposed to do with eternity?

We remain silent for the rest of the ride home. When we pull up to the driveway, I can see my father's car. I look at the dashboard clock and see it's only seven thirty. I'm not sure why he would be home this early, but the last thing I feel like doing is talking anymore.

Brent turns the ignition off, and before I can jump out of the car, he grabs my forearm. The sensation from his touch almost burns my arm, but I refuse to look him in his eyes.

"I don't think it's a good idea that we tell your father just yet. Do you mind if we just keep this to ourselves for now?" he asks, still not removing his hand.

"Fine," I answer without looking back.

I open the car door, snatch my arm back, and speed to the porch. To my surprise, my father is at the front door, waiting.

"Hi Daddy." I give him a kiss on the cheek.

I notice him looking past me as I greet him. "Hi, honey. I made some dinner if you're hungry."

"No thanks, Daddy. I'm tired. I'm going up to bed." I head up the stairs, skipping every other step to avoid being in Brent's sight when he walks in.

Eternal Mixture

It has been a very long and awkward day. I can't think or wonder or question anymore tonight. If I do, my head will explode. I have probably been in this same position a million times throughout my other lives, but I can't connect to those ones. This life is what I have right now, and right now it feels like my first time going through this.

All I hope for in this moment is a good night of sleep and maybe when I wake up, this will all be a dream.

Shevaun DeLucia

# Chapter 12

I crack my eyes open at the sound of the piercing alarm, roll over, smack it twice to shut it up, and rub the sleep from my eyes. I lay here a moment, wondering if yesterday was all a dream.

Immortality? Ha! That is just completely ridiculous.

But, the longer I lay here awake, the more I realize yesterday wasn't a dream; it *was* real. I am immortal, and Brent is my friend, my lover, *and* my true other half.

I almost rip my covers off to run to him, but then I remember why I was so upset with him last night. I won't give in. I swing my feet to the floor and sit up in my bed immediately, squinting my eyes from the blazing white light that filters through my window. I suddenly realize that today is Friday, which means I have my date with Jaime.

Why not go through with it? I mean, maybe I could learn to have feelings for someone else. I already like him enough to go on another date with him, so that must mean something, right?

I hop into my pants, then brush through my nappy hair. I hear a faint knock at my door, and my stomach sinks to know Brent is on the other side.

I whip open my door with fury and cross my arms

against my chest. "What?"

Brent looks me over slowly with his eyes. "Um, are you going to say something, or are you just going to stare at me all day?" I ask.

"I would love to stare at you all day," Brent jokes. I huff in annoyance. "But I was coming to tell you I will be waiting in the car for you. Just make sure you take your vitamin."

Is he serious? He must have spoken with my mother, and, of course, I should have already known he is aware of my mother's vitamin obsession.

"Fine," I growl, gritting my teeth.

I grab my vitamin, lock up the door and sink into Brent's car. The exquisite aroma of fresh soap and soft cologne fill the air, making me thirst for him. I feel warmth and wetness in places that are so adult and foreign to me. I'm almost embarrassed, and I hope he doesn't notice my face burning with desire.

"How did you sleep?" Brent asks.

"Fine."

Brent smiles. "Is that going to be the only word you say to me all day?"

"Yes," I reply, irritated.

"Ah, good. A new word," Brent teases.

I scowl, hoping he will feel my animosity towards him.

"Listen, I am just not in the mood to talk to you right now, okay? Now can you please turn the music on?"

"You got it!" he says, amused.

Once we hit the school parking lot, Brent insists on taking me to my class. Bailey is already waiting for me at her seat, and I already know she has an interrogation planned for me.

"Hey, I've missed you!" Bailey admits. "I texted you last night; what happened to you?"

Shoot! I totally forgot. "I'm sorry. I just got caught

up with homework, and my dad came home early, so I spent some time with him," I inform her, only telling half of the truth.

Here I go, lying again.

"So, tonight is your date with Jaime. What are you going to wear?"

I watch the students pour into the classroom as the first bell rings, and I realize I haven't even really thought about my attire for the evening.

"I don't know."

"Oh no, Raina! We can't have you looking ... *normal.* I will be by after school to drop off a dress. You're going to look damn good in it!" Bailey shrieks with excitement.

"Thanks B."

Sometimes I don't know what I would do without her. She has always been my biggest fan, and that's just what I need these days.

Math trudges along, and before I know it, the bell rings and it's time for next period. Before attending my next class, I make a pit stop to the ladies' room. When I enter, I see Jenna standing by herself in front of the mirror. I almost gasp when she turns my way.

She looks morbid and sickly. Her skin is no longer a milky white; it is now a pale yellow. Her eyes no longer shine with life; they're dull with pain. Jenna's lips used to be a vibrant red, and now I see chapped lips and a bruised, sunken face.

I walk up to her, wanting to comfort her as she looks frightened by her own appearance.

"Jenna, what happened?"

For a moment she looks as though she wants to embrace me, but then her expression turns cold again.

"Nothing, Raina. Just leave me alone!" she growls, then faces back towards the mirror.

My heart aches for her. "Whatever I did, I am *so*

sorry. I'll make it up to you—whatever you want me to do!" I beg.

She turns back to me, emotionless, "Jason told me you would do this."

My face wrinkles with confusion. "That I would do what?"

"You would say anything just to get close to me," she blurts out.

Has this girl gone mad? I have done absolutely nothing to Jason, and yet he has a vendetta against me. I need to find him somehow and talk to him without Jenna being present.

"Jenna, of course I am willing to do anything, because I love you. You're my friend, and we've never let anything or anyone get between us before. I just want my friend back, that's all."

I can see the recognition of our friendship in her eyes. For a moment she looks ashamed of what's become of us, but then her face is wiped clean of any possible emotion, as if someone just whispered in her ear.

"I have to go," Jenna says, bumping my shoulder on the way out.

I don't know what to do with her or how to get back on her good side. She has obviously been completely brainwashed against me, but why? I feel like my whole life right now is just full of questions, and it's up to me to get the answers.

My next couple of classes fly by, and as I am heading to the cafeteria, I see Brent with Casey in what looks to be an argument. I figure now is my time to claim my love once and for all.

I walk up behind Casey, and watch as Brent's face lights up with curiosity. Casey eyeballs me as I walk past her to give Brent an intimate peck on the cheek. "Hey," he says, returning the affection and smiling down at me in amazement.

Shevaun DeLucia

When I turn to face Casey, I can clearly see the fury spread across her tomato-red face. "I see. So this is why you are breaking up with me?" she screeches, arms flailing.

"Casey, we were never together. That was the illusion you created in your own head."

I almost feel a little guilty as I watch a tear slide down her cheek, and then I remember who I am looking at: a narcissistic, sad excuse for a human being.

"No, Brent. We were together. Don't you remember what happened at my house?"

Immediately his eyes bug out of his head like he's caught red-handed.

"What happened at your house?" I ask, my arms folded across my chest, looking back and forth between them.

"Why don't you ask him?" Casey smirks and then walks away, pleased with herself for putting a damper on our happiness.

I turn and face Brent, waiting.

"Raina, it's not what you think-k," he says. Brent never stutters, so I'm starting to believe that some of what Casey implied is true.

"Oh, I think it is, Brent. You should have told me." I scold him and walk away feeling hurt, *again.*

He doesn't follow me to the lunchroom or even enter the cafeteria. Maddie and Bailey are the only ones sitting at the lunch table; Jenna is nowhere to be seen. I am starving. I grab my lunch and head over to my table.

"Hey girlie," Maddie pulls out a seat for me.

"Hey."

They both take one look at me and realize something is completely off.

"What's the matter? I just left you, and you were fine!" Bailey says.

I take a bite of my pizza, trying to fill my mouth so I don't have to answer. I just shrug my shoulders hoping they will just leave it alone.

"Bailey, she must be stressed about tonight's date with Jaime, that's all," Maddie covers for me, knowing I don't feel like talking. I just nod my head up and down in agreement.

"Well, I will be at your house by three thirty to drop off that dress. I'll help you get ready, so no need to feel stressed." says Bailey.

"I ran into Jenna in the bathroom earlier," I announce.

Bailey and Maddie both look at each other, then at me. "We saw her, too. She looks horrible, Raina. I don't know how to help her. She won't even talk to us anymore or answer our calls," Maddie says.

"I tried calling her last night, and I just got forwarded to voicemail," says Bailey.

"It looks as though her energy and youth is getting sucked right out of her. Everything that came out of her had to do with Jason somehow. He even told her I would try to apologize just to get in her life again!"

Both their mouths hang open in shock. "I told you that something was off about them," Maddie comments, taking a bite of her pizza.

"I want to talk to Jason—*alone*," I say. "Where do you think I can find him?"

Bailey looks at me like I've lost it. "Why would you even want to speak with him?"

"I don't know. Maybe I can figure out why he has something against me."

"I think you should just forget about Jenna. If this is how she wants to be, then let her be this way," Maddie says, trying to convince me.

I just don't want to forget about her. I wouldn't forget about Bailey or Maddie, so why should Jenna be any different? I think Jenna is in trouble, and she needs someone to help her. She's just too deep in it to ask for the help.

"Regardless, she *was* our friend, and I am still going to figure out a way to get ahold of Jason," I decide. "Are you guys in or out?" I ask them, hoping they will change their minds.

"Raina, you know I am here for you, whatever you need," Maddie offers.

I look in Bailey's direction next. "Okay, okay," she laughs. "I'm in."

"Thanks guys."

The bell rings, and we head out to our next period class. Gym goes by quickly, since I forgot my sneakers and couldn't participate. Jaime is not in school today, which will make History a lot more bearable. And, of course, I haven't forgotten the Casey situation either.

Brent is waiting for me in the hallway when I walk out of the gym. I walk past him, clearly showing my anger towards him, and head to History. He catches up with me and walks at my speed.

"Raina, *come on*! Don't ignore me like this. Please, just let me explain," he begs, but I refuse to listen and keep walking.

I take a seat at my desk and see Casey giving me the evil eye. She has a devilish grin on her face, as though she has something in store for me. I remember what Brent said when I asked him how he felt when he found out he was immortal, and his answer was "powerful" and "untouchable." As I sit facing Casey—who yesterday I might have been intimidated by—I realize I am immortal. She can't touch me, because *I* am untouchable. And she has no power over me, because *I* am powerful. She has no idea who she is messing with. So if she has something in store for me, I am ready.

I give Casey a return smirk, suggesting her to bring it on. If she wants to battle, let's battle.

Brent leans over his desk and pokes me on the

shoulder. I turn around. "Please let me explain, Raina," Brent continues to plea.

"Can't we talk about this later? We're going to get in trouble," I whisper, but unfortunately, it doesn't matter. Mr. Jones has already targeted us.

"Ahem. Is there something you two would like to share with the class?" Mr. Jones asks, putting us on the spot.

I feel my face burn with fever as the whole class turns to look. Casey seems satisfied that we have been called out, and Brent seems more than amused. "No sir, we were just discussing our study plans for the upcoming test, that's all," Brent lies with pride.

Mr. Jones looks pleased with his response. "Good, now let's discuss those plans *after* class. What we talk about today will benefit you for Monday's test."

"Yes sir," Brent agrees.

The remainder of the class we stay to ourselves, but that doesn't stop the flow of tense energy in the room. Casey continues to glance back in Brent's direction every now and then, and she must not be getting the response she is hoping for, based on the emotion on her face.

At this point, I have no idea what to think about Brent versus Jaime. I have no idea which one I want to spend my time with. I feel lost and jumbled, with too many types of feelings. I need to make it an obligation to give all my thoughts to Jaime when I am with him tonight, that way I give him an even chance on the playing field. Brent has had decades of my time; he can stand to lose a couple of hours.

Class ends and, of course, Brent waits to walk me to his car. I am a little nervous. I have a feeling that Brent thinks I am not going on my date with Jaime because of what happened yesterday. Now I am going to have to break the news to him.

He opens the car door for me, gets in the driver's

seat, and starts the car. After we're on the road for a couple of minutes, Brent starts in. "Raina, I just really want to explain myself. I have absolutely no feelings for Casey; she was just someone to pass the time with. The only thing we did was kiss and that was because I was so angry with you for leaving with Jaime. I was hurt, and I messed up. Please forgive me?"

Well, if that's true, I wonder what he will do when he realizes I am going tonight.

"I can forgive you, but what will you do tonight?"

He looks at me, baffled. "Tonight? What's tonight?"

"My date with Jaime."

His face turns from baffled to irritated. "I thought you would have cancelled that with him," he says, clearly miffed.

"Why would I do that? I already told you I was going."

I can see his knuckles turn white from squeezing the steering wheel extra tight.

"Because things have changed now."

"Brent, I am confused more than ever right now. I like Jaime, and I need to see where my feelings stand with him. I can't just go on your word that we belong together. What if life has another purpose for me this time around?" I watch his face melt with pain.

"I'm sorry if this hurts you, but can't you just allow me to figure some things out for myself?" I ask him, hoping he can understand.

"Fine, Raina. Whatever you want," he agrees coldly.

"Does this mean you are going to run to Casey?"

Maybe it's not right for me to ask this, especially since I will be out with another man, but I feel if he truly loves me like he says he does, then he will give me some time. Time to figure my feelings out on my own. He may

Eternal Mixture

have known how I felt in the past, but he doesn't know who I am in the present.

"You know, that's a little unfair of you to ask that, considering your plan for tonight. But, I am willing to prove my love for you. So if that means letting you go on this date, then I will take a step back and wait for you at home," he says sweetly.

How can I be mad at that?

"Thank you," I say, giving him a kiss on the cheek.

We reach home, and I head upstairs to change and take a shower. Bailey shows up like she says with her dress in hand. When she holds it up, I see that there's barely anything to it.

"Um Bailey, where is the dress?"

"This is it. You are going to look hot in it!" Bailey winks at me.

The dress she is holding is a red halter-top mini dress with an open, low-cut back. She expects me to wear this at night, when it will be cold enough to see my own breath?

"Bailey, I am going to freeze to death!"

She throws the dress down on the bed and reaches in her bag for the black shawl to cover my shoulders with. I look at her like she is crazy.

"Um, do you have one for my legs too?" I tease.

Bailey just laughs and grabs the curling iron. I work on my makeup while she works on my hair. After a couple hours of prepping, it's time for Jaime to pick me up. I open my bedroom door and peek out the hallway to see if Brent is lurking. If he sees me in this dress, he may just make a scene to prevent me from going.

I make it down the stairs and look out the window to see if Jaime is in the driveway, but he's nowhere in sight yet. Bailey gives me a big hug and sneaks out the door, hoping not to bring any attention my way. Unfortunately, Brent is already standing behind me as I turn around.

Shevaun DeLucia

"Uh, you're not wearing that, are you?"

I watch him looking me over, and it is clear his jealousy is going to get the best of him.

I turn around, flaunting the low-cut back, and he rushes up to me, covering me up with my shawl. "There is no way I am letting you leave in *that* dress!"

I stomp my feet like a little kid. "Stop, Brent! It is just a dress! I am wearing it, so just feel lucky you got to see it first."

Before he can respond, the doorbell rings. Our eyes grow wide, and we both turn towards the door.

Shoot!

We already made promises to each other that no one was to come in the house. I rush to answer the door and turn to Brent to ask him to please behave. He looks like he wants to kill me for even asking.

I open the door and Jaime stands in front of me with a bouquet of flowers in hand. He is dressed semi-formal in nice black slacks and a tan button-down shirt that goes perfectly with his olive skin tone. He immediately notices the dress, eyes caressing every inch of my body.

"Wow, Raina, you look beautiful!" he says with a punch-drunk smile.

Brent grabs the door and opens it as wide as it will go, purposefully staring Jaime down to cause intimidation. I hate to admit it, but it works. Jaime looks shook.

I immediately take charge before my date runs the other way and wrap my arm into Jaime's, leading him down towards his car. "Are you ready?" I ask, batting my eyes.

"I am definitely ready to get out of here!" he chuckles, glancing behind him quickly. He opens my door like a gentleman.

I see Brent standing in the doorway as we pull out of the driveway. He looks miserable, and my heart twinges with pain. I almost think I might feel what he feels

Eternal Mixture

sometimes, and then I shake my head. Impossible.

I promised myself I would clear my mind of Brent to give Jaime an equal chance, and that is just what I plan on doing.

"So, where to?" I ask.

His eyes are like magnets as I cross and uncross my legs. He can barely keep his attention on the road. I didn't realize I could have this affect on anyone; this may be a gift I never knew I had.

"Ahem," I clear my throat to get his attention.

I can see his embarrassment. "Oh, sorry. Yes, we are going to my uncle's restaurant. Best food in town!"

"Oh yeah?" I smile. "What's it called?"

"The Bistro."

"Is it that new restaurant that just opened?"

He nods.

He pulls into a parking lot in front of a small cape house. It looks quaint and cozy, with Christmas lights sparkling in the windows and couples laughing and holding hands as they walk out. He opens the car door for me and places his hand into mine.

We walk through the door, and he is greeted with hugs and kisses from what seems to be some family members.

They turn their attention to me. The older man smacks Jaime in the chest. I can only assume it is his uncle trying to say he approves as he looks me over.

"Uncle, this is Raina. Raina, this is Uncle Vito."

He pinches my cheeks and shouts "Bella!" He then gives me a tight hug. I don't know what else to do but laugh and give him a tight squeeze back. They sit us down at a private table in the corner near the fireplace. Before I can open my menu, Jaime grabs my hand.

His eyes sparkle with giddiness, and his smile is as vibrant as the morning sun. "I am so glad you are here with me tonight, Raina."

I feel my cheeks begin to burn like fire.

"Me too," I tell him, squeezing his hand in return. "Is your uncle always that vivacious?"

Jaime laughs. "Yeah, he's what you consider an old Italian—full of life and love for his family."

I like that. It's nice to talk to a guy who seems to have good family values, but how would his family react if they found out Jaime was dating an immortal? In fact, how would Jaime react?

"It's nice that you're so close with your family. What are your mom and dad like?"

"My mother is the typical Italian mom. She cooks huge meals every day. My father is gone a lot. He owns a small car lot across town, so he's always busy with work and keeping the money flowing," he explains.

"Are they happy?"

He takes a moment to think. "You know, I think they're just comfortable. They've been together since they were kids. Of course they love each other, but sometimes life takes a toll on relationships and families."

I think I understand his underlying message. They must have been in love in the beginning, and then family, work, and the everyday stresses of life got in between them. And instead of trying to rediscover their lust and desire for life, they became complacent.

Do I want a safe and comfortable life, or do I want to strive for the gold at the end of the rainbow? It's obvious that Jaime is calculated and cozy. When it comes to Brent, there is a wild thirst for love and for the unknown. He is *everything* I have ever feared. I always wanted to stay under the radar and just glide through life with no bumps or hiccups, but since he's come along, I feel more alive than ever. I am beginning to have a drive to be seen and a lust to be heard, and I kind of like it.

Our waitress comes by to drop off some appetizers and drinks that must have been pre-ordered by Jaime.

"I hope you like artichoke french," he says, placing some on his plate.

"Yes, I do. Thank you," I grin, not really enjoying the idea of someone ordering for me, but I suck it up so I don't come off as rude. "So, you said you wanted to be president, what else do you look forward to in life?"

He gives me a warm smile. "You know, what everyone else wants," he shrugs his shoulders. "A wife, kids, and a family to grow old with," Jaime answers, as though he read it off a manual.

Of course he mentions the one thing I will never be able to give him: the ability to grow old together. The more this date goes forward, the more I realize I may never be able to be with a normal man. And honestly, I am not so sure I want to be. I am by no means a normal woman, and I feel as though I am beginning to accept my fate.

"That's a good answer that many girls would love to hear, but that's not what I see in my future," I open up to him honestly.

He takes another bite of his artichoke and sips his Coke before responding.

"Okay, what do you see in your future then, Raina?" He almost seems a little irritated when asking this.

"Well, I'm not so sure I want the whole family and kids thing. I just know I have lots of time, so why plan now?" I finish, taking a sip of my drink.

Before Jaime has a chance to reply, my cell phone rings. The number on the caller ID is one I know all too well. I ask Jaime to please excuse me and walk out of the dining area and into the girl's bathroom.

I press the green answer button. "What is it, Brent?" I demand to know, placing my hand on my hip.

I hear only silence across the line.

"Brent, what's going on? Is everything okay?"
I begin to feel a little worried.

"I just wanted to make sure you are having a good

time," he lies.

I exhale deeply. "It's going okay."

"You don't sound okay, Raina."

I hear the worry and adoration in his voice.

"Do you want me to pick you up?"

I just can't help but shake my head with a smile. Sometimes he can be so sweet and so annoying in the same moment.

"No Brent, I have to go back to my date. Don't wait up for me."

"I love you, Raina."

It crushes me that I am not able to give him what he wants. I can't say it back.

"Goodbye, Brent."

I have to take a moment to collect myself. I turn on the water, lightly splash my face, dry off, and head out of the bathroom.

Jaime looks a little irritated when I sit back down.

"Is everything okay?" he asks.

I feel a little distant after my phone call with Brent.

"Yes, I was just being checked up on," I tell him as I pick up a piece of bread.

Our dinners arrive. He ordered the rigatoni with meatballs for himself and the chicken parmesan for me. We eat in a strange silence. I get the sense that he has something to say but he is holding back. I decide to call him out on it.

"Jaime, you seem like you have something on your mind," I say calmly.

"Who was checking up on you?"

I knew that was what he was thinking about, and I'm guessing he already knows the answer.

"Brent."

"I don't understand it, Raina. He lives with you, and he watches your every move when I drop you off and pick you up."

Eternal Mixture

"What are you getting at, Jaime?" I finish a bite of chicken.

"I just feel that there's something you aren't telling me," he finally spits out.

I take a moment to gather my thoughts and to figure out how I am going to respond to him. "I am sorry you feel that way. Brent is a part of my life now. I'm not sure I really need to explain it to you. He just is," I tell him, leaving no more room for discussion.

Jaime seems a little thrown off by my response.

I think he figures he's not going to win this conversation, so he changes the subject. "So, do you want to go see a movie?"

I decide to accept his offer. After the movie ends, he drives me home. We make small talk on the way, avoiding the topic of Brent altogether.

My house is pretty dark except for the light on the front porch. Jaime doesn't pull all the way up the driveway. He stays far enough back so we can't be seen from inside the house.

"Well, it definitely has been an interesting time," I admit.

"Yes, it has," he agrees. "You looked amazing tonight, too."

The way he looks at me makes my heart race, not in a sensual way, but more in a nervous sense.

"Thank you."

Jaime leans forward, placing his hand on my knee. I watch him inch closer, entering my personal space, as he begins to slide his hand up my thigh. I place my hand over his, stopping him from going any farther. My nerves are trembling inside, and I begin to feel panicked.

I'm not sure if I feel this way because of what is about to happen between Jaime and me or because Brent is only yards away.

I decide to give in to Jaime, only to see if there is

something more between us. He smashes his lips against mine, forcing his tongue inside my mouth. I let go of his hand and tangle my hands through his hair on the back of his neck, trying to allow myself to give in.

Unfortunately, the kiss feels forced and empty. I feel no passion or emotion, and when I try to back off, he just grabs me tighter. His fingers have traveled up my outer thigh and are now tugging on the side of my underwear in an attempt to pull them down. I now have the overbearing urge to separate myself from him and exit the car, but his grip has become stronger.

I turn my head to speak and can feel his lips against the skin on my neck. I lay both my hands on his chest to push him away. "Jaime, stop!" I screech, but he doesn't stop.

"Come on, Raina," he begs, almost like I am purposely teasing him.

I feel trapped, and I am beginning to exhibit signs of fear. Before I have a chance to plead for him to stop again, my passenger door swings open and I'm lifted up and out of my seat.

Brent sets me behind him and reaches in the car, slamming his fist against Jaime's face. "What the hell, man?" Jaime yells, his nose now gushes blood.

"If you ever touch her again, I will kill you!" Brent threatens.

Jaime backs the car up and peels out of the driveway. His tires leave hot, fresh rubber marks against the asphalt. Tears begin to pour from my eyes and my body trembles. I have no idea how the situation escalated so fast, and to think what might have happened if Brent hadn't come makes me tremble even harder.

Brent turns to me. I bury my head in his chest, and he holds me tightly while rubbing my hair. I feel safe in his arms.

"Raina, you're okay now. I'm not going to let

anyone hurt you," he assures me softly.

My legs are still shaking, and I can barely walk. Brent lifts me up in his arms and carries me inside the house and up to my room. He lays me on top of my bed, removing my heels, and covers me with a blanket.

I wrap my body inside it, and the warmth begins to calm me down.

I watch Brent pace back and forth. "I *knew* I should have picked you up. Next time I am going to listen to my gut feeling," he mutters under his breath.

I reach my arm out to him. "Brent, come sit down. Please?"

He stops immediately and sits down next to me on my bed. I gaze into his eyes, and I feel so much love. This feeling swarms through my veins. I realize he is my protector, my friend, and the love of my life. I can't deny it any longer, and I can't explain it either. I just know, with every inch of my being, that I am crazy for this man.

He brushes the hair from the side of my face, and I feel the brand on my cheek that his fingers have left behind. I know what I am feeling is love, but I am afraid to say it out loud.

"Will you just lay with me?"

Brent doesn't hesitate. He climbs over me, tucks my blanket under me, and wraps his arm over my waist. I grab ahold of his hand and entwine my fingers into his. The rhythm of his breath and the heat from his body lulls me into a deep sleep.

# Chapter 13

I open my eyes, and my room is pitch-black except for the faint, illuminating glow allowing me to only see the outline of the objects in front of me. I didn't realize I had fallen asleep; it must have been the incident from earlier that drained my emotions. I look down at my waist and can see Brent's arm is still wrapped around me. I crack a smile, happy to see he is still by my side.

I roll over, keeping his arm nestled around me, and face in his direction. He slowly opens his eyes. When he sees me, his eyes light up.

We lay here for a while, in quiet serenity. The energy surrounding us is heightened with an intense yearning for each other. I suddenly have this deep urge to release my feelings to him. I finally feel a *need* to tell him how I really feel.

I place my palm against his cheek, and I can feel a warmth flare up under my touch. He smiles, urging me on.

"Brent?"

"Yes, mon amour?"

He stares back at me with a look of dedicated love.

"I-I love you."

Brent doesn't even take a second to let my words sink in. He glides his hand through my hair and brings my face to his, touching his lips delicately against mine. This time he kisses me with a gratifying surrender. His tongue massages mine gently, moving in circles of sweet enjoyment like he wants to savor every last moment of this.

Our breath is rugged and intensifies with every second passing. I slide my hand down his side to the curve of his back, digging my fingers into his skin and bringing him closer to me. I *want* him. I *need* him. I feel like I have too much lost time to make up for, and I want to show him how much I love him at all costs.

I grab a hold of the bottom of his T-shirt and begin to slowly lift it up with desperation. Brent slows his kisses down and gives me little pecks on my lips.

"Raina, we have all the time in the world for that. You don't have to prove anything to me. There is no need to rush. Okay, mon amour?"

I give him my pouty lip, and he happily leans down to kiss it.

"I love you, Raina," he whispers in my ear. My heart melts, and I grab his face to begin another kissing session.

After what seems like eternity of kissing, I see my father's headlights in the driveway. Brent gives me one last kiss to remember and sneaks off into his room. Brent obviously has the respect and trust of my parents, but he has made it clear to me that courtship shouldn't fly out the window just because we have spent lifetimes together. My parents are from another era and still have those beliefs, no matter what century or decade it is. At least that is what Brent has told me.

**I** wake up to the aroma of bacon and eggs under my nostrils. My belly growls as I stalk the scent down the stairs. I walk into the kitchen and my father is cooking breakfast with Brent.

"Hey honey, are you hungry?" my father asks after giving me a kiss on the cheek.

"Yes, I'm starving!"

I look over at Brent, and he gives me a quick wink while buttering the toast. I take a seat at the kitchen table and my father brings me my vitamin along with a glass of orange juice. Brent brings the food over to the table and hands me the plate of bacon.

"Wow, this looks yummy," I complement them. "Why aren't you at work, Daddy?"

I see a quick meeting of the eyes between my father and Brent. "Well, I think it is time we talk, Raina."

I look between them both and can read the formality in their gaze. I admit, this makes me a little unsettled.

"O-okay, what is this about?" I ask. "Brent, is this about what you have told me?"

He smiles and his face warms. "Yes, mon amour. I thought it was time that your father answer any questions you may have."

I never realized Brent spoke French, but I guess I still don't really know everything about him.

"Daddy, how could you have not told me? How could you and Mom keep this from me for so long?"

I look to my father and wait. He looks conflicted, trying to come up with the best way to explain this all. "I promised your mother we would wait for the right time to tell you, and she and I have already spoken, and we both agree that it is that time now. She wanted to be here so badly, but she still has some work to do." He pauses for a brief moment. "Let me just start at the beginning.

"You were our first-born. Your mother and I were so happy when you came into this world. You were so full of life and possibilities. When we married you off, we were of the belief that you were going to live a fairytale and be treated with the utmost respect by your husband. He promised us that!" my father explains as his closed fist pounds against the table in anger. I jump back, startled.

"It had already been over a year, and we hadn't heard from you. You promised before you left that you would write to us every month. We wrote to you every single month but never received a letter back. We wanted so desperately to visit you to make sure you were okay, but your sister and brother had gotten sick with fever and we couldn't leave them."

I sit up, not believing what I have just heard. "What? I had a sister and brother? What were their names?"

"Hannah was your little sister—she passed away first—and Benjamin was only three years younger than you. He passed away on the first snowfall."

"That was when Brent's father had found me: on the first snowfall," I whisper to myself.

I zone in on the corner of the table, trying to make sense of this all. I had a brother and sister who I will never know again. If only I could remember, just recall one split second with them, it would mean the world to me.

My father continues. "As soon as we were able to take care of things back home, your mother and I packed up in search for you. It took us weeks of travel, and when we reached your husband's land, you were nowhere in sight.

"We had a feeling something was wrong, so we made sure not to make ourselves noticeable. Your husband had already found a new wife, and there were rumors from the townspeople that you had fell sick with fever. Your mother was a wreck—just lost two children and now her third. She fell into a deep depression. I didn't know how to help her," my father admits, shaking his head.

"How did you find me, Daddy?"

His face lights up. "We went deep into the woods to stay incognito, and that's when your mother came across you and Brent bathing in the lake. She was ecstatic and couldn't believe her eyes. She thought she was seeing an illusion; it had been years since we saw you."

My fathers looks worn down just having to dig through those memories.

"So, you knew Brent's parent's then?"

"Yes, they were wonderful people, and they loved you very much," he tells me.

I look over at Brent, and he nods his head in concurrence.

I soak everything in before getting back to a question that Brent refused to answer for me. This time I look directly at my father to ask. "So tell me, how does someone get reincarnated to the same parents over and over?"

My father rubs his eyes with his fingers and then takes a drink of his coffee. "It was the oddest thing. You became ill out of nowhere, like someone was sucking the energy right out of you. Then you became pale and extremely frail, your face and body had sunken in, almost like a ninety-year-old. We couldn't stop it or slow it down, and Brent, here, refused to live without you. So, we went in search for a witch."

All I can do is blink. I'm confounded, unsure if I just heard that correctly. "Wait, witches exist?" I ask, leaning forward in my seat.

Brent and my father laugh together. "Not in the way you may think, Raina," Brent jumps in.

"Okay, then how?" I ask, confused.

"Well, they don't wear the black pointy hats and ride on a broom," Brent teases, almost as if he is mocking me.

My lips draw into a straight line. I glare with fury, and I fold my arms against my chest.

"Brent, why don't you let me have at it, huh?" My dad takes the reins in an attempt to calm me down.

"What Brent was attempting to explain," my father

clears his throat and Brent snickers, "is that witches are like everyday people. If you passed them in the street, you would never know. There's a power that lies deep within their heritage, though, and to be a witch is to be a seeker, a teacher, a giver, a healer, and a protector of all life's things. They are more connected to nature and Mother Earth than any human being, and because of this, sometimes the impossibilities of the world become possible."

"So, where does the witch come into play with me then?"

My father takes a bite of his eggs and another big swig of his coffee. Brent has already scarfed down his plate, and I've suddenly lost my appetite.

"Brent's parent's knew of a woman, Eve, who practiced witchcraft. Your mother couldn't bear to see you go, though she knew you couldn't hold on any longer. When we got to Eve, she connected your soul to your mom's so you would always be born to her in future lives," my father divulges.

I sit for a moment, trying to wrap my mind around this. But I can't get past the question flashing in my head like a lit-up billboard: if my soul belongs to my mother, then where do Brent and I fit in with this whole eternity thing? How would we *truly* know we are eternal soul mates if I keep coming back to the same parents?

This is just way too much. I feel like I'm on overload, and I am about to come to a crashing halt. I excuse myself and run out to the front porch. I wrap my arms around my stomach, waiting for the fresh, crisp air to soothe me and take away my aching pain. My stomach is turning in knots and the vomit burns up my esophagus and protrudes out of my mouth without warning.

Tears rush down my cheeks as I'm bent over, hacking my lungs out. Familiar hands rest on my back with comfort while handing me a towel. I can't stop the tears from tumbling down. My body is finally releasing all the

Shevaun DeLucia

bottled up stress and anxiety that I have been holding in for the last couple of days.

"Raina, baby, are you okay? Do you need anything?" Brent tiptoes around me.

I slowly calm down enough to speak. "Brent, is this why you didn't want to be the one to tell me?" I yell angrily, tears still pouring down my face.

"What do you mean?" he responds defensively, snapping his head back. "I don't understand..."

"You said that my reincarnation is because of our love for one another, because we beat the odds. Now my father is telling me my soul belongs to my mother? Do I get a freaking say in anything in my life or *any* of my lives for that matter?! How do we know this is real, Brent? How can we really know if we were given the gift of eternity when you *know* I will keep coming back to the same parents? All you have to do is wait, and then line me up with all this bullshit about our souls belonging together!" I shout, ripping my hands through my hair and pacing the front yard.

I see the hurt in his eyes. "Raina, do you truly believe I would do that to you? I know you can feel what I feel when we're near each other. Now tell me, is that something I made up? God, Raina!" Brent leans into me, pain smeared on his face. "None of us knew if you would actually come back. Do you know how hard the next twenty five years were after you passed? Do you know how many times I wanted to just end my own life because it wasn't worth living without you? *Every* freaking second of *every* freaking day!" he reveals as tears roll down his face.

I stand in slight disbelief. I have never seen him in such dismay.

"I had to believe in us—believe in our love—and when your mother became pregnant, it was like a phenomenon. Immortals can't bare children, Raina. If she didn't have your soul bound to hers, you would have been born to someone else somewhere else in this world, and your mother would have remained childless forever.

"Don't you see, just the fact that you came back into this world proves that our love is for eternity. It doesn't matter who you would have come back as, because we would have found each other eventually. The universe would have lead us to each other, Raina," he says, sweating, arms raised in the air. "I guess there is nothing else I can say. It's now up to you to believe, mon amour."

He kisses my forehead and turns to walk away. My heart is mangled into a million messed up pieces. I don't know what to believe or how to even untangle and make sense of the information. I guess I need some time, but what I really need is my mother.

I take out my cell phone and dial her number.

"Raina?"

"Mama? When are you coming home?"

I *need* her, right now. She is the only one that knows what I need to hear. I know she will be able to guide me in the right direction, and direction is what I need, since I feel so lost right now.

"Aww baby, I won't be home for another week or two. Daddy told me he spoke with you this morning, and you didn't take it all that well."

Is she out of her mind? How did she think I was going to take it? With rainbows and flying pigs?

"Mama, how did you think I was going to react to all of this? This is all just crazy!" I say with my voice raised.

"Listen, baby. I know this is a lot for anyone to take in, and personally I think you are handling it a lot better than in the past. But, more than anything, just know that me and Dad love you, and we only did what we did for that reason. We were going to tell you, but we needed the right moment."

"I guess there is never a 'right' moment to tell

Shevaun DeLucia

someone they are immortal, huh?"

The faster I stop placing the blame, the faster I can
learn to accept my fate and begin my new life.

"Oh, Raina. There is just so much to tell you and
talk about. You have always been taken from us way too
soon, but I know this time will be different."

"But, how do you *know* this, mama?"

She takes a moment before she responds. "I know
because you have changed. I just feel it in my gut that you
will be with us for centuries to come, baby. You and Brent
are going to be so happy together."

It's obvious that my mother loves and respects
Brent or she would never say this. But what if Brent
changes his mind and doesn't want to be with me after
what I have just accused him of? I basically told him that
everything he believes in when it comes to us is a lie. More
importantly, what if I have changed so drastically that I
can't be the woman Brent believes me to be? He may
eventually realize I am not that same woman he fell in love
with.

"I don't know what to do about Brent," I admit.

"What do you mean, sweetie?"

I pace back and forth on the front porch, almost
denting the concrete with my footprints. "How do I know
what I feel between us is real? Maybe I am just feeling this
way because he's told me this is what I have felt in the past.
How do I know what he is saying is true?"

I stop pacing and stand quietly, waiting for her to
bring the hammer down and put me back in my place. My
mother is sweet as pie, but when she is passionate about
something and knows I am in the wrong, she is not afraid to
say it.

"Raina, sweetie, nobody can answer these questions
but you. You have to look inside yourself for the answer.
The only thing I can tell you is that Brent adores you, and
he has from the moment he laid eyes on you. I am sure he

168

will be willing to wait as long as you need."

"Mama, I do love him. I know with every inch of my body I do, but I'm not sure if that's enough right now."

I think what I need right now is some time and some space. But with Brent living in my home, that will be nearly impossible.

"Just give yourself some time."

I sigh. "I know. You're right, mama."

We hang up and I sit in the rocking chair behind me. I have a lot to think about and a long day ahead of me. Tonight was supposed to be my date night with Brent, but I'm sure that's all null and void now.

I sit for a moment longer, taking in the late morning light. The sun beats its golden beams against my skin, and it feels rejuvenating. I could use the extra energy right about now. I feel drained, and I feel I've lost control. I need to take my life back and own it, but how do I own something I know nothing about?

I hear the squeak of the door, and my body immediately freezes. The adrenaline I have been living off of the last couple of days is now depleted and another conversation might throw me over the edge.

I slowly peek my head over my shoulder and sigh deeply in relief as my father takes a seat next to me. We sit in a silence of understanding. My father makes no attempt to speak. We just listen to the rustle of the leaves skittering across the ground, aimlessly, and the whistle of the wind as it swirls through my strands of hair. Through the grumpy sky, I can almost hear screams of sunshine wanting to reclaim the fall sky, a little like my mood.

I look over at my father, welcoming the conversation now.

"How are you holding up?" he looks at me with deep concern.

I shift in my seat before speaking. "I'm letting it all sink in. How are you holding up? I mean, you have to be afraid of losing me all over again. How do you do it?"

He takes a long gaze at the world in front of him while pondering my questions.

"It has always been bittersweet. You take a piece of my heart with you every time you pass into the next dimension. It's gut-wrenching to let you go, but when you come back to us, we get the joys of watching you grow all over again," my father explains.

He looks very conflicted as he explains this to me. I can see the ripple of pain my deaths have caused him along with the pure blissfulness he has found with watching me grow each and every time. I think there is an underlying numbness to him, and I am sure all these years of having to watch a child die over and over again has caused him to build up a barrier. I mean, who wouldn't in his situation?

I do have to say, though, my father never once faltered from allowing me complete and total access to his heart. He has given me an amazing childhood to look back on, and I can only be grateful for it. But no matter how hard he tries to conceal it, I can still see the worry in his eyes. It must be the unknown that continuously tugs at him.

"I can understand how you see it that way. I just hope this time is different. I hope we don't have to worry about planning my funeral any time soon." I can't believe how easily that slid off my tongue, as though my death is an everyday occurrence. "Tell me how Mom is holding up."

My father shakes his head softly. "You know your mother puts on a strong façade, but deep down inside she is a mess. As soon as you hit sixteen, she always goes downhill."

"Why sixteen?"

"That seems to be the age where it all has the possibility to begin. Your sickness never seems to pick a particular time or age, but it just always seems to happen after the age of sixteen," he says matter-of-factly.

Eternal Mixture

This must be why Brent has chosen to come here, to make sure he spends enough time with me before he loses me.

"Is this why Brent has decided to come here?" I wonder, knowing my father will tell me only the truth.

My father puts his hand over mine. "No, Raina. He's has been begging us for years to come here, but it has been your mother and I who have denied him. We felt you weren't ready or mature enough for these heavy grown-up issues. But, most of all, we know how deeply he loves you, and we just wanted you to be old enough for that type of love."

I jumped to assumptions, and I was obviously wrong. Brent has been waiting years to steal a moment with me and now that he has finally gotten permission to, I do nothing but push him away.

"Daddy, tell me about my other lives. Have I always felt this way about Brent?"

My father stands up and leans down to kiss me on the cheek. He then faces me and says, "Just follow your heart, sweetie. It will lead you to the answers you are seeking. The heart never lies." He gives me a wink and turns to walk back into the house.

# Chapter 14

The hot water runs through my hair and down my spine, thawing my skin from this morning's brisk air. The scent of the rose soap fills the steamed air, soothing my muscles and releasing some of the stress left from the morning's conversations.

I can't help but replay my father's last words through my head: "the heart never lies." This may be true, but is my heart leading me in the right path? Just because my heart may feel something, doesn't always make it right. Brent seems to have always been the right choice for me in the past from what I am told, but is he the right choice for me in this life?

These are all questions demanding my immediate attention, yet part of me just feels that following my heart *will* somehow guide me to these answers, as my father has said. And that is just what I plan to do, for now.

I step out of the shower after reaching my decision and dry off. The mirrors are thick with condensation, and the hot steam still clouds the air. I thrust my towel around my naked body, holding it closed with my hand, and open

172

the bathroom door to head to my bedroom. I exit the threshold, and I bump right into Brent. I jump back, startled, towel slipping from my hands as they fly in the air. Here I stand, nude, in front of the man I love. I'm completely mortified. I try to cover myself as I lean down to grab my towel.

"Oh shit!" Brent says, eyes wide open. Stunned by the sight of my bare skin, he immediately covers his eyes and turns around.

"Oh my God! I am so sorry!" I screech, trying to quickly wrap the towel back around myself.

Brent turns around, eyes still covered. "Are you okay? Can I uncover my eyes?" he asks as he stands in front of me, laughing.

"What is so funny?" I growl through my teeth.

He takes his hands away from his eyes, and I can see a twinkle of excitement gleaming through them—along with the excitement showing through his sweatpants. He must have realized where my eyes have traveled to, because he places his hands in front of his bulge.

"Raina, I didn't see anything," Brent lies, still smiling from ear to ear.

"You are such a liar! The proof is practically poking me in the eye!"

His face turns scarlet, but this doesn't stop him from continuing to crack up, his eyes filled with tears.

"Okay, okay, you got me. But, *wow*, how could I not look?"

I continue to scowl at him.

He takes a step toward me and strokes his finger down my cheek. "Raina, you are beautiful."

I don't know whether to melt under his touch or to be embarrassed that he's talking about my birthday suit.

"Thank you," I respond, not sure what else I can possibly say after this horrifying moment.

"So, I was hoping we were still on for our date," he

says, completely changing the subject.

"I figured you wouldn't want to go through with it after today."

I crushed him this morning, and he still wants to go on our date? I don't get how he would even want to spend time with me after questioning our love or his love, for that matter.

"Listen, I know you have questions, confusion, and doubt. And I am okay with that; it's only normal. I also know that in time you will figure it all out, and I would never hold that against you. But, while you're trying to figure things out, I want us to spend time together and get to know one another on a different level. So my response to you is yes, I still want to follow through with our date."

He is being nothing but patient with me, and I owe it to us *and* our past to give us time.

I give him a soft smile. "Okay, what time are you picking me up?"

"I'll be at your door by six o'clock."

He gives me a kiss on my forehead, walks past me, and shuts the door to the bathroom.


**I** decide to get out of the house for a little while and head over to Maddie's for some much-needed girl time. We head into the kitchen where her mother is getting together some lunch.

"Hi Mrs. Lakes," I greet her as I enter the kitchen.

Maddie's mother, Gina Lakes, is a little older than most mothers with children our age. She has the strands of silver throughout her hair and wrinkles that years of life provide, along with the smile lines that come with a lifetime of laughter. Maddie's parents tried for years to have a child and finally got blessed with Maddie after her mother's fortieth birthday.

Mrs. Lakes is a lot like my mother: amazingly

patient, full of wisdom, and just simply thankful for the gift to look after another life. For a moment, I think of myself. I am immortal, and immortal beings aren't supposed to have the ability to have children, from what Brent tells me. Now, because of a choice far beyond my control, motherhood may never be an option for me. It saddens me that this choice has possibly been taken from me, but at this time in my life, I have no urge to dwell on the issue.

"Hi, Raina. Are you hungry?" Mrs. Lakes asks, already putting Maddie's sandwich together.

We take a seat at the kitchen counter. "Yes, starving! I didn't eat much breakfast this morning."

"How are your parents doing, dear?"

"They're good. My mom's out of town right now for work and my dad is relaxing at home today," I tell her, hoping she'll move on to something else.

Mrs. Lakes sets down two plates full of chips, a sandwich, and a pickle each, and comes back with drinks in hand.

"Thanks, Mom," Maddie says before she takes a huge bite of her turkey sandwich.

My stomach growls before I can even put the food to my mouth. "This is great! Thank you." I praise Mrs. Lakes.

"You are welcome, dear."

Mrs. Lakes takes off to the grocery store, and Maddie looks over at me with raised eyebrows and a sly grin.

"What?" I ask, feeling a little put on the spot.

"Um, this time you are so going to tell me what happened between you and Jaime. I am *dying* to know!" she says, accentuating her point by waving her hands in the air.

Yesterday seems like a century away already. I almost forgot that Jaime and I even had a date last night. I am a little embarrassed about how it ended, but I have to remind myself it wasn't my fault. It was Jaime who was being the jerk.

I take a deep breath and dive back into last night.

"It started out okay. We went to his uncle's restaurant, and we were having great conversation. But I couldn't take my mind off Brent. He called me during the date to check up on me, and Jaime got upset. When we got back to my house, we kissed, but then he was trying to take it too far. Brent came out and punched him, and then Jaime sped off."

Maddie's face right now is priceless. Her mouth is hung open with no words to follow. She is speechless, and it's sort of fun to watch.

"So, wait, let me get this straight. Brent came to your rescue, and you still don't want to be with him?"

"Well, we're sort of going on a date tonight."

Her face lights up as though she has been secretly cheering for him all along.

"*Okay,* and what exactly do you mean by 'Jaime was trying to take it too far?'"

Her eyes are steady, and she waits for my answer. "We were kissing, and he kept putting his hand up my dress. And at one point right before Brent opened the door, he tried to pull my panties down."

"Are you kidding me, Raina?" Maddie freaks. "I always saw him as a gentleman. Not the type to push sex on a first date!"

"Yeah, well, he was pretty pushy. I was thankful that Brent came when he did."

In fact, I had never been so glad to see someone. It makes me nervous to think how far Jaime might have tried to take it or how far I would have had to go to stop him. But luckily for me, I didn't get the chance to find out.

"*And* how did you show your gratefulness to Brent?" Maddie hints. No one needs to know the intimate details besides Brent and I.

Eternal Mixture

"He was great, Maddie. He just laid with me until I fell asleep. He was a perfect gentleman," I inform her. I'm not lying, but I'm also not telling her the full truth, which is that *I* was trying to seduce *him*.

"Raina, I am so happy he was there for you. I want to kill Jaime right now!"

I just adore her. She is always so passionate when it comes to her friends. I couldn't ask for a better person to be best friends with.

"Yeah, well, wait until B finds out about that. She was completely rooting for Jaime. She is going to be pissed once she finds out what actually went down."

"Oh, you're right about that!" she agrees, chuckling to herself.

Right now, in this moment, I can't stop thinking of Jenna and how she should be here with us. We were always the four amigos, the four musketeers, and now she has just simply jumped off the face of the earth. I *have* to find a way to speak to Jason alone.

"What are you thinking about? You have that faraway look on your face," Maddie notices. She knows me oh-too-well and knows when I get this look on my face that something serious is brewing.

"Jason."

"You're thinking about *Jason?*"

"Yes, I still need to figure out a way to talk to him, *without* Jenna," I inform her.

I watch as a light bulb turns on in her head. "Well, I think I might know a way," she spills with a devilish grin.

I lean in a little closer with excitement. "How?"

"So, the other day I did some investigating. I followed Jenna home and saw Jason's car in her driveway already waiting for her. I waited until he left and then followed him home. You won't believe this, but he lives by himself in the motel behind Billiards."

I can't believe this. This doesn't make any sense.

He must be older than what he led us to believe. I mean, no parents *and* he can afford a room without having a job? Just seems very odd.

"Maddie, are you sure that he wasn't meeting someone there?"

"No, I am definitely sure. When he went in his room, I crept outside his window and watched him. It was definitely his room, and no one else came to visit him," she says in confidence.

"Okay, so that's where I will have to confront him. I will wait outside in the parking lot, and he will have no choice but to speak with me."

My plan feels solid. I just have to convince him to keep our conversation between him and I, Jenna seems to be in a fragile state and I don't want to give her yet another reason to hate me.

"Maybe you should wait until you see him in a public place."

"No, then I am risking the chance of Jenna being there."

Maddie stands up and walks towards the sink to place her dishes inside. "Okay, maybe you're right. But I am coming with you when you decide to talk with him. I won't let you go alone," Maddie insists.

"Fine. Come with me, but stay out of it. I don't want Jenna taking it out on you if she finds out."

Maddie holds her hand out to me, and we shake on it.

I look over at the time on the microwave and realize I only have roughly three hours until date night. I brought my things over in hopes that Maddie would help me get ready.

"I have my things in the car; can you do my hair for me?"

Maddie begins to jump up and down in her seat with excitement while clapping her hands together.

Eternal Mixture

178

"Yes, of course! Go get your things and meet me upstairs!"

I was indecisive about what I wanted to wear, so I grabbed a number of different outfits. I have my stonewashed skinny jeans along with my sexy black sweater and black stilettos. I also brought my tan sweater dress—tight in all the right places, not leaving much to the imagination—and my dark brown knee-high hooker boots to go with it.

When I pull these out to show Maddie, her mouth drops. She never even knew I owned this type of clothing, and I think the pure sex the clothing puts off shocks her.

"Um, Raina, where did you get these?" she asks, holding the boots up with her two fingers as if they were poisoned.

"I bought them at the mall. Just never had a reason to wear them until now. So, what do you think? Casual or sexy?"

She bites on her bottom lip while looking between the clothing and then back up at me, trying to decipher. Finally she holds up the skinny jeans and black stilettos with a smile.

"These heels are going to drive him crazy. Believe me, men love a sexy pump." You would think Maddie's had a ton of experience with this.

I slip off my beige everyday bra and slip into my black lace brassiere feeling an overwhelming surge of power and confidence. This is a foreign feeling for me, and I get the sense that this is what a hungry New York businesswoman feels like on a Friday night: sexy and controlled, with a deep-down craving that is dying to be fulfilled.

My sweater is cut low, illuminating the softness of my skin and bringing immediate attention to my breasts—something Brent's already viewed firsthand. But, I am sure the image of me has been replaying in his head since this morning, so any glimpse of my skin will now just heighten those images. This, of course, will give me the upper hand in my attempts to seduce him.

My jeans hug me in all the right places, and Maddie gives me a loose curl so he'll be able to slide his fingers through my hair without any resistance. My makeup is flawless: a natural pink to my lips and eyes outlined like cat eyes to reel in my bait. With a squirt of Versace perfume and a dab of lip gloss, I am ready for my date night with Brent.

"Raina, you look beautiful. Brent is going to melt when he sees you," Maddie comments in awe.

"Thanks."

I give her a hug goodbye and head out to my car. When I get back to my house, my father has already left for work. Whether it's Saturday or Wednesday has no meaning when it comes to my father and his work. He is dedicated, and I am grateful for the time I had with him this morning.

The house is quiet upon entering. I head up to my room to put my things away. I hear a quiet knock on the outside of my door. The blood in my body rushes to my heart, and the butterflies in the pit of my stomach begin to flutter furiously. My palms feel slick with sweat and my armpits feel warm and moist.

I take one last deep breath and open my bedroom door to Brent.

His eyes immediately bulge out of his head. "*Wow*, you look amazing!"

I can't help but smile with satisfaction. This is the exact response I was hoping for. I want to be his friend, his lover, and his seductress all in one. We still have so much to learn about each other, but no matter how hard I try, I can't deny the need to be with him in *every* way.

"Thank you."

Brent grabs my hand and brings me close to him. I breathe in the smell of fresh soap and sweet man, a combination that makes my knees weak and my inner thighs wet. I try to gain my control back, but it's useless when I am in his hands.

My eyes lock with his. Brent's lips are only inches from mine, and instead of joining as one, he snickers and chuckles with amusement as he turns and pulls me towards the stairs.

"Are you ready for tonight?" he questions with a smirk as we walk towards his car.

He opens the door for me. "Are *you* ready for tonight?" I throw the question back in his face.

Brent grins and closes my door.

He gets in the driver's seat and starts the engine. He peeks my way, eyes sliding up and down every inch of my body until they land on my lips. I see the thirst in his eyes as he drinks me in, and all I want to do is ravage his inner thoughts and his body until my desire is fulfilled.

Instead, I break from his gaze, knowing this might frustrate him, and ask what is on the agenda tonight. He slides his fingers through his tousled hair, trying to gain a grip on my quick maneuver. But, instead of allowing himself to fall for my attempt to gain control, he throws me a curveball.

"Raina, kiss me, please?" Brent pleads unfairly with his bright golden stare.

My lips part with every attempt to be defiant, but I surrender to him instead. I surrender to him, to our love, and to my longtime itch that has been dying to be scratched by him. So I dive into pure ecstasy.

Shevaun DeLucia

# Chapter 15

We have been driving for over an hour, and Brent still has not given me any clue as to where we are headed. Surrounding us along this windy road are trees engulfed in blackness, and yellow dashes on the road flash before us as we trudge along to our destination.

I'm not sure I dressed appropriately for the occasion, due to the fact that Brent is dressed in casual attire: ripped blue jeans and a perfectly fitted muscle T-shirt that grips the curves and contours of this chest.

He must sense my uneasiness and quickly lays it to bed by assuring me perfection is all he sees. I, of course, roll my eyes at his mush and dare him to speak nothing but the truth.

"You're too hard on yourself, Raina. You just don't realize how beautiful you are. You look bangin', with or without clothes," Brent comments, throwing me a wink.

I quickly smack him on the arm and promise to ease up on myself a little. He is right. I *am* too hard on myself. I need to start believing in myself and my intuition. I always second-guess myself, and that's when I end up in a bad situation. I mean, look what ended up happening with

Jaime. A good situation gone bad, and I only have myself to blame for not trusting my own doubts.

"You are such a pervert!" I hiss jokingly. "So, what is the deal, are we almost wherever we're going or what?"

Brent shakes his head and laughs. He grabs my hand and rubs his thumb over mine. After another thirty minutes, he nudges his head forward for me to look ahead. We pull up to a small cabin hidden deep in the woods. I look in all directions and see nothing but trees.

"Where *are* we?"

Brent turns the ignition off and reaches behind my seat to grab a large paper bag.

"We are at my Aunt Lilly's cabin. This is where I first laid eyes on you as a baby."

Talk about throwing me for a loop. I grab his arm before he can hop out of the car. "Wait, what did you just say?"

"I said, 'Here is where we first meet in this lifetime,'" Brent repeats and then jumps out of the car.

I quickly follow behind him. The cabin is small and petite with a cozy quality. We step onto the small front porch, and I see two wooden rocking chairs facing our wooded surroundings.

Brent unlocks the door and pushes it open, allowing me to be the first to walk through the threshold. A sort of calmness rushes through me, giving my veins a crystallized sweetness. This place is original—a time warp, never faltering from its genuine purpose—and a real monument to the past.

To my right is a pull-out couch with a wooden frame. On top, a mattress stuffed with down feathers and a fluffy oversized rug warming the ice-cold floor in front of a small brick fireplace. Behind me, the kitchen holds a rusted old bubble fridge from the '40s, a wood-burning stove topped with a dingy old tea kettle, and a table only big enough for two.

I stand here for a moment, taking it all in. The beauty is in the essence of age and time and the simple décor that sends one back into the past. It all feels perfect, considering the circumstances, and when I feel the little hairs on my skin stand up, I realize I almost forgot that Brent is standing right next to me, watching me intently.

I turn to him. He smiles. "What are you smiling at?" I ask, amused at his amusement.

"You."

I walk in farther, placing my purse on the table. When I turn, he is standing in front of me, eyes gleaming and filled with hunger like a wild animal. He makes me nervous when he looks at me this way. I know what is passing through his mind, because I have had the same thoughts myself. But, knowing it is just us here in the middle of nowhere means *anything* is possible. We are really and truly alone. Now *that* makes my stomach turn and twist into a million frayed knots.

I try to say his name, but my voice squeaks instead.

I know he can sense my uncertainty, and deep down inside, I know he only means well. Still, he *is* a man with needs, *especially* after 150 years of life.

Brent smiles at me with adoration. "Raina, I didn't bring you here to seduce you, if that is what you're worried about. I brought you here because this place means a lot to me. This cabin was where I held you for this first time in this lifetime. Here was the first moment I knew I would be whole again, and *here* was the first moment that I knew our lives would be different this time."

I'm trying to grasp all that he has just said, but I can't seem to wrap my head around it.

"Whoa! Okay, hold on a minute," I tell him, lifting my finger up for him to pause as I ponder his words. I turn and begin to pace. "What do you mean you *held* me?" I start with question number one while halting my pace to face him eye to eye.

Eternal Mixture

Brent takes a deep breath and then begins. "When you were first born, Lillian and I came here to see you. Raina, you were beautiful and *so* perfect. I got to hold you when you cried. It was the sweetest sound I ever heard. I rocked you to sleep night after night. You would wrap your little tiny finger around mine and your mother had to pry it from mine," he explains with a far-away dazed smile. "When you were young, it was a different type of love I had for you, more like your protector, big brother, a parent. It wasn't until I saw you for the first time at thirteen when my love changed, but even then I knew you were too young to love. So, I waited patiently until now."

I tuck my hair behind my ear. "You saw me at thirteen? How come I don't remember?"

I shift through my memories, trying to find one with his face before he answers, but I come up empty.

Brent takes the kettle and runs the tap water into it. He must have already came up here earlier to prepare, because the wood has already been placed in the stove. After lighting the wood burner, he has me sit down at the table.

"You don't remember because you never saw me. I begged your parents to allow me to come visit you, but they wouldn't. They were afraid you weren't ready for me and maybe they were right, but I had to make sure you were okay, regardless. They couldn't always be there for you because of their work, and that worried me. I never stayed long. Just until I was sure everything and everyone surrounding you was positive," he explains while holding my hands. I see the slight fear he has with opening up to me like this, so I squeeze his hands to reassure him it is okay.

"So you're good with babies, huh?"

I have no idea why I just asked that. This is a subject we are probably never going to have to worry about. I wonder, though, if he is okay with this void in life.

"Yes, I am *very* good with babies. I helped raise you

Shevaun DeLucia

many lifetimes over," he admits, proud gratification pouring out of him.

"Brent, you told me immortals can't have babies. I know my parents were the exception, but where does that leave us?"

I whacked him right in the face with the big pink elephant in the room. There is nowhere to run and nowhere to hide. His only option is to answer this question head-on.

"Hmm, I knew this subject would eventually come front and center. I just didn't think it would be so soon," he confesses, with a sort of sadness taking over his eyes.

My heart plummets with the thought of possibly causing him pain. I'm sure this is a wound we have had to revisit many times before, and here I am, reopening it.

"I'm sorry. Is it hard for you to talk about?"

I can almost taste the overbearing sadness I see beneath his surface.

"Maybe a little. We never really talked about having a family all that much. You usually leave me before we get that far ahead."

Now I really feel awful. Why didn't I think of that? Now I have caused a dark, gloomy cloud to hover over our beautiful night together.

Brent squeezes my hands. "This time is going to be different though. I *know* it. Let's just cross that bridge when we come to it, okay? I strongly believe where there is a will, there is a way."

He always knows just the right thing to say. The clouds break, and I can see the sun again. He is right. If immortals can exist, then anything is possible.

"You know, my parents really adore you," I inform him. "They already think of you as part of our family."

Brent laughs. "I don't think they ever really had a choice."

"I don't believe that for one minute," I contest. "The love that I see is not forced—it's natural and authentic. This type of affection only comes from years of earned respect and loyalty."

Brent looks as though he is reflecting back to a certain moment in time. A time where I might not have existed. "Your parents and I have been through great ordeals together and have overcome many obstacles."

"Tell me about one, *please*?" I beg of him.

I need to know something, *anything* about my past. I feel a void that needs to be fulfilled, and he, along with my parents, holds the key to make me whole again.

Brent walks over to the stove with two coffee mugs in hand and pours the steaming water into them. He then heads over to the couch and sets the scorching hot mugs down on the end table. I stand up and follow him to the living area while he works on the fire.

Immediately, I can feel a deep warmth caress my insides as the crackle of the firewood snaps, and I sink snugly into the couch's mattress. I hold my mug full of hot cocoa in my hands, waiting for him to begin a story from our past.

Brent grabs his cup and sits down next to me, facing his body my way.

"It was the early nineteen hundreds on Christmas Eve. We were having dinner with your parents. They lived in a small cottage on the outskirts of town. We were watching the snowfall while listening to Christmas music on the radio box. The fireplace was crackling, stockings hung from the mantle, and candles flickered a golden light throughout the room. It was an ideal, perfect night.

"During that era, it was unheard of for a couple to live together unwed, but we were no ordinary couple. Your parents allowed me to stay with you in their house until we decided to marry. They knew I couldn't stay away from you, and we couldn't live apart. We were inseparable. We told the townspeople I was your far-away cousin who came to visit."

Shevaun DeLucia

"Did they believe us?"

He takes a sip of his cocoa. "Honestly, we barely went into town. We kept to ourselves. We stayed close enough to the lake to make sure the water was available for our mixture, but far enough away from the town so questions wouldn't be asked. We made sure to cover all our bases.

"Your parents didn't stay up too late that night. They left the fire going and allowed us to spend some of the holiday alone. We snuggled up on the couch together. I was waiting all night to give you your Christmas present, and the time finally came. You looked so angelic, Raina. Your nose and cheeks were a rosy pink and your hair smelled like vanilla from the cookies you and your mother were baking earlier that day. I wanted to remember you in that moment forever.

"My mother, of course, had already passed in the tragedy, but somehow I came across her ring. I was walking along our lake where the incident had happened, and there it was in the mud, as though it was calling for me: her wedding ring. She had one simple diamond encrusted in a small silver rose. I had it cleaned and added a couple of diamonds around the band. I put it in a small red velvet box and placed it in your hand that night.

"You opened the box and immediately gasped. Tears rushed down your cheeks as I got down on my knee and asked for you hand in marriage," Brent reveals, completely blowing my mind.

I sit up in my seat, back straight and eyebrows pointed to the ceiling. "You mean to tell me we got married?"

Brent's face drops and a tear releases down his face. A moment goes by before he answers. "No, you passed away before we could get married."

I slump back in my seat, all excitement gone. I should have known it was inevitable. We both sit here in

Eternal Mixture

silence, letting the moment sink in. How can he possibly think this time will be different? Every good moment has been followed by a bad one. Where does he scrape up the hope?

"Raina, look at me," Brent asks, placing his fingers under my chin. "I wouldn't trade any of those moments for the world. They are part of us, and they made us. Whether you remember or not, I do believe one day it will all come back to you, and when it does, I'll be right there by your side," he pauses for a moment. "That's only if you will have me, of course."

I press his hand against my cheek and close my eyes. Just the warmth from the heat radiating off his skin soothes me. My mouth waters with the scent of his manly aroma mixed with hot cocoa as it roams past my nose. It's a delightful combination. And just knowing that I told him about my doubts upsets me. I wish I could take it all back, the constant questions and uncertainty, the second-guessing of his love for me. I finally believe in him and in us. All I want to do is start our life together and work on the future.

I open my eyes, looking back into his. "I am not going anywhere. You're stuck with me."

He lights up, grins ear to ear, and leans in to kiss me. His lips are so plush against mine. The electricity surging between us is magical, and as he slowly thrusts his tongue deep into the moist cavity of my mouth, I let out a quiet moan of satisfaction. Just the taste of him soars through my body and the silky warmth of his tongue ignites every nerve ending, lighting me on fire.

I scoot myself closer to him while tangling my fingers through his thick, sexy hair. I can't seem to get enough of him. My head falls back with his tug and his lips cover my neck, giving me love nibbles that drive me into pure ecstasy.

I remove my hands from his hair and feel my way under his shirt. I pass through the swollen ripples of his

Shevaun DeLucia

stomach and slowly inch my way up to his mounds of pecks. His body is perfection, and the burn I feel from his skin to my fingertips is buzzing through me, making me warm and tingly inside. These feelings are strange, yet so familiar to me, almost like déjà vu.

Brent pulls back just enough to meet my eyes. "Raina, look at me," he begs.

I know I shouldn't feel self-conscious, but a small part of me is. Maybe it's because I'm inexperienced, or because I fear I may be doing something wrong.

"Don't be shy."

I gather the courage and bring my eyes to his.

"I love you. I want to spend the rest of my life with you, and I don't want to wait. We've waited so long already," Brent explains, making absolutely no sense whatsoever.

I try to comprehend his words. They're all jumbled in my head. "Brent, I don't understand what you're trying to say."

He sits up straight and puts his hands on my shoulders. "Raina, do you love me?"

He sounds ridiculous.

"Of course I do."

"Love is all that matters in life. We are soul mates. We belong together, so why wait? Marry me," he blurts out, steadily watching and waiting for my reaction.

I shimmy out of his grip and stand up, needing some air and some space. I'm trying my hardest to grasp what he's just asked me. I mean, did he really just ask me to marry him? I am only sixteen. Is he crazy?

I rush my fingers through my hair, trying anything to stop myself from going into pure panic mode. I stand in front of the fireplace, watching the flames lick the chimney as they convert into multiple layers of colors. I am not a flame. I can't just transform into something because it's what I am supposed to do. And just because I love him doesn't mean marriage should be the next step.

I turn to him calmly now. "Brent, I can't marry you." I walk back to the couch and sit down next to him. "I'm too young. I need to live life first. *We* need to live life first. I'm not saying that I don't see that in the future for us, I am just saying not right now. You have lived a long and full life. And I know you're ready for the next step, but I am not. Can you please understand? I love you Brent. I am ready to spend the rest of my life with you. But, I need you to just slow down a little."

Even though I just denied his proposal, he still has that twinkle in his eyes.

"That's what I am asking for, the rest of eternity together. I just got a little ahead of myself, I guess," he admits, chuckling at himself. "I have waited this long, what's another couple of years?"

I laugh and move myself over to sit on his lap. I wrap my arms around his neck and lean my head down on his chest. "Why rush forever? Anyways, you might soon realize that I am not the person you fell in love with."

He kisses my forehead. "Impossible."

He says that with such faith.

We sit like this, watching flames glisten with the colors of sunset while listening to the fire crackle for what seems like forever until we hear a grumble from my stomach. It's now eight o'clock. The time has flashed by. Brent jumps up, sets me on the couch, and heads to the kitchen. I follow. The refrigerator is already stocked with veggies, meats, and other ingredients for us to cook.

He bangs through the small cupboard, gathering the pots and pans. He hands me a knife and sets the tomatoes and cucumbers on the cutting board for me.

"What are we making?" I ask as I cut into the tomato.

Brent's already busy seasoning and chopping the chicken. He turns to me, grabs my hips, pulls me close, and

Shevaun DeLucia

applies his sweet lips to my right cheek. "I thought we would eat light and healthy tonight: a chicken salad," he tells me. He gives me a wink and turns to finish his work on the chicken.

"*Yum*, that sounds perfect!"

I could go for something safe right about now. I just don't know if my stomach can wait. It's ripping and roaring like a hungry tiger.

"*Oh*, I forgot. I brought a little pinot grigio for us to drink. If you're okay with that, that is?"

Is that alcohol? I've never even tasted alcohol before. *Or* have I?

"I've never even tasted that before, *I think*," I inform him, hoping he won't see me as child-like.

He takes a glass out of the cupboard and pours me a small amount. "I keep forgetting you are not as experienced as I. *Actually*, you are, but you just don't remember."

I take the glass and sniff the liquid. He watches me in amusement, and when the bitter sweet wetness slides down my throat, I shiver. I can't decide whether it stings me with disgust or warms me with delight.

Brent is too busy laughing from the reaction on my face. He's not able to get his words out. I stand here with my hands on my hips, waiting for him to simmer down.

"Are you done yet?"

"Oh my God, Raina. You should have seen your face. It was priceless!" he chuckles, still out of breath from laughing.

"Ha ha, hilarious," I reply sarcastically.

He pours me some more but this time and adds some Sprite to cut the bitterness. He watches me carefully as I take another sip. This time it tastes like grape pop, and the sizzle slides down my throat with ease.

"Hmm, much better."

Brent gives me a quick kiss and turns to place the chicken in the frying pan. There's a quick snap and pop as the chicken browns from the sear. I finish the salad and garnish it with croutons. The wine is beginning to take some effect. I feel warm and fuzzy inside, my cheeks are flush, and my giddiness is showing front and center.

Brent takes one look at me and informs me that this will be my last glass. I laugh at his commanding voice and then walk over to pour myself some more. He gives me a disapproving look, but ultimately, if I get drunk it's his fault for bringing the alcohol here.

I get out the plates and set the table. He dumps the chicken in the salad and mixes it up with some oil and vinegar. I can't help but stuff my face as fast as I can swallow. I forget about my surroundings as I inhale the food, until I hear a snicker from across the table.

I pause in the middle of chewing and feel my face begin to burn.

"Is it good?"

I swallow and take a sip of my wine. "Ahem. Sorry, I was starving," I giggle.

Brent takes a sip of his drink and then pauses, just staring.

"What?" I ask.

He shakes his head slowly. "You're just so beautiful."

He always does this to me. He makes my insides melt. I'm never prepared for his systematic charm.

"Oh, *please!*" I burst out. I get up from the table to place my dish in the sink. I turn and lean my body against the sink. This night we are having gives me a glimpse into our future, which automatically drudges another thought up. "Brent?"

"Yes?"

"What are we supposed to do for eternity?"

There have been many days where this thought has crossed my mind, and to be honest, it worries me. What can someone possibly do with forever?

Shevaun DeLucia

He stands up, leans in, and locks me in with his arms on each side of me. "Whatever our hearts desire."

The muscle in my chest begins to pump on overload. Every neuron in my body lights with a crazed energy. My thighs burn and my knees feel as though they might give out. I reach my hand to his face and bring him into me. Our breaths are ragged, and I can feel the beat of his heart from under me.

"Your heart is beating fast," I inform him.

His eyes never waver from mine. "So is yours," he whispers back, leaning into me.

"I love you," I say.

He sweeps me off my feet in one swift movement, brings me over to the rug and lays me down. His body lays next to mine, the heat disseminates from him, making me overheat. I can't restrain myself. I want him, I want *all* of him. My body is screaming to be touched in every womanly way possible.

He must sense my impulsive urge as he locks in to my eyes. In this moment, I can *see* him. I can see *every* piece of him down to the depths of his blackest secret. All his darkness and all his sadness disappears when I am with him. He is the darkness and I, his light. My soul is entwined to his, and when my body has moved on to another dimension, all promise and meaning of life is lost within him.

Each and every time he loses me, he sinks deeper down the abyss of nothingness. Every time I soar back into his realm, it's that much harder for him to return to my light. What happens if he is wrong and this life is no different from the others? Will he be able to overcome darkness, or will he become a prisoner to it?

"Brent, I'm scared," I admit, my voice shaking from what I have just witnessed.

He grazes his finger down my cheek. "What are you scared of, mon amour?" he asks me so softly.

Eternal Mixture

A teardrop falls across my temple. "What happens if you can't come back to me? If somehow this life shows to be no different from the others? How will you relinquish your depression? I know what it does it you, Brent. I *see* you, and I saw the hold it has over you when I am gone. I am afraid for you."

He takes a long deep breath and then kisses my forehead. "You still don't believe, do you?"

I let his word sink in for a minute. "Believe what?"

"That love conquers all. It doesn't matter how immersed I become. I can always find your light. It is you who guides me out, Raina. Don't you see? Our love is invincible! There is nothing or no one that can come between it."

I immediately grab his face and smash my lips against his in a desperate attempt to be melded with him. I can't get enough of him. I want to crawl inside him and stay there forever. Now *this* is what love is.

Love is not selfish or conditional. Love is neither jealous nor resentful. Love forgives with the power to overcome all obstacles. I have finally been touched, and *I* am in love.

# Chapter 16

A little over a week has passed since that night together. Halloween has come and gone, and the leaves on the trees have fallen, leaving their limbs open and vulnerable. The first snow is said to fall sometime late in the week, which means the holidays are coming near.

My mother and Lillian have run into some complications and are not intending on coming home for another couple of weeks. That day will be bittersweet for me; my mother will be home, but the room across the hall from me will be empty.

Brent had opened up to me the night we were at the cabin, and I've had a lot of time to think some things through. First, he proposed to me. He was heartbroken when I denied him, but he covered it very well. Unfortunately, because of our strange bond, there is very little he is able to hide from me. Second, he opened my eyes and showed me what real love is supposed to be about. Third and most importantly, I have had a revelation: I am head over heels in love.

I get butterflies in my stomach when I think about it. I am in love. *Me*, actually in love! I want to scream this to the world while jumping up and down on my bed. I want to dance like a happy child on Christmas morning. But, most of all, I want to dive into his arms and ravage him like a hungry lion. How am I ever going to keep myself under control?

I hear my phone vibrate against my nightstand. When I lift it up, I see my mother's number on the caller ID.

"Hey, Mom."

"Hi sweetie, are you getting ready for school?"

I know my mother has been gone for a little while, but she has never called me this early. I wonder why it couldn't wait.

"Yes, what else would I be doing? Mom, is everything okay?"

I hear only silence for a moment.

"Well, I'm just worried about you. Have you been taking your vitamin?"

I can't help but huff with annoyance. "Yes, Mom. This can't be what you're calling about."

"Listen, there are some things I will explain to you when I get home, but in the meanwhile, can you just stick close to Brent?"

There's nowhere else I'd rather be, but she's making me a little uneasy.

"Okaaaaay. You're scaring me a little, Mom."

"I know, sweetie, but just do me this favor for once and don't be a hardhead about it, okay?"

I know my mother wouldn't ask this of me unless it was important to her. But if she can't tell me what's going on, I'm sure Brent can.

"Okay, Mom. I will. I love you."

"I love you too, sweetie."

I can't help but sit here for a moment and let the conversation sink in. I hope my mother isn't in any danger, but then again, I know my father wouldn't be here if she was. Now how am I going to get Brent to spill it?

Hmm, I think I might know a way.

I think I'm beginning to catch on to the fact that women have powers that we are never formally informed of. A secret club that you may enter once you've hit a certain age and reached a certain level of maturity. I crack a smile.

I finish getting dressed, take a look in the mirror, and for once I feel happy about what I see. The more time I spend with Brent, the more confident I am beginning to feel. I think it has something to do with love. Love does unimaginable things.

I apply my lip gloss, grab my bag, and head out my door. Waiting for me in the kitchen is a note with one single rose next to it and, of course, my vitamin.

*Please take your vitamin, mon amour. I will be waiting outside for you*, the note reads.

My mother must have already gotten to him, which means he is already prepared for my questions, and he will be that much harder to crack.

I hold this little purple pill in my hand, rolling it around while studying it. What is so important about this little pill? And why in God's name must I keep taking it? I am immortal. *You know*, never die, never get sick, and live forever. There is absolutely no reason for me to have to keep taking this day after day.

Today I am taking control. *I* am in control of my own destiny, and I am no longer taking this damn pill! I toss it in the sink and wash it down. There. I feel so empowered. Who knows what else today may hold, but I am feeling optimistic.

I lock up the house behind me and take a seat in Brent's car. He is jamming! He has the music cranking, his head bobbing while he's singing to the words and drumming on the steering wheel.

"When we were young, oh oh, we did enough.
When it got cold, ooh ooh, we bundled up.

I can't be told, ah ah, it can't be done."

I can't help but giggle. Before the next verse, he makes a pretend microphone with his hands and continues to sing in my direction.

"It's better to feel pain, than nothing at all.

The opposite of love's indifference."

He closes his eyes, getting deep into the words while still singing on his pretend microphone.

"So pay attention now, I'm standing on your porch screaming out.

And I won't leave until you come downstairs."

He lets the rest of the song continue as we both laugh together.

"What band is that playing?"

Brent backs out of the driveway.

"The Lumineers."

"I like that song, but I *especially* like you singing that song," I admit, still giggling over it.

"I don't know, but I feel like they made the song for us," he tells me, with a cute smirk and a quick wink.

I think about the parts that I heard, and I can see why he might think that. Of course I will have to listen to the beginning to completely agree. Regardless, he was unbelievably adorable singing it, and I wouldn't mind a redo.

"So, you know what I've been meaning to ask you but keep forgetting?"

"What's that?" he asks, eyes still on the road.

"When did you learn French? Have you been to France?"

He looks at me with a perplexed expression.

"No, never been to France. French was my native language."

My eyebrows crease. I run my hand through my hair. "Please elaborate," I insist, watching his movements, waiting to see how he might respond.

"I was born in Alberta, Canada. You *loved* it there."

Did he just say Canada? Isn't that where Jason said he was from? Oh, what am I even thinking? Canada is huge. There would be no way in hell Brent knows who Jason is.

"I did, did I? Tell me about it," I ask with excitement, knowing this is another chance to get to peek into my past.

"Hmm, where to begin?" his eyes drift off to a faraway place. "It was a whole other world back in the eighteen hundreds. The streams and lakes were crystal clear, the air was clean and fresh, and the trees were plentiful and vivacious. The world belongs to nature, and we were gifted to live among it.

"My mother was a student of Mother Nature. She learned from it, she healed from it, and she respected it. Sometimes I think that's why she was given the golden egg, so to speak. It was not in her nature to abuse such a privilege. Unfortunately for my mother, not everyone was as pure-hearted as her.

"It was only a matter of time before someone discovered the mixture and the powers it held. Once it fell into the wrong hands, all chaos was heightened, and our world as we immortals knew it was forever changed."

"I don't understand. How was it changed?" I ask, providing my complete and undivided attention.

We pull into the school parking lot and Brent parks in the very back. He keeps the car running for warmth and continues on with the story while looking far into the past.

"Things like eternal youth cause people to do unimaginable things, Raina. Family becomes estranged, friends become enemies, and strangers become assassins. There are no boundaries when it comes to greed and domination. People give up their souls for these sorts of things. A moment of eternity is worth walking hand and hand with the devil to some.

Eternal Mixture

"Our very first life together—*your* very first life as an immortal—was the most serene. My parents were alive and happy. The mixture had only touched a few of us, including my brother EJ. Innocence was still among us."

I notice a bright glow on his face for just a slight moment, and then it fizzles out within seconds. I wonder what that was about.

"Every day was a learning process for you. Raina, you haven't even *begun* to touch on the powers you hold as an immortal. There are no limitations to what we can do."

"Brent, how old was I when I passed?"

He turns to me and reaches his hand to my face and tenderly grazes his fingers down my cheek. "You passed away on your eighteenth birthday," he speaks so quietly and then looks back out the windshield.

"But we were happy the couple of years we had together, right?"

He nods his head. "Very."

I feel satisfied with his answer.

The last of the kids are dwindling through the parking lot, and if we don't leave now, we are going to be late for first period. Brent exits out of the car first and comes to my side to open the car door for me. Perfect gentlemen. That is what I am beginning to love: no matter how many centuries and decades have passed, he still has proper etiquette.

We hold hands as we walk side by side.

"So tell me about your brother. Where is he now?"

I remember him mentioning a brother a while back, but he never spoke of him again until now.

His expression becomes stone-cold and his eyes glaze over with something I have never seen in him before: pure hatred. I almost take a step backward. The look just sent goose bumps rolling down my spine, and *not* in a good way. I am afraid to pry any further, so I give him a moment.

"EJ is no longer my brother. We parted ways decades ago. He is the meaning of destruction, greed, and betrayal," he finishes so matter-of-factly.

And there it is: this is him shutting me out. I have been barred from his secret brothers club. No women or humans allowed.

We reach my math class just as the first bell rings. He stops and gently grabs my chin, pulling it up so my eyes are to his.

"I'm sorry, baby. I don't mean to shut you out. But that is a dark topic for me. Do you understand?"

How can I not when his golden eyes are piercing through mine?

I give him a smile and agree. The last of my classmates file into the room, giving us disgusted looks on the way in. Brent pays them no mind, though. He leans down and touches my lips with his. I can't help but bring my body in closer to his. He has this magnetic pull I can't resist, and he makes me feel as though it is just him and I here alone.

He laughs and straightens my hips out just as Mrs. Liberty comes to the door to signal the start of class.

Why in God's name does he do this to me? It's bad enough that I have Bailey grinning from ear to ear as I head down the aisle to my seat. I just roll my eyes, anticipating the time it takes her to blow. I know it's coming, and she can't hold it in much longer. And knowing her, she is plotting for just the right moment, knowing that Mrs. Liberty must turn her back at some point.

Minutes pass by, and Bailey finally gets her shot.

"Psst. Raina," I hear her squeak in a wispy voice.

I try my hardest to ignore her, but she makes it impossible as she throws a spit wad at my face.

I snap around in her direction, giving her the attention she is demanding. "What?" I mouth back to her.

She leans in to me, hoping not to be heard. "There

is a rumor going around that you and Jaime messed around together," she informs me, waiting smugly for my explosion.

I shake my head in disbelief. "That's impossible."

She just nods her head in confirmation.

"Are you freaking kidding me? Does he really want me to tell everyone what happened?" I am freaking out at this point, because once Brent hears this, it's going to be "game on." He has been waiting for a reason to go after Jaime. "Brent's going to *kill* him!"

At this point, it is unbelievably hard to keep my voice down. My classmates around me begin looking our way, and the worst part is I can hear Janet talking crap loud and clear.

Janet is Casey's best friend. We used to be friends back in our elementary school days. Then Casey moved into town and things between us got weird. By the time we hit junior high school, I was no longer cool enough to be a part of Janet's crowd. So, here we are, strangers running side by side in different packs. The only difference is her pack has one alpha leader, Casey. In mine, we are all equally worthy.

I turn my head in her direction, and it's obvious she can see me, but she refuses to acknowledge me. She proceeds to send a subliminal message while speaking with her friend.

"Karma's a bitch. Stealing boyfriends catches up to people," Janet sneers in my direction as though I am contaminated.

I'll be damned if I am going to remain quiet about this! I may have rolled over in the past to avoid situations like this, but not today. Not anymore.

"Janet, you can't steal something that was never yours to begin with. Give that message to your owner, slave."

Bailey, along with the whole class, bursts into

laughter while Janet's face turns beet red with embarrassment.

"*Yeah!* Boo-ya!" Bailey yells.

I can't help but giggle at her ridiculousness.

Mrs. Liberty begins lecturing the class on how outbursts are unacceptable and makes sure to direct her attention to Janet and I. I try my hardest to hold a stern face, but with Bailey still snickering, it's nearly impossible.

I have never been one to purposely enjoy someone else's demise. In this case, though, I'll make an exception. She had it coming from years of abuse and pretending I don't exist.

Class continues on, and I remain silent. I stare up at the clock with dread. In a matter of minutes, I am going to witness Brent snap. Once he gets a whiff of the rumor going around, he is going to lose all control, and that scares the crap out of me. I know what he could possibly be capable of. A human is no match for him; Jaime doesn't stand a chance.

I hear the buzz of the bell. I grab my book bag and fly out of the classroom door before anyone has the chance to get out of their seats. Bailey is running behind me, trying to keep up.

"Raina, wait! Slow down!"

"I have to find Brent!" I yell, still slithering my way through the now-crowded hall. I almost make it to Brent's locker, but I am blocked by a mass of students huddled in a heaping pile together. I push my way to the front, shoving through the students with their cell phones out and fingers ready to record.

I finally reach the front, and it's my worst nightmare come true. Brent's got Jaime backed up into a locker, fist solid and ready to punch while Jaime pleads his case. I run up behind him and try to step in front of him to simmer him down. He needs someone to talk some sense into him before all hell breaks loose.

Eternal Mixture

204

"Brent, it's not worth it. *Please*, let's go home," I beg in a low tone so no one else can hear.

I see some sensibility returning to him—some recognition of humanity—that is, until Jaime taunts him with a bold-faced lie.

"If you didn't come to play the savior that night, I would have been in your girl's pants," Jaime sneers with a smug, crooked grin.

It's as if Jaime just stabbed a dagger right through Brent's heart, the sacred spot that triggers any man in love to call out a duel to the death. In one swift movement, Brent carefully shoves me aside, winds his fist back, and slams it into Jaime's face. Blood pours from Jaime's nose, splattering all over the front spectators. He's face-down on the floor, knocked out cold.

The crowd rips and rumbles with excitement and disbelief. Let's face it, Jaime has never been one to compete for a girl, nor did he ever hold a reputation in martial arts. This time his cockiness got the best of him, and I think he will walk away with a lesson learned. Brent is no one to fuck with.

**B**rent spent the remainder of the day in the principal's office until my father was able to get to the school and take him home.

Thank God it's time for lunch. I have been a complete mess since the fight, and all I want to do is forget about it.

I walk into the cafeteria, and the buzz of this morning's event still hasn't died down. My stomach sinks as I pass by tables full of reenactments. It's loud. The energy in here is alive and upbeat. To think this all stemmed from a simple bruised ego.

Maddie and Bailey are already sitting down at the table. I take a quick scan around the room, and I don't see

Shevaun DeLucia

Jenna anywhere. Where can she possibly be? I ran into her last week in the hallway, and her face was even more sunken in, her cheekbones were protruding, and the skin under her eyes was deeper and darker. I wanted to reach out and shake her. It feels as though she is in a deep trance, sinking into quicksand without a life raft. Each time I see her, she is presumably worse. I'm beginning to wonder if she is hooked on some sort of drug and Jason is her pusher.

The thought of that makes my blood boil. It is time to confront Jason, and today I have the perfect chance, with Brent out of my shadow.

"Hey girlie, do you see everyone? They're still going bananas over the fight. How are you holding up?" Bailey asks, concerned.

I pull out the chair and take a seat at the table, empty-handed. I have no appetite. "I'm okay. I just wish it didn't have to get to that point. I haven't gotten a chance to talk to Brent yet."

"Well, I am happy he stuck up for you. Jaime deserved what he got," Maddie tells me, dipping her fry in ketchup and popping it into her mouth.

Bailey sips her soda, nodding in agreement.

"You think he was sticking up for me? It was more like his male ego got bruised. Don't get it twisted."

It's true. Men can't stand when anyone belittles what is theirs, whether that's their looks, cars, or girls. If Brent confronted Jaime because he was disrespecting me, he could have made Jaime apologize to me instead of knocking him out.

"Of course I do!" Maddie blurts out, slamming her fry down. "He loves you. You don't even have to ask him; it's written all over his face. You're just being too hard on him, Raina."

Is she really serious? She must be blind.

Bailey just shakes her head at me with disappointment. "What?" I question her, calling her out on her unspoken thoughts.

"Raina, you're going to push him away with those thoughts like you do with every other guy," Bailey opens up, taking the bait.

"What the hell are you talking about, B? There have never been other guys! I'm sorry, was it just me or did you not also notice the lack of men standing in line to date me?"

"Open your eyes, Raina! There have been many guys interested in you. You just opt not to notice. Wake up and smell the coffee. Men drool over you; they just know you won't give them the time of day. They get intimidated by the barricade you've put up. You think they are looking at you with pity or revulsion, when really it is the *complete* opposite. Why do you think Janet and Casey despise you so much?" Bailey finishes, looking slightly proud of herself.

Maddie looks at me, too. "She is right, you know. You don't give yourself or the people around you enough credit."

What the hell is this, Bash on Raina Day? First Jaime and now them?

Casey and Janet sit at the table behind us. I can hear Janet filling Casey in on this morning's extravaganza. Casey still insists that I stole her man, as though Brent is some trophy or thing she owned. Doesn't she know that men can't be stolen unless they want to be? She is clearly delusional.

It is obvious that Bailey and Maddie hear them as well. "They are such losers. Don't even pay attention to them. I told you, they are just jealous of you," Bailey reminds me.

This is why I started going to the library, to avoid drama like this. My life was much easier before Brent, but that doesn't mean it was better. A life without Brent is something I can no longer imagine.

I decide to change the subject.

"Have you guys seen Jenna lately?"

A flicker of sadness runs across their faces momentarily. "She wasn't in our science class today. I tried calling her cell phone the other day, but I just got her voicemail," Bailey tells us.

"Bailey, maybe you should try to go over to her house after school today. I bet she will talk to you since she isn't mad at you," I try to convince her.

"Wait, you want *me* to go over there? I may not come back alive!" Bailey jokes while picking lint off her black shirt.

I can't help but roll my eyes. She is ridiculous sometimes. Thank God the bell rings. Bailey heads off to class, and I ask Maddie to stay behind so we can talk.

I wait until the halls have cleared out before I begin talking.

"I am going today after school. Can you drive me?"

"Going where?"

"I am going to speak with Jason. Brent is at home, so this is my chance. Plus, Jenna is getting worse by the minute. We have to figure out a way to help her."

Maddie bites her nails, seemingly nervous. "I don't know, Raina. I just have a bad feeling about this."

She is absolutely dead-on, because I have the same feeling. Regardless, Jenna is our friend, and we need to do something. If that means dealing with Jason, then I will do it.

"I know, Maddie, but you won't have to talk to him, okay? Just drive me there and wait for me in the car. He is going to have no choice but to talk with me."

The last bell rings, and we are now late for class. We part ways, agreeing to meet in the parking lot after school. I have to admit, with Brent gone, I have a big void that cannot be filled by anyone else. He is now suspended for the rest of the week for this morning's incident. My father has him going into work with him for the rest of the week to help out. The separation is going to be hard on both of us, but Brent enjoys dabbling in my father's work. It's far from a punishment.

The rest of my day goes by in slow motion, and, finally, the last bell rings. I head out to the parking lot to meet Maddie, and my nerves are beginning to get the best of me. I have a million questions running through my head, but I need to straighten them out and decipher the most important ones. He might not give me the time I need to get through them all, so it is imperative that I get the important ones out first.

"Are you ready?" Maddie asks.

"As ready as I'll ever be."

I hop into her car, and we head over to Billiards. It's quiet here, the place doesn't come alive until after dark. There are the normal regulars inside shooting pool, but for the most part, the parking lot is empty.

We drive to the back where the parking lot to the motel is located. I see his car parked in front of one of the rooms. The pit of my stomach begins to churn with an acid fire. I look over at Maddie, and the blood has drained from her face. She bites her nails when she is nervous or stressed, and her fingers haven't left her mouth since we pulled up.

"Okay, stay here. I will be back."

I open the door, but before I can get out, Maddie yells, "*Wait!* Raina, what if Jenna is in there?"

I guess I didn't think that part through. "I'll just say I came to talk to her instead."

"Okay, if you need me, just yell."

"Okay, Mom. I will," I agree with sarcasm before heading off across the parking lot.

It feels as though every step I take closer to his room makes my heart gallop harder and faster. I try to remain calm. I repeat the questions I want to ask in my head so I won't forget. I can't let him distract me in any way. I need to stay focused and in control at all times.

Shevaun DeLucia

I finally reach the front door. I stand there for a moment in silence, listening for any voices, but I hear none. This is a good sign. I gather my courage, take a deep breath, and knock.

I hear the sound of footsteps making their way to the door. The doorknob turns and Jason is standing directly in front of me.

"*Raina?* What are you doing here?" Jason asks, skepticism passing across his face. It is obvious that he doesn't trust me or believe that I am here for anything good.

Before I respond to his question, we seem to lock eyes momentarily. His irises have the identical honey-brown color as Brent's eyes. There is something that is so familiar about them, something that my inner self seems to recognize, but I can't put my finger on it. The buzz of energy engulfing us is strange, and it is clear he feels it too, just by the expression on his face.

His stare is intense. It's as though he is trying to figure something out or trying to read me. He waits patiently for me to speak.

"I came to talk with you about Jenna."

His eyes continue to bore into my flesh, never faltering from me. His eyebrows crease with questions and confusion. I can't help but wonder what is going through his mind.

"What about Jenna?" Jason wonders as he leans his shoulder against the door frame.

"I'm worried about her. She looks sick, and she refuses to talk with any of us anymore. Is something wrong with her, Jason? Is she sick?"

I try to explain my reasons in the nicest way possible. I don't want to scare him off with accusations before hearing his side. I watch him aggressively, taking in his every move, hoping he might give something away.

"She is fine. What you see is a lack of sleep. She

Eternal Mixture

has insomnia, and she is working with a doctor. Is there anything else you must know?"

Jason remains closed and in control, never showing any sign of weakness. There is just something else I sense that I can't put my finger on. I know for a fact he is hiding something. I just don't know how to prove it.

"Well, I was hoping maybe you could speak to her, and let her know that it is okay to talk to us," I say in a subtle manner. I don't want him to know that I think he's caused the rift between Jenna and I.

He doesn't answer or comment right away, because he is too busy studying me. It is now becoming weird, a little uncomfortable being under his constant scrutiny.

"Jason, is everything okay? Is there something you want to ask me?"

I can't take it anymore, so I call him on his bull. If he has something to ask, then he needs to just ask it.

"I am sorry if I am staring a little too hard, but you have this amazing energy about you. I just wonder where it came from. I have never seen you with this force before. You're usually like the rest of us. I mean, you are normally so negative and downright mean like the rest of the girls."

I take a step back, a little thrown off. "Whoa, excuse me? You don't even know me!" I snap, unbelievably angered. Who the *hell* does he think he is? "I came here to ask for your help in getting my friend back. I miss her, and regardless of what you think, I care about her deeply. Will you talk with her?"

I am done. I have made my plea, and if he won't help, I will just have to go to her house. If that doesn't work, I will go to her parents. I won't stop until I know what is wrong with her. I know my friend, and she is in desperate need. I can feel it.

He thinks for a moment before answering. "Okay, I will talk to her. I can't promise anything, though. I will call you if she wants to meet with you."

*Phew!* I think I have finally talked some sense into this kid. "Thank you."

I turn to walk away, but he stops me with a question. "Hey, you are dating that new kid Brent, right?" Jason asks.

I turn back around. "Yeah, what's it to you?"

He shrugs his shoulders. "Just wondering, that's all."

I stand still, perplexed, watching him descend into his room. I can't understand why he would be concerned with who I am dating. He has never asked me anything personal before. Strange.

I head back over to the car, and Maddie begins to bomb me with questions.

"Raina, OMG! Did you see the way he was looking at you the whole time?" Maddie freaks out.

"Yeah, he was gawking at me the whole time. It was weird. He did say he would talk to Jenna, though," I explain.

We pull out of the parking lot and head over to my house. I have already missed a million calls and texts messages from Brent. If I don't get home in the next ten minutes, he is going to send out an APB on me.

"Is it eerie to see him again after looking at those paintings?"

"He looks identical. What was odd, though, was I picked up on a slight accent. Almost as though he's from another time. It must be something you pick up when living in another country. I just never noticed it before."

Maddie listens intently. "I told you the whole situation with that family painting is weird. There is just something off about it," Maddie reminds me. "What did he say is wrong with Jenna?"

"He said she has insomnia, and she is seeing a doctor for it. I'm not really sure I believe him, though. He wasn't too convincing."

212

"I'm sure her parents would clarify it if you asked them to," Maddie suggests.

I *know* they would, but getting her parents involved doesn't seem right. Not yet, at least. "I am not getting them involved. Not unless I have to."

We pull up to my driveway. Brent must have heard us pull up, because he is already waiting on the front porch. His face is stone, and he looks irritated. Maddie must notice this too, because when she says goodbye, she adds a "good luck" at the end and drives off.

I walk up the steps, and he crosses his arms in front of him.

"Where have you been?"

Is he kidding me? I was gone no more than an hour, and I get the parent treatment from him? This is absolutely ridiculous!

"Um, you just saw Maddie pull away. I was with her, obviously!"

I push myself past him, annoyed with the interrogation he is giving me.

He follows me into the kitchen. "Then why didn't you answer my calls or texts? Don't you remember your conversation with your mother this morning? She told you that you need to stick by my side!" he yells, frustrated.

I snap around to face him, eyes slit, and ready for a fight. "Well, maybe if you weren't such a hothead this morning, you would have been with me after school! Oh, and speaking of my conversation with my mother, I want to know what she is keeping from me. I deserve to know!" I demand, sticking my ground.

I wait for him to come back at me with some smart comment, but he doesn't. Instead, he is studying me with the same look that Jason used. He looks puzzled, perturbed, and it's making me a little uneasy.

I shift in my stance. "Why are you looking at me like that?"

Shevaun DeLucia

"Raina, you look different," he comments as though it's a bad thing or something.

"What do you *mean* I look different?"

He takes a step closer in disbelief. "Your aura's *glowing*. I see a faint purple surrounding you. I don't understand what it is." His eyes paint my body.

I scan over my arms and hands, but I cannot see a thing. How can he see this, and I can't? I look up at him and say, "I don't see anything. Are you sure you are feeling well, Brent?"

I am beginning to feel worried about him. Maybe he is low on energy and needs more of the mixture. Out of nowhere, his eyes bug out of his head, he runs his hands through his hair with stress and then begins to pace through the kitchen in deep thought.

"Brent, what is the matter? You're scaring me!" I screech.

"Raina, did you take your vitamin today?"

I freeze and think for moment, and then it hits me. I totally forgot that I flushed it down the sink this morning.

"No, I decided not to take it. Why? What is the big deal?"

He begins to pace again, but this time he stomps in anger. He begins swearing and tugging on his hair to the point of almost ripping it out. I can't move. I stand still as a statue, watching and waiting for him to calm down.

"No, no, *no*! I can't believe I let this happen!" he mumbles to himself under his breath, still walking back and forth. He then turns to me unexpectedly and asks, "Who did you see today? Anyone out of the ordinary?"

"I don't understand what this is all about, Brent. What does my vitamin have to do with this so-called aura?"

He grabs my arm aggressively and brings me to the bathroom mirror. What I see is indescribable. My mouth drops, and I can barely get a thought to form enough to make sense in my head. I finally take a breath to collect

Eternal Mixture

myself, and my voice squeaks when I finally speak. "This can't possibly be me." I continue to move my body around in disbelief. "I look magical, dream-like. And my skin glistens like the North Star."

Brent comes up behind me and wraps his arms around my waist, staring back at me in the mirror. "You are beautiful, Raina." He moves my hair to one side of my shoulder and leans in to kiss my neck with his silky lips.

I respond by closing my eyes in complete bliss. A slight moan escapes my lips. He slides his tongue up to my earlobe and nibbles gently. My skin crawls with energy. He then whispers in my ear, "Raina, who have you seen?"

I immediately push him from me, upset that he has just ruined a moment. "Why? Why does it matter?" I question, annoyed.

"Please, come sit down." I follow him to the kitchen and take a seat on the barstool. I watch as he carefully chooses his words before speaking. "Your parents left our town before you were born. They thought maybe if they could keep you a secret from the others, you might be able to live a normal life. At this point, after decades of losing you, they were willing to try anything. So they moved to the cabin, 2400 miles away from home.

"When you were born, I was in my glory. I was dying to come see you, but your parents wouldn't allow me. I couldn't help myself. I needed to be with you, so I showed up at their doorstep on my hands and knees. Your father could never say no to me. He already thought of me as a son, and he knew my intentions were only pure.

"I remember walking up to your bassinet for the first time. Each step I took towards you sealed my fate, and when my eyes finally touched your tiny self, I knew you were blessed with a life of preservation. You glowed as an angel would, with a pure light of innocence surrounding you, as though you had been touched by God himself. I fell to my knees in this moment of realization; my prayers had

Shevaun DeLucia

been answered.

"We had to keep you from the mortal world. Mortals get scared of the unknown and react in horrible ways with things they cannot explain. Shortly after you began to crawl, we discovered your gift of healing. You cut your knee on the wooden floor. When I brought you to the sink to fix you up, your cut was gone and your skin was clear. In that moment, your father fell deep into his research, and we rid of all trails that could possibly connect you to the immortal world.

"You see, Raina? Your light is the emblem of immortality. We immortals depend on the mixture, but when the lake dries up someday, we will diminish. With your blood, an immortal will no longer need the mixture and will truly live for all eternity. The world revolves around power, and by having your blood at their disposal, they would hold the key to domination. Do you realize what that means, Raina?"

I can barely wrap my brain around all of this. He told me about my blood, but having to worry about other immortals coming after me is a whole other ballgame.

"It means I am in real big trouble," I realize. A tear falls down my cheek.

Brent comes to me, wipes my tear, and kisses my forehead sweetly. He then leans down to look me in the eyes.

"It means you have to protect yourself by taking that vitamin and keeping a low profile, baby. Your father spent years coming up with something that would dilute your glow. We were so relieved when he found a formula that worked," he explains, speaking low. He grabs my face in his hands and tells me, "I will *never* let anyone hurt you. I will give my life to protect you. Just *please*, help me with the part that I cannot control and take your pill, okay?"

"Okay."

At this point, it seems wrong to even argue. He has

216

made his point, and it is a valid one. I lean up and touch my
lips to his. My body responds to him immediately. A deep
fire spreads across my skin, awakening my insides. My
heart no longer flutters, it pounds with the need to devour.

He thrusts his tongue deep into my mouth, moving
in a rhythmic pace. The taste of him drives me wild. My
fingers glide through his hair, and the deeper he kisses me,
the more I dig my nails into his scalp. He leaves my mouth
and makes his way down my neck. My body arches, dying
for him to put out my fire. His sweet manly aroma fills my
nostrils, and the strength of his masculine hands makes my
entire body want to quiver under his touch.

He leans down, eyes full of hunger, and sweeps me
up into his arms. I giggle. Just knowing I drive him mad
turns me on. He leaps up the steps and carries me to his
room. The air explodes with his scent, envelopes my body,
and almost pushes me over the edge. I am laid gently on his
bed. He stands above me, ravaging me with his thoughts
while taking me all in.

I reach up, begging him to come to me. I see the
uncertainty in his eyes as they graze over me. If one more
moment passes, I might lose him. But he surprises me. He
lifts his arms up over his head, his washboard abs flexing
individually as he removes his T-shirt and disposes of it on
the floor. I knew it was only a matter of time before he
gave in to me. I smile with prevail.

Brent slides his body in between my legs. A
sweltering heat burns beneath him. He shifts his body onto
his left elbow, pressing his bulge against my pelvis as he
brushes my hair back with his free hand.

"I love you," he whispers hoarsely.

I feel his love radiate through my skin, soaking into
my pores. With our love, we can conquer the world. We are
indestructible. We are invincible. And we are two halves in
dire need to become one.

"And I love you."

Shevaun DeLucia

I stroke his cheek, baring my soul to his. I am ready to expose my inner self to him in every way possible. But just as he begins to unbutton my shirt, my father calls up the stairs to us. My gut drops to the floor. Before I can blink, Brent has his shirt back on and is already out the door.

So much for my fairytale ending. I button my shirt back up and tiptoe my way across the hall. I lunge onto my bed and graze my fingers along the parts of me still burning from his touch.

# Chapter 17

Brent had no choice but to let my father in on my decision to wash my pill down the drain. My aura is powerful, and I will need a couple of days for the vitamin to dilute it down again. I am now dealing with the consequence of my decision to rebel by being held a prisoner in my own home.

It's really not as bad as I am making it seem. The long days spent with Brent have actually been beneficial to us. The last couple of mornings, as soon as my dad leaves, Brent crawls into my bed and snuggles with me until mid-morning. We kiss, laugh, and simply lie in each other's arms until the grumble of hunger rips through one of us.

The afternoons we spend on homework. My father advised our teachers that we were heading out of town, and they were nice enough to email us the work so we wouldn't fall behind. Brent spends most of the time tutoring me, since he has already mastered everything there is to know. He has already lived through the Civil War and the Great Depression. He's met Albert Einstein in person and studied alongside Charles Darwin at Cambridge University in England before the scientist took off to sail on the HMS Beagle.

Brent tells me stories from his past by my request. I

only ask for the details of his life that he has had to endure without me. He is worldly and educated and has been to places I have only read about in books. He paints me a picture of contentment to pacify my curiosity, but I know deep down these stories carry suffering and misery. I wish he would open up to me, allow me to see in again. For a slight moment at the cabin, he allowed me to glimpse into the darkest part of his soul, but ever since then, he has shut me out.

I know he feels he is protecting me by filtering out the unpleasant parts of his life. I get that. But it *is* part of him and part of who he is today. By no means do I want him to embrace it, but I want him to heal from it.

He did tell me that it's my light that leads him out of the darkness. Maybe it can mend his broken pieces as well. This light that surrounds me has impeccable strength and endurance. It surges through the tissue of my skin and penetrates deep into my bones. I have been gifted with something beyond anything any of us can imagine. I know it. I can *feel* it. I am just not sure how to seize it.


Today, the first snowfall has descended. The white flakes drift aimlessly down until they reach the soil, and then they dissolve, leaving a wet shine behind. Even though the snow isn't sticking, it's a reminder that the holidays are near.

Thanksgiving is only a couple days away, and this will be the first year my family will not be together. Brent's here, but he does not fill the void my mother has left. I always look forward to watching my parents dance around the kitchen together so gracefully. My mother works on the pies while my father chops and mixes the sides, and together they turn the turkey into a masterpiece.

With my mother gone and my father working long

Eternal Mixture

hours, it may just be Brent and I left to create our own memories. I watch him sleep peacefully and smile at the thought of beginning our life together: just him and I.

Brent's eyes flutter open, and when he sees me, he smiles.

"Good morning. Did you have a good sleep?"

He raises his arms above his head and stretches his body from head to toe. "Yes I did, actually. I was having dreams of you."

He wraps his legs around me under the covers and slides me close to him.

"Oh, yeah? What was your dream about?"

He pauses a moment before replying. "Our honeymoon."

My cheeks blaze as that dream passes through my thoughts. This may be the opening that I have been waiting for. With his thoughts of intimacy running through his mind it may be easier to persuade him into more than a kiss. My body is on fire, and he is the only one that can extinguish the flames.

I slide my hand through his hair and lean in for a kiss, hoping he is on the same page as me. But before we continue any further, my stomach growls. He wiggles out of my arms and jumps out of bed. An ice-cold breeze now replaces his hot body, and I can't help but feel defeated.

I don't understand. I practically throw myself at him, and he springs away as though I am diseased. A small tear falls down my cheek.

"Raina, baby, don't cry. Believe me, it's not that I don't want to, because I do. You don't know how bad I have been waiting for this moment, but I want it to be more than just sex. I want that memory to last us an eternity."

"But what if you are wrong? If I die tomorrow, we will never get this moment back. I don't want to wait another lifetime to be with you, Brent."

He climbs onto the bed, and lies down on his

Shevaun DeLucia

stomach, facing me. "I promise you it will be in this lifetime."

His reassurance doesn't soothe me one bit. In fact, it makes me wonder what he has done with his time when I am not around. Who has occupied his time and his manly desires?

"Brent, how many lovers have you had?"

He almost chokes on his own spit.

"Are you really asking me this?"

I cross my arms and just wait for his answer.

"Raina, you are the only one on my mind."

He thinks he's slick, trying to appease me with a half-ass answer.

"You didn't answer my question, Brent."

"I *told* you, you are the only one."

"Are you saying we have slept together before?"

"Yes."

"And I am the only one you have been with?"

"Yes." He smiles. "Is that so hard to believe?"

"Well, yes it is. You are a man, and you do have needs. It's just a lot of time to pass by with no comfort. Besides, you have already mentioned keeping your mind busy with other girls."

He grabs my hand and traces my fingers with his. "I have waited decades for you, and I would wait a million more. I only told you that because I knew telling you the truth would only drive you away."

Another tear rolls down my cheek. "I love you."

He kisses me softly and then drags me out of bed. My wood floor is ice-cold. I step into my slippers and grab my sweatshirt before he pulls me down to the kitchen. Brent is an amazing cook, so I leave breakfast up to him each morning while I observe and learn.

"Does bacon and scrambled eggs sound good?"

"Sounds perfect. I am starving!" As I say this, my stomach growls in agreement.

Eternal Mixture

Brent laughs, and then he lays the bacon on the sizzling pan. Steam clouds over the stove and evaporates, leaving a mouthwatering smell. I have just entered food heaven.

"Do you want some orange juice?"

"Yes, please."

He sets down my vitamin and a full glass of juice. His eyes remain locked on me until the pill has sunk down my throat. I stick out my tongue and roll my eyes.

"Good girl," Brent teases. He loves to drive me crazy in any way he can.

"What was our sex life like?" I ask him.

This time he almost chokes on his orange juice.

"What's wrong? Did I shock you?" I tease.

He swallows. "Um, yeah, shock isn't the word." He fills our plates with the steaming hot food. "We had amazing sex. Each time was like the first—no point intended—and each time is still burned into my memory like it was yesterday."

My cheeks flare up. I look to my plate and shove a huge forkful of food into my mouth.

I decide to dig a little deeper. "When was our very first time?"

Brent finishes chewing. "The year was 1948. You were twenty-one years old. It was a hot summer's night, and we decided to take a dip at the falls. The stars lit the sky, casting just enough light to glisten off the water. You were mesmerizing: the way the light wrapped around your bare body, highlighting your womanly curves and bringing the water around me to a boil.

"The sight of you was more than I could have imagined, but the feel of you—there are no words to describe it," he finishes, eyes sparkling with love.

"Was I nervous?"

Brent takes his last bite before picking up our plates and placing them into the sink. I carefully watch him, waiting for the answer. I can only imagine what it must have been like — to be in love and know for the first time what love literally feels like. I can imagine his light, gentle touch and his passion and need for me pouring from his soul as we made love for the very first time. It must have been beautiful.

He takes his seat back at the kitchen table.

"Yes, I think we both were. But once our eyes connected and skin touched, I think all worries flew out of our minds. We became natural, like we had been making love for centuries already.

"After that first night we met, every single night after that was like clockwork. We couldn't get enough of each other. I think your parents might have suspected what was going on, but they turned a cheek to it, because they knew we were in love. That was one of the best summers of my life," he stares out the kitchen window, mind in a different era as he finishes.

I can't help but feel eager to have those feelings and memories again. Even though I have no recollection of what he is telling me, somehow my body does. The burn from deep within is awakened, licking every inch of my body, overheating me and releasing the moistness in forbidden places.

What is he doing to me?

All of a sudden, I have turned into this hormone-crazed teenager who has lost all sense of reality because I am in love. I promised myself I would never be consumed with putting someone else's needs before myself. I told myself I would never be that girl. Now look at me—completely drenched in thoughts of only Brent.

"I hope you can replay those moments for me this summer," I hint to him, giving him a flirtatious wink. I get up from the table and immediately feel him behind me, his hands against my hips and his bulge protruding stiffly behind me. I have obviously excited him, which makes me feel accomplished inside. I feel womanly.

He kisses my neck before he turns me around. His lips are soft and moist, heavenly on my skin. I can't help but want more.

"Whoa, whoa," Brent laughs, holding me at a distance. "You gotta slow down. What if your father comes home?"

Shoot! He's right. My father could walk back in at any moment. This is not an ideal situation I want him to walk in on.

"Sorry," I laugh. "I just get carried away."

Brent lets go of me, and my skin suddenly feels empty and cold. It scares me sometimes, how much I need him in my life. Brent likes to remind me that it's okay to depend on someone else besides yourself. He says that's the human inside of me still.

"So what is on the agenda for today? Homework? Yahtzee?"

"Yahtzee sounds good to me. We can work on our homework later," I say.

He pulls the Yahtzee game out from the hallway closet and sets it up on the kitchen table. He hands me a score sheet, and I put my name on the top. We roll to see who is the first to go. I roll a five and he rolls a two.

"Ha! Guess I get to go first!" I tease, rolling the dice.

I roll a five, three, three, two, and a four: a small straight. I clap and re-roll the second three dice. The dice now lands on four. I re-roll one last time, and this time the dice lands on one. I jump up and down with excitement: a large straight. Brent tells me it's just beginner's luck.

I check the box next to the large straight on the score sheet and hand the dice over to him. He rolls and gets three fives, then re-rolls the three and the one, and ends up with all fives: a Yahtzee.

"Woohoo! Beat that!" he screeches, jumping up and

down in his seat.

We play for another couple of hours. I won the first round, and he won the last two. I look up at the time, and its almost three o'clock. Maddie and Bailey should already be out of school by now. I feel as though it's been weeks since I have spoken with them. I could really use some girl time right about now.

Brent must sense this as well, because before I know it, the doorbell rings. I get up to answer it, but Brent has already beaten me to the punch. To my surprise, Bailey and Maddie are standing in front of me. I am completely stoked but also feel a little uneasy. I told the girls I was going out of town and wouldn't be back for a little while— now here they are, standing in my foyer.

"Hey! We've missed you!" they both say ecstatically, jumping up and down.

I look to Brent. "I called them as soon as we got back. I figured you needed some girl time," Brent hints.

Okay, he must have read my mind! He just knows me too well. It's the little moments in life that make me happy. Brent has definitely hit the mark on this one. As Maddie and Bailey enter the living room, I thank Brent with a sweet kiss.

To the human eye, my aura cannot be seen—that was proven true the other day at school, when I was surrounded by mortals. So my girls are able to visit whenever they would like. It's the immortals that Brent and my parents are worried about, so I am ordered to stay under this roof.

With this same thought, Jason comes to mind. How was he able to detect my aura? Is it possible for him to be an immortal? No. No way. There must be some other reason, something I still have to learn about the aura's capabilities. I quickly shake the thought from my head.

Brent excuses himself from the whole "girl time" and leaves to run some errands. I turn to Bailey, and she is bursting out of her seams with gossip. I grab us some drinks and take a seat in the living room.

"Okay Bailey, I know you have some gossip for me."

Maddie laughs, knowing it's true.

Bailey tucks her feet under her butt and sits up straight. "Okay, so Jaime comes back to school, and who do you think goes after him?"

I tap my finger on my lip trying to think, but I give up. "Who?"

"Casey."

I look to Maddie, and her head is nodding like a bobblehead. I'm not surprised this happened. Casey is grasping onto anything at this point. Anything to bring her self-esteem back up since Brent rejected her.

"I am not surprised. They may actually make a good couple," I reply.

"I think you are definitely right!" Maddie agrees.

I take a sip of my iced tea, wondering what else Bailey might have in store.

"So, is that the *big* gossip?" I ask.

Bailey shakes her head, and her face turns a little somber. I can tell she has something serious to talk about next.

Bailey sips her tea, and Maddie looks down towards the floor. "Jenna hasn't been in school for the last week. I overheard some teachers talking, and they said she wasn't doing very well. They mentioned her being in and out of the hospital, and they aren't sure when to expect her back," Bailey says, breaking the news.

We all sit in silence for a moment.

I decide to break the ice. "What do you think we should do? Should I talk to Jason again or go to see her parents?"

Maddie speaks up this time. "No way! You are *not* going back over there to talk with Jason. He is a creep!"

Shevaun DeLucia

She surprises me with her outburst, and I can't help but laugh. "Okay, okay, I won't go see Jason again. I'm just not so sure what to say to her parents, though."

"Maybe all three of us should go, so if Jenna is there, she won't freak out as much," Maddie suggests.

"Honestly, from what it sounds like, Jenna doesn't even have the energy to fight us on this. She's probably bedridden. We might not even have to deal with her," Bailey assumes.

Bailey might be right, and if she is, I know Jenna's parents will be more than happy to speak with us. I'm sure they are just as worried as we are, if not more.

"You may be right. Let's just give it until the weekend. Who knows? Maybe Jason will call me and tell me Jenna is willing to see me," I say.

Maddie just rolls her eyes at the idea, and Bailey agrees. We spend the rest of the time chitchatting and gossiping over some pizza I ordered. Brent hasn't came back yet, and the sun's beginning to set. I texted him ten minutes ago to see where he is, but he still has not responded. That's not like him.

It's late, and the girls take off because they have school in the morning. They asked if I would be there, and I had to lie. I hate lying. But until my aura has completely dissipated, I am stuck in this house.

Brent finally calls me to tell me he's right down the street and on his way. It felt good to have some girl time. I got it out of my system, and now I am ready to spend the rest of my night with Brent.

I throw out the pizza box in the garage and sponge down the counter. We used paper plates, and the cups are already in the dishwasher. I take a seat on the couch, kick my feet up, and open my book. I may only have a couple of minutes to read, but it's more than I get in a week's time lately.

This *Blood Thirst* book now sends chills down my

Eternal Mixture

spine. The thought of living for thousands of years scares me. The way the world changes in just a hundred years is unbelievable. I can't image how it changes over thousands of years. Maybe vacations will be taken out in space instead of the Bahamas, cars will no longer drive on pavement but in the sky, and sex will no longer be an act, it will be a thought.

It may be a blessing that immortals can't have children. The thought of outliving my child or, even worse, telling my child that they have to endure life for thousands of years—so buckle up for the ride—doesn't sound like happiness to me either. But maybe I am wrong. I'm sure if I ran a poll on a choice between dying or living forever, most people would pick forever. I am sure it would only be for the superficial reason of never getting old, if anything.

Brent pulls up like clockwork. Over the past couple of weeks, my hearing has become impeccable. The more in tune I become with my body, the more I am able to unlock the secrets of my gift and perfect my newfound craft.

If I concentrate and listen real hard, I can hear the scratching of squirrels scurrying across the limbs of trees, the subtle whoosh from the wings of the hawk in the sky, and the humming rhythm of the motor on Brent's Infinity as he pulls into my driveway.

It's an amazing feeling to be able to push myself to these extreme superhero capabilities. Each day I inch closer to a new discovery of my immortal gifts on my own. I haven't let Brent in on the fact that I have uncovered this. I am enjoying my own little secret, and I am beginning to understand why he felt so powerful and godly. I mean, who wouldn't?

I hear the key rustle in the door. "*Raina?* I'm back. Where are you?" Brent calls from in the foyer.

"I'm in the living room!" I yell back.

The butterflies flutter wildly in my stomach with the thought of his smooth manly scent caressing my nostrils

Shevaun DeLucia

and knowing that soon I will be engulfed in his strong, loving arms. I need to be knocked back down to reality, of course. I'm not so sure this is the best way to go about it— knocking down a dream with a dream.

"Hey, baby. Did you miss me?" Brent greets me with an enormous smile.

I can't help but smile at his glow. "I *did* actually," I admit.

He flops down on the cushion beside me and turns in my direction. "I missed you too. I hate being away from you, even if it's just for a couple of hours."

"Did you get anything accomplished while you were out?"

He kicks his shoes off, wraps his arm behind me, and gives me a kiss on the cheek. "I did. Your dad called me last minute, so I swung by the lab."

"What did he need?" I ask, eyebrows furrowed.

"He needed me to give some blood."

I sit up, confused. "Why would he want *your* blood?"

Brent slides his fingers through his hair. "Raina, your body doesn't seem to be responding to the pill any longer. Your father thinks you have grown immune to it over the small amount of time it was out of your system."

What is he telling me? I can't stay in this house for the rest of eternity. What am I supposed to do? I begin biting on my nail, panicked, and in complete remorse for my actions.

"Brent, I don't understand. How do I fix this? I can't stay in here forever," I stand up, stressed, and slowly pace the room.

Brent stands up and stops me. "Raina, its not all your fault. It would have happened eventually. Your father has been tweaking the pill since he created it. Your aura is so potent that one remedy is never enough. That's why he has been working day and night. He has been trying to come up with something more permanent for you, but now he's run out of time."

I take a deep breath in and exhale. "How close do you think he is?"

"Right now he is trying to compare our blood to see what sets yours apart from ours."

"That's why he needed yours?"

"Yes."

"Why not just use his own?" I wonder.

Brent grabs my hand and pulls me down to the couch. He takes a moment and gazes intensely into my eyes. "Because we are two parts of a whole; we're bound to each other. Your dad has the idea that the bond of our souls has to amount to something. Alonzo feels God had to have created a shield for your gift, and he won't stop until he figures it out."

I now look to the ground, recalling all my memories of my father being void during most of my life, telling me his commitment to his work was all for me. Now I finally understand the meaning behind those words.

"And my mother, am I the reason for her leaving?" I ask, remembering all that my mother has said to me as well. She asked me to stay close to Brent while she is away for work, and I could hear the distress clearly behind her voice. I know there is more that Brent is holding back from me.

"You are your parent's reason for existing, Raina. Everything they do is because of you and for you. Your parents would have left this world a long time ago if they were certain you would never come back. You are the center of *our* universe. I couldn't go on living either if I knew I had to live a life without you," Brent informs.

"But you have already lived without me, Brent."

"Years, yes. But a life, no. I have *always* known it would be only a matter of time before you came back to me. It's like the certainty of breathing in air. I know the next breath I take will fill my lungs with oxygen, just like I know you are coming back.

"Your mother has the same intuition, but for a different reason. She fears you will be discovered. She believes in your father's work, but also believes that sometimes nature has a different plan for us. Do you remember what your father told you about the witch?"

"Yes."

Man, he is beginning to make me a little nervous.

"Well, that is who your mother and my Aunt Lillian have been looking for."

*Whoa!* What in the heck is he trying to say?

"Are witches immortal too?" I question, snapping my neck back.

Brent laughs. "No, but this one is. We gave her the mixture in return for her bonding your soul to your mother's," he explains.

"Oh, I see." I can't help but wonder what exactly this witch can do for us now. "But why now?"

Brent's eyebrows crease together as he thinks about his next words. "Eve, the witch, is tied to nature like I explained to you before. So your mother is hoping she might be able to reverse what nature has done and cast a spell to cover or reverse your aura permanently." Brent clarifies.

Reverse it permanently? My heart begins to bang against my chest with this thought. I just discovered this part of me, and I don't know if I am ready to give it up yet.

"Brent, what if I don't want her to reverse it? I feel like there is so much to learn from it. This aura has powers that I have yet to discover. I *feel* it, just like you knew I would come back to you," I confess.

I haven't told Brent about what I have been feeling, because I wanted to keep it to myself. But he needs to know so he will be able to stand behind me when I refuse Eve's help.

Eternal Mixture

"Why haven't you told me any of this?"

"I wasn't ready to," I admit.

Brent puts his arm around me and pulls me into him. His aroma permeates the air and calms my worries. "I just want you to know that you can tell me *anything,* and if you are not ready, I will wait until you are, okay?"

I just nod my head up and down, relieved he is not upset.

"We'll figure something out. I have faith, mon amour. "

We sit on the couch, embraced in one another for hours until my mind fades into the background and my dreams take over.

# Chapter 18

The days have passed by quickly, while the nights have been long and restless. I can't help but worry about Jenna and my mother. Jason still has yet to call me, and my mother is still searching for Eve. I, on the other hand, am becoming more antsy as the days go by.

I've spoken to my mother a couple of times since Brent revealed her real reason for being gone. Brent came clean to her and let her know that he told me everything. He didn't want me to feel guilty when talking to her, and my mother was relieved but aggravated with him for not allowing her this moment. She was hoping to explain this all herself, in her own way.

I'm happy that the secrets between us all are starting to dwindle down and honesty is popping up in its place. I just wish for one moment that I could peek inside my other lives and get to know my other selves. I feel the singe from the missing pieces of me, and I'm afraid I may never feel completely whole.

My father, like every other morning, has already left for the lab, and Brent is downstairs working on breakfast. I stretch my stiff muscles and sit up, hanging my legs to the side of the bed. Brent has laid my slippers in place and my hoodie across the side of my bed. I can't help but smile at his thoughtfulness.

Before I make my way downstairs, my phone vibrates against my nightstand. I pick it up, scroll through my notifications, and sit for a moment, heart throbbing with disbelief and excitement all in one. The text says Jenna is ready to talk and gives me directions to meet her, *alone*.

Now the question is, how am I going to pull this off with Brent calculating his every move around me?

Maybe my father will call for his assistance again, or maybe I can beg him to go grab me some snacks. I huff in defeat, knowing both possibilities will never happen. At this point, the only option left is to wait until Brent heads in the shower and lathers up before I head out the door.

He will hear my wheels grind against the pavement as I pull out, but the shampoo in his eyes will buy me some time. Once I convince Jenna how silly she has been, I will come home and explain it all to Brent. He'll understand and will forgive me for running off.

As I make my way down the stairs, the delicious combination of eggs and bacon tickle my nose. My stomach immediately growls with anticipation of what's to come. I take a seat on the barstool and watch Brent at work. He acknowledges me with a loving smile before flipping the bacon one last time.

I laugh as the pan spits out stifling spats of grease, causing him to dance in anguish. "Are you okay?" I ask between giggles.

"Maybe you should do this next time," Brent challenges me, obviously annoyed at my frivolousness.

I take him up on his challenge. "Maybe I *will*," I reply, staring him down with a scowl.

"Well, good then. Tomorrow it is! I will lounge in bed, and you can serve me breakfast." Brent winks as he slides some scrambled eggs and two pieces of bacon onto my plate.

Shevaun DeLucia

*Man*, what have I gotten myself into? Instead of diving into another pride-filled challenge, I shove my mouth full of food. This time, it is Brent who snickers at my arrogance and stubborn ways. I decide to change the subject.

"Have you gotten a chance to speak with my father?"

Brent finishes his bite. "Yes, I actually spoke with him this morning. Why? What's up?"

"Has he come any closer to a remedy?"

I can't help but sit in this house and count the seconds, minutes, and hours that pass me by. Something has *got* to give. I miss my girlfriends and the freedom I once had: shooting pool, going to the library, or even just hanging out at Maddie or Bailey's house. But, most of all, I miss my thinking spots. The places I would go to feel the fresh crisp air against my skin and the peacefulness that allowed my mind to wander.

"No."

Panic is filling my lungs and suffocating my airflow. I get up for some space, and turn my face from Brent so he can't detect the trepidation in my eyes.

Brent must sense my anxiety. He jumps off the barstool to be by my side. "Raina, are you okay?"

I feel his arms wrap around my waist. "I just need a minute." Actually, I need some freedom.

"I know this is hard for you. I'm sure you feel trapped. I would feel the same way. It won't be for that much longer, though. As soon as we can figure this out, I can take you away for a much-needed vacation—anywhere you want."

I snap around, indulged by his words. He always knows just the right thing to say. My mind has now switched to thoughts of him and I on an exotic beach together, with no one around for thousands of miles.

"I would *love* that."

Eternal Mixture

I can't help but meld my hips into his, wishing that he would do the same. I stare up at him in desperate need to feel his lips against mine and his hands against my skin. He must sense this need, because in the next moment, his lips are smashed against mine. His tongue opens me up and dives deep into my warmth. I match every thrust of his, making him aware that I am ready for anything he is willing to give. My head feels dizzy, swarming with adult thoughts, but before I get carried away, he stops me and slowly tears us apart.

"I have to take a shower," Brent says, ragged and out of breath.

I can't help but sulk.

"Okay, I'll clean up."

He gives me a lingering kiss on the cheek and heads upstairs. This is it. This is my only chance to meet up with Jason and Jenna. I run up the stairs quietly, skipping every other one, get into my room and change out of my nightclothes. I stand in the hall, carefully reaching my hearing out for a moment. Brent is happily whistling to himself as the water is still barreling down his naked body. I quickly shake that thought from my mind.

I tiptoe down the steps, grab my keys, delicately open the front door, and close it behind me with as little force as possible. My blood is rushing through my veins and my heart is going bananas with the thought of Brent running out the door after me.

I know as soon as the ignition is fired up and I back out of my driveway, I am alone. The emptiness swallows the car, reminding me that every inch I take is an inch farther away from my love and deeper into the unknown. My mind wanders to a million scenarios about how this visit could possibly turn out. But Jenna's willingness to meet with me has to be a good sign, right?

Something deep down under disagrees with me. I have this unnerved acid burn in the pit of my gut. This is never a good sign. Fortunately for Jenna, I don't care. I will do whatever it takes to help her. I would jump through fire and dive into a tank full of sharks if that's what it took, because that is what friends do. I would like to think she might do the same if the tables were turned.

Jason gave me directions to a cabin located about forty minutes away, past Ontario County. I plugged it into my GPS this morning so I wouldn't waste any time messing with it in the car. The farther in route I go, the more isolated my surroundings are. The houses are getting farther apart with each passing minute, while the trees and brush get thicker, engulfing the road and denying any bit of sunlight the ability to seep through.

I can't help but wonder if there are any police officers that survey this area or how many cars pass through here in a day's time. I finally pull onto a small cobblestone road hidden deep in the brush. If it hadn't been for the navigation, I would have never known the cabin was back here. Immediately, I begin to think of creative fast getaways if need be.

The crackle and snap of the rocks against the tires seem to last forever until finally I pull up to a small beat-down wood cabin. The porch looks fragile and worn, the roof is smothered in lime-green mold, and the house seems to lean to one side, tired and begging to be torn down.

The trees surrounding the structure hang low, limbs stretching for earth and giving the illusion of evening instead of day. I bundle my jacket tighter against me for warmth and comfort before I take a step out of my car and onto the moist earth. My senses become heightened with each step I take, striding deeper into the dark mist. The air is hazy and thick, and my conscious is screaming for me to turn around. For a split moment, I look to the house, and I see red. Bright fire-engine red. I slam my eyes shut, shaking the vision from my head and attempting to refocus. When I look back, it's gone.

Eternal Mixture

I think my fear of the unknown is getting the best of me. I need to grasp ahold of my imagination and get this visit over with. I swallow enough courage to take a step forward and knock on the door.

Jason swings the door open without saying a word. He gazes at me in silence as I walk through the door. I am uncomfortable. Jenna is nowhere in sight, so I take a step in, a little farther towards the small brick fireplace. Still no Jenna. I turn to him, hoping he might start the conversation by explaining where she is, but he doesn't. Silence is his forte.

I cross my hands behind my back to shield my nervousness. "Jason, where is Jenna?" My hands are shaking behind me.

He draws himself closer, studying me like he did before, only this time he doesn't look confused. He looks intrigued, fascinated, and envious. Once I meet his gaze again, I can't help but feel this odd familiarity. It's strange how much he repels me while compelling me in the very same moment. I'm not quiet sure what that is all about, but it feels natural, like we have danced to this song before.

"Why are you looking at me like that?" I ask, wanting to veer our conversation towards Jenna's whereabouts.

"You have this magnificent aura surrounding you," he says while taking another step forward. "Where did it come from?" He reaches his hand out to graze my perimeter with his fingers, but I back away.

Oh my God! I am completely spazzing out inside! I don't understand this. Brent told me mortals would not be able to see my aura, so how can this be? Maybe he is just talking about a womanly glow. I *have* been taking better care of my skin, but something tells me that's not what he's referring to.

"What are you talking about, Jason?"

"The illumination is a vibrant lilac tone that radiates

off of your skin. You have never, in your many lives, had this before. I just don't understand," Jason trails off, rubbing his eyes.

I am completely floored. Did he really just say what I think he said? My *many* lives? How could he possibly know this information? Maybe he has been spying on me, or maybe he has overheard a conversation between Brent and I. But, that's impossible. There is just no possible way.

I try to gather my thoughts together, to make sense of them quickly. "Did you just say my many lives?" Jason looks down at me as I'm now fiddling with my hands.

"Yes."

"Are you out of your *mind*, Jason?"

"No."

"Then why are you talking crazy?"

"He hasn't told you, has he?" Jason shakes his head, smirking.

I don't know where this is going, but he is making absolutely no sense at all. I need to see Jenna so I can get the hell out of here. Although I must admit, I am intrigued to know who he is talking about.

"Who is *he*, Jason? You're not making any sense."

"Brent."

"I don't understand. You don't even know Brent."

Jason cracks up out loud, smacking his hand on his thigh. "You silly little girl. Have you not listened when he's spoken? Have you not picked up on anything surrounding you?"

My fingers ball up into a fist. "I don't know what you're talking about! You're not making any sense!" I shout.

Jason folds his hands behind his back and begins to pace slowly against the weak, creaking floor. "Lets just start at the beginning, shall we?" He continues without waiting for a response while keeping his eyes on the floor.

"The day was coming to an end and twilight was

upon us. My younger brother and I were very competitive from a young age. First it was skipping rocks, and then our father introduced us to chess. By the time we hit our teenage years, we were masters. Shortly after that, hormones kicked in, chess was forced to the dust, and lust set us into a whole new type of competitive edge. But I'll save that story for another time," Jason chuckles. "This night still burns in my head like it was yesterday. My brother and I were playing chess on the table next to the blazing fire, he was just about to beat me—until my father burst in, that is."

Why does this sound so familiar?

"My father was screaming, face stricken with horror, sweat dripping down his sideburns as he barked orders to my mother, a limp body in hand. It was total turmoil in a matter of seconds, with chess pieces clinking, scattered about the hardwood floors, the dinner table turned into a rescue operating station with my father frenzied over this battered and beaten girl.

"My mother was always the opposite from my father: she was the calm and serene one. She was always able to keep her cool while maneuvering gracefully through stressful situations. You could imagine my brother and I, being young and inexperienced with life's crises, how monumental this was. It was an absolutely terrifying moment."

My mind is spinning rapidly on overload. I know Brent told me he had a brother long ago, but what did he say his name was? AJ? No. Or was it MJ? I shift through my memories until I come upon it: EJ.

"Your first name isn't Jason, is it?" I whisper with hopes that I'm wrong. He shakes his head and halts his pacing. "Then what is it?" I ask.

"Edmund."

"Edmund Jason?"

This name I have heard before. I just can't place

from where and when.

"Yes." He answers, eyes gazing fiercely into mine. And then it clicks.

"Edmund Jason Alexander," I whisper to myself.

Jason hears with his impeccable ears. "Yes."

"I saw you in a picture. I thought it was one of your relatives, but it was you, wasn't it?"

His eyes turn soft before looking away. "That was the last picture I took with my parents."

I remove my eyes from his. His gaze is fiery and stings with unknown emotions. I have no idea why he continues to look at me in this way, as though I am his long lost lover. It's making my skin crawl, but the scariest thing is I can't decipher between this feeling being good or bad.

I almost feel a twinge of guilt, as though my emotions are being hijacked by this fool, and I am becoming more confused by the minute.

"So you are Brent's brother?" I let it sink in, attempting to gain control of myself.

"Yes."

"And you are immortal?" I question, hoping I didn't hear him right a moment ago.

"Yes."

"Where was Brent? He wasn't in the picture."

"He didn't agree with the way I took charge. After we mutilated the mortals and took over their land, he felt I was taking things too far. He said I was blinded with greed and it was going to ruin me. But boy was he wrong! It was just the beginning," he replies with an evil smirk.

The book of *Immortels* floods my head page by page. "The Louise family. Victor Louise, he was my husband, wasn't he?" A tear falls down my face.

"Yes. He was the monster who threw you away to the wolves. He was too close to finding out the true beauty of our lake. We had to do something, and what better than to avenge you? Brent was my right-hand man. I moved, he moved," he smiles. "We destroyed his whole army of guards in a matter of minutes. We were *amazing* together. And by the time we reached your husband, we did things to him you couldn't even imagine," he says proudly.

I wince at the thought.

"Does he know you have been here in town this whole time?" I only ask because of Brent's last comment to me about his sibling, "EJ is no longer my brother."

"No, he doesn't know I am here," Jason confesses.

I furrow my brows, confused. Why wouldn't he want to make his presence known to his brother? What *exactly* is he up to? From the way Brent made it seem, his brother turned to the dark side a long time ago, which means he can't possibly be up to anything good.

"Why not?" I cross my arms, annoyed.

He looks into the distance for a moment. "It's complicated."

It's obvious he doesn't want to go any further into detail, but I feel compelled to know. "Life is complicated. And as far as I know, so is you and your brother's history. So tell me, EJ, why is it you and Brent don't get along?"

He begins pacing again. After a couple of minutes, he turns to me. "My brother is a weak excuse for an immortal. Such a waste of space. He has been blinded by love for the last hundred and fifty years, when we could have taken over this world together. *You* are his downfall!" he barks with deep anger.

His eyes penetrate deep into my flesh, scorching my skin with the look of pure evil and one hundred and fifty years of hatred. This can't be good. The veins in his neck bulge while blues and greens paint the muscles on his forearms from his tense, balled fists. He wants to hurt me. I am afraid if I don't speak to Jenna now, I will never have the chance again. She is in danger; I have no doubt about it.

In this moment, I gather every ounce of strength I have to stand up straight, puff out my chest, and show no fear. "At least he has the courage to love! A man who has never loved is a man who will never be completely fulfilled in life. He will always be just a fingertip away from his conquest and just a second too late for his dream. I feel very sorry for you, Jason."

I watch as his hatred turns to hesitation with where I am heading. "Now, if you will excuse me, I am going to speak with Jenna."

I turn and walk to the small hall with only two doors. I open the first and a bathroom lies ahead of me. I close the door and head on to the next. In front of me lies a sturdy oak door separating me from my current archenemy. I can't help but wonder what is to happen once I walk across this threshold. Will she forgive me and wrap her arms around me, or will she still shun me? My palms become clammy with anticipation.

The door gives a protesting shriek as I push it open. The image I see is feeble, sickly, and child-like. Jenna lies on the bed in a curled-up fetal position. Even soaking wet, she could only weigh about ninety pounds. She has been wasting away in Jason's care over these past couple of weeks. Now she lies frail and unhinged as death creeps over her. Her face is no longer plump with flesh, and her cheeks are no longer rosy with life. She has been replaced by a skeleton wrapped in skin—a corpse-like shell. My gut twinges with pain as I take her in.

I move to her bed slowly, hoping not to spook her. "Jenna?" I take a big gulp. "It's me, Raina."

I see a small flutter of her eyelids, but she is so weak that she has no strength left to open them. The floorboard squeaks behind me. I snap my body around in protection mode.

"What have you *done* to her?" I accuse maliciously.

"Only what she has allowed me to do," Jason replies.

"What the hell does *that* mean?" Is this kid crazy?

Eternal Mixture

In one moment he's dark and creepy, and then in the next he makes my hormones go haywire, and now I've never wanted to rip someone to shreds as much as I do him.

He remains planted in front of me. "It means she is fully aware of what is going down."

My right eyebrow lifts. "And what is going down, Jason?" I grit through my teeth.

He grins. "She wanted to become immortal. So I am giving her the opportunity."

Oh my God! My mouth drops with shock. Why does he think immortality is his to give? Does he even realize what he is condemning her to? He doesn't love her, because if he did, he would never have offered this to her. She will be left with an eternity of disappointment. He'll leave her in the dust while he strives for world domination.

I take a step closer. "You should have never offered her immortality. You don't even *love* her! What are you getting out of this?"

There has to be a reason behind his madness.

"I'm getting you," he says so matter-of-factly.

The skip of my heart picks up with adrenaline and my mouth turns sour with the taste of fear. "I don't understand. Elaborate, please?" I need to buy myself some time. I have got to get Jenna and I out of here.

Jason walks around me to look out the window. "I will grant your friend her mortality back if you come with me. If you choose not to, she will die. But let me remind you, the eternal mixture is nowhere in proximity," he discloses, leaving an impossible offer on the table.

I leave with him, and Jenna's life goes on as normal. Or I refuse and she dies or, even worse, becomes immortal. There is only one right option here. "If I leave, will she remember any of this?"

He grins with an emotion I do not recognize. "Once I refuel her with my energy, she will only have memories of a faded dream."

"What do you mean by your energy?"

I wish he would just come out and tell me the facts. All the guessing and innuendos are tiring me.

"Ah…if I told you, I may have to kill you," he jokes.

"This is not the time for a joke, Jason!" I huff, slapping my arms down to my side.

"I assume you have heard of vampires?"

"Who hasn't? Are you trying to tell me you are a vampire?" I ask, laughing. He has definitely lost his mind.

He chuckles. "No. But sometimes you need to go to extreme measures in order to gain the supremacy that I seek. I'm sure Brent has mentioned that people do crazy things for a life filled with youthfulness, and I tend to find just the right ones who have a need in common and are willing to trade in order to gain the upper hand. That is just what I did with Lula. She's a witch who had all the powers in the world under her belt, *except* for one: immortality. That is the ingredient I held."

"Okay, so what did she hold?"

"She gave me the power to feed off of people's energy. An energy vampire is what it's called. The more energy I feed off of, the less I need the mixture. Unfortunately, it kills my donors," he explains.

I look over at Jenna, and my heart weeps for her. She was willing to put her life into this man's hands out of love. "You are sick! How could you take advantage of her? She loves you!" Tears stream down my cheeks. Jason walks over to me and grabs my wrist. "Let go of me!" I shriek, trying to snatch myself from his grip.

"See, I knew there was something different about you this time around, and as we can both see, I was right. Usually, it's simple. I just kill you off. Slowly replacing the ingredients within the mixture. I had to be careful at first. See, when my mother was alive, it was hard to alter the mixture without her knowing, so I had to choose something

Eternal Mixture

to replace the Astragalus with something that had the same smell and taste or she would know.

"After my mother died, there was no need to try as hard. Brent was so concerned with finding a cure that he never stopped to look right in front of him."

"You asshole!" I cry with disbelief. How could he? How could he be so cruel as to kill me over and over, century after century? He is so cold and removed from any feelings whatsoever. All I can think is, what happened to make him this way?

Jason chuckles. "Yes. Maybe you're right. But I had my reasons. Only it never seems to work quite as I plan. I always hoped my brother would come to his senses and would join the dark side, *my side*. Unfortunately, he just wouldn't let you go. I never did understand how you continued to resurrect yourself decade after decade, and honestly, it pissed me off!" he sneers, face contorting with anger. He quickly quiets his emotions. "I think this time around you may be useful instead of merely an obstacle. So, here we are."

I recall my father explaining my deaths in detail: "You became pale and extremely frail, your face and body were sunken like someone was sucking the energy right out of you." And now I know what was happening.

"You not only switched my mixture, but you also stole my energy, causing me to deteriorate faster. That's why no one had time to figure out what caused my sickness. All this time it was you." I shake my head in disbelief. "Did you really hate me that much, Jason?"

"My reasons were far from that. One has many sides, and there is not always a rhyme to one's reasons."

I roll my eyes with his nonsense of an answer.

"You know Brent's going to come after you once he finds out, don't you?"

He glares. "I'll be waiting for it."

"What did you say to Jenna to turn her against me?"

"When I consume my victim's energy, I am able to control their thoughts. That is how I am able to keep them remaining calm while I take what I need from them."

"So these weren't her real feelings towards me?"

"No."

Jenna stirs. "Jenna? It's me, Raina."

Her voice is a scratchy whisper. "Raina?"

I rush to her side and sit on the bed next to her. "I'm here. How are you feeling?"

"Weak. Where is Jason?"

I look to Jason. "You need to *fix* her! She doesn't have much time. I can hear her heart, and it's barely pumping!"

He stands there in a deep stare, not budging a bit. I want to shake him, slap him into having some real human emotions. Just because he has lived for over one hundred and fifty years doesn't give him an excuse to become dehumanized. Yes, it may have numbed him a bit, but if anything, it should have brought him closer to humanity with all this time he has invested.

"Are you just going to stand there?" I screech.

He crosses his arms. "How do I know you're not going to run once I do this?"

I want to run. I want to run *so* badly, but I can't. Jenna needs me in order to survive. I would never be able to live with myself knowing I chose my life over hers. Besides, nothing that was said these last couple of weeks was real. I knew he was behind it all along. I'm just happy he gave me confirmation of it.

I stare him directly in the eyes and give him everything I have left. "You have my word. I will leave with you."

# Chapter 19

Something in my eyes must have convinced Jason to believe in me, because he quickly springs over to Jenna and crouches over her, coming nose to nose with her frail body. Her face is soft and filled with a look of adoration. Little does she know, he was almost the cause of her demise.

I study his moves carefully, storing the memory deep into my mind for a later time. His eyes lock with hers, and immediately—like a snap of the finger—she is taken over. Her eyes are blank, and her expression is empty. As soon as his mouth opens, a brilliant white light escapes and bolts like lightning into her mouth. His energy is seeping through her, integrating and melding with her own tissue.

I watch her transform in front of me. The darkness under her eyes begins to fade, and her sunken cheeks fill in again with plump, pink flesh. Her lips moisten and redden to a healthy shade. I can hear every breath getting stronger and each beat of her heart pumping faster. Within seconds, she is almost back to her vibrant self.

She sits up, groggy and confused like she just awoke in a strange new place. She takes a moment to look around, and she lays her eyes on me. "Raina? What are you doing here?" she asks. "Jason? Where *are* we?" She continues to look over the room.

My eyes dart to Jason as I take a seat on the bed next to her. I slide my fingers through her hair, brushing it from her face. "Jenna, how are you feeling?"

She takes a moment to answer, still seeming dazed. "I feel sort of rested. Have I been asleep long?"

"Yeah, I guess you can say that. Jenna, what is the last thing you remember?"

She looks over at Jason, furrowing her brows while she thinks. "Um, I'm not really sure. I think Jason asked me if I wanted to get out of town for a couple of days." She turns to him. "Jason, how long have we been here?"

"A week," he responds coldly.

Jenna runs her hand through her hair in deep thought. She almost has a look of panic on her face.

"A *week*? How is that possible? I can't seem to r-remember," she replies, dumbfounded and a little nervous.

"Jenna, it's okay. You have been extremely sick, and that's why you're having trouble remembering." I want so badly to tell her everything that scumbag has put her through, but I need to be careful. I don't want to throw her into shock or worse, have her rebel against me.

"*I* have been sick? Funny, I don't feel sick."

I glare up at Jason. "That's because Jason fixed it." She looks more confused than ever. "I know you're confused right now, but just know I came here to help you. I'm leaving my cell phone here for you. Call your parents and have them come get you. The address is in my GPS."

"I-I don't understand. Where are you going?"

"We need to go, Raina. Now," Jason barks.

"Give me a minute," I growl.

Jenna looks between the both of us accusingly. "Jason, what is going on? Where are the both of you going?"

"Jenna, it's not like that. There's just some things I

Eternal Mixture

can't explain."

Jason grabs my upper arm and pulls me up aggressively. I try to snatch it back, but his grip is too tight. "Let *go* of me!" I snarl.

"Jason, don't touch her like that! What's the matter with you?" Jenna yells, but because of her condition, it sounds more like a kitten's cry.

Jason ignores her and drags me out into the living area. "Let *go of me!*" I shout. "I told you that I would leave with you. There's no reason to put your hands on me."

"She's asking too many questions. We need to leave—*now*."

He lets go of my arm, and I gather my composure. I hear Jenna calling us from the other room. She's still too weak to get up, and this gives us enough time to get out of here without her following. I am grateful he kept his end of the deal, and now it's my turn to follow through.

"Okay, let's go."

He leads me out of the cabin, twilight now upon us, and opens the passenger door of his metallic silver Camaro. I slither into my seat to avoid any physical contact with him. My eyes are like daggers that never leave his, and even though I am filled with an underlying hatred, I still feel an intense static electricity. It doesn't make my knees weak or my heart thump, it makes my skin crawl and my fist ready to meet his face.

He slams the door, closing me in. I feel claustrophobic and sick to my stomach. Every last inch of my being is telling me to open this car door and run. If I make it out now, I may have just enough time to jump into my car before Jason can stop me. The thought of running into Brent's arms soothes me, but ultimately saddens me as well, knowing he is miles out of reach. Deep down inside, I know he's looking for me, and that gives me a little hope.

The driver's side door opens and a cold gust of wind knocks away thoughts of Brent. Instead, I'm left with

Shevaun DeLucia

a chill down my spine and the aroma of expensive leathery musk. Everything about Jason is cold: his body, his stare, and his heart.

Jason doesn't waste any time. He takes one quick glance my way, shifts the car into drive, and faces ahead, slamming his foot on the gas pedal and launching us forward into the night.

My head slams back against headrest as though I am on a rollercoaster. I grab the assist handle above the car door for support.

Jason looks over at me. "Sorry," he says, but I refuse to look over at him or acknowledge his apology. I won't show him any weakness or lead him on to the fact that I'm deathly afraid of driving this fast. He knows more about me than I know about myself; I'd like to keep my secrets from this life mine. This is the only thing I have left that is my own.

"Where are we heading?" I ask.

"Canada."

"Are we going to the lake?"

"Not yet."

"Then where?"

"A cabin."

A cabin? I take a look out the window to see if I recognize anything about the scenery. I remember the void of houses and the abundance of trees, but other than that it all looks the same. The blackened sky above us makes it even harder to decipher anything.

"Your Aunt Lillian's cabin?"

His head snaps in my direction. "How'd you know?" he asks, surprised.

"I was just there with Brent a couple of weeks ago."

His grimace expresses something I haven't seen in him before: hurt. The look is gone in the blink of an eye as he gains control and once again appears emotionless.

"Well then, I am sure you will feel right at home,"

Eternal Mixture

Jason comments sarcastically.

I am not sure where the sarcasm is coming from. If I knew him better, I might mistake his sarcasm for a little jealousy. But that can't be the case in our situation.

"And once we get there, then what?"

"Raina, do you remember anything about your past?"

I look down, fiddling with my hands. "No. Why?" I ask softly.

"Has Brent filled you in on anything?"

"Some." I can't imagine why he is asking or what his agenda is.

Jason slides his fingers through his vanilla-stroked hair just as Brent does. "Let me guess, stories of the two of you?" he asks.

"Yes. Why are you asking?"

His mouth is rigid and his eyes stare out the windshield, glazed over with an icy coldness. I look at him, studying him, wondering what made him this way. What was the final moment that sealed the deal and stopped his heart from beating?

"You've lived many lives, Raina. Brent wasn't the only one you ever shared time with." Jason throws me a bone, but has no intention of giving me any explanation as to why.

I let that sink in for a moment. "Are you suggesting there was someone else?"

"I'm just saying there is more to his stories than he is willing to admit."

I huff softly with impatience. "Jason, stop with the antics, and just say what's on your mind."

His brows furrow just slightly, enough for my immortal eyes to take notice. "You know, you and I weren't always enemies. At one time we actually enjoyed each other's company."

My annoyance begins to rumble underneath my

skin. "Was that before or after you killed me?" I snarl at him.

Jason chuckles. "Yes. Ok, I deserved that. I think in time, though, it will all come back to you."

Extremely annoyed by his implications, I decide to refrain from any further conversation with him and turn my direction to my window. He must pick up on this as he offers no more conversation. I can see him through my peripheral view, however, stealing fleeting looks at me.

He seems to be taken by my illuminant aura. I can't fault him for this, because I too was mesmerized by it. I contemplate his words very hard and continue to get this nagging inkling that the details behind his comments may be more than I can handle at the moment. I'd like to believe that what he said was a lie, but my gut is saying otherwise.

After almost two hours, we pull onto the dirt road leading up to the cabin. I sit up in my seat, praying that Brent may have beat us to the punch, but as I see the cold darkness spewing from the cabin, I know all hope is gone. I'm on my own.

Jason removes the key from the ignition and slams the door behind him as he exits the car. I sit in complete silence for a moment, pondering what lies ahead for me. My door opens, and the cold air rushes in. Regardless of Jason's stone heart, he still remembers how to be chivalrous. He holds his hand out for me to take, but I ignore his offer and lift myself out of his car on my own. The thought of touching him makes my skin crawl.

He shakes his head and chuckles once to himself while slamming the passenger door after me. I wait for him as I stand on the small stoop and hug my arms around myself to keep away the chill. The air is crisp, the bare trees rustle in the light wind, and the moon gleams brightly overhead, giving us a hint of light. Jason pulls his leather sleeve over his hand, smashes the small glass square in the door, and reaches in to unlock it. I jump back, caught off-guard. He opens the door and waves his hand in front of him for me to enter first.

"After you," he says.

I walk past him. "What, you had no key?" I chuckle.

He closes the door behind him. "Unfortunately, my Aunt Lillian and I do not speak. We haven't seen each other in decades," he reveals.

I watch him closely, and even though his face is smooth and controlled, I see a glimmer of sadness in his eyes. In the next moment, it's gone. Under his hard exterior, I can actually see something real and human-like. I think he has played this tough, emotionless role for so long that it has just become him. What he has done to Jenna is completely inexcusable and unforgivable. I will never be able to get over that. Seeing her lying in front of me on her deathbed is still front and center in my mind.

Now I have to figure out how to get myself out of this mess. If I can convince him to allow me to go free, we can all walk away unscathed. No harm has to come. I just know that's not going to happen, though.

"Jason, what is it you want from me? Why am I here?" I sit down on the couch, waiting for his explanation.

He unzips his backpack that's laid on the kitchen table, grabs a bottled water, and throws it in my direction. "I figure you could use some nourishment."

I open the bottle and take a sip. "Thanks." The mixture tastes sweet like a Crystal Light iced tea and does the job of quenching my thirst. I can't lead him on to the fact that I don't require this to survive, so I close my eyes as the mixture slides down my throat. "I needed that," I lie. "So, I thought you didn't have any of the mixture in close proximity?"

"I lied," he admits bluntly with his back turned toward me.

It's clear that I cannot trust anything he says. He is

extremely good at lying. He figured if I was aware that the mixture was available, I might have chosen immortality for Jenna rather than leave with him. I know I wouldn't have.

He walks over to the front window to scan the area. "I've been following my brother's tracks for years. He must have sensed me close behind, because I lost his trail. He's very good at getting lost, but when it comes to you, he tends to get a little blinded. It took me a while to locate him again and when I did, you weren't too far away.

"My plan was to get rid of you and to give my brother one last shot, but when I saw you, there was something different about you. Your aura, your radiance, and your strength all tell me there is more than what meets the eye."

I swallow.

I gather a tight composure over my emotions, because deep inside I am panicking, and I *cannot* allow him to see this. Brent warned me about what will happen if the gift of my blood is discovered, and I'm sad to admit that I didn't take him seriously. I haven't done a great job protecting myself thus far, and now I'm paying the consequence.

A tear escapes me, and I quickly swipe it away before Jason notices. I miss my love. I know he is in turmoil right now trying to find me, but if I had to make this choice all over again, there would be no doubt that I would put Jenna before myself.

"Well, I'm sorry to let you down. Maybe you'll still have a chance to live out your plan. Unfortunately, Jason, you are wrong about my aura. There's nothing special about it other than it has grown with my love for Brent."

"Bullshit!" Jason states aggressively.

I notice him watching me through the reflection in the window. He studies my every move, which forces me to be more calculated with my movements. Is he curious about me? Or does he want to use my own mannerisms against me?

I stand up quickly. "It's not bullshit!" I growl back loudly. I pause, close my eyes, and take a moment to breathe. I need to connect with him on a different level. "Listen, Jason, if you ever cared for me as a friend, you'll let me go. *Please?*"

"Brent wasn't the only man you ever loved, you know. You loved me as well, lifetimes ago," he reveals.

Bingo. This is what he was hinting at earlier. My mind drifts off for a moment as I stare at the fireplace. I take a slow breath in, trying to allow my body to remember him. I wait for a tingle or a spark, *any* sort of recognition that my body and soul once connected with his. I get nothing. Sure, there was a bit of static electricity earlier, but that was nothing more than misplaced anger and hate.

He took my best friend from me and turned her against me. He sucked her dry from almost all of her human life, and I'm supposed to believe I would have fallen in love with someone like this?

If we were as intimate as he says, shouldn't I feel some sort of underlying emotions for him? With Brent, there is this immediate irrevocable attraction that floods through my veins. My body knew it before *I* really knew him.

"I'm sorry, Jason, but I don't think that's possible," I break it to him. "I love Brent. I see how you are. I've seen what you're capable of. There is no way I ever loved someone like you."

I see the rage fill his eyes as he stands only a couple of feet away from me. I'm scared. I have no idea what I have just opened myself up to. I sit down. He hasn't moved, and his eyes haven't left mine. Finally, I drop my eyes from his stare and look to the floor. I hear his shoes clack against the wood floor as he moves. I look up, and he grabs a blanket from his bag and throws it in my direction.

"I'm going to start the fire. We should get some

sleep. Tomorrow we have a long drive ahead of us," he tells me before walking outside to grab some firewood.

I look quickly to the door and then to the kitchen window, trying to decide if I should run or not. In the next second, Jason walks back through the door with the firewood.

I curl up on the couch, bring the blanket up to my chin, and hunker down. Tears slide off my cheeks, making a puddle on my pillow. I close my eyes tight. The only thoughts I have are of Brent. His gentle kiss and ambrosial aroma put me to sleep every single night. I grab ahold of those memories with all of my might and drift off to a faraway place.

# Chapter 20

"Raina, mon amour, wake up," he whispers sweetly in my ear. "Wake up, baby. I'm here."

I hear the familiar voice of my love far in the distance, and I know I am dreaming. This wouldn't be a dream if he weren't in it. I can smell his sweet manly aroma as if he were right in front of me, and I can feel his warm fingers against my skin as though he's really touching me. I smile as his lips graze my jawline, and then I hear him again.

"*Please*, baby. Wake up."

This time it's closer and more vivid, as though he is truly right in front of me. I smile and reach out to him as I would in any of my dreams. His skin is warm under my touch. He brings my hand to his face. I can feel the softness of his cheeks and the plush of his lips as they graze each of my fingers slowly, one by one.

I can't deny myself any longer. I need to *see* him, if only for one moment before I awake. This will provide me with enough strength to continue on. I open my eyes to a foggy darkness. I reach for him. His face glows in front of me, cast with a golden shadow. He looks like an angel, staring at me with adoration.

"Brent," I whisper with a loving smile.

He shakes me softly. "You're not dreaming, Raina. Wake up!" he whispers.

His words echo through my head. You're not dreaming.

I sit up, rubbing my eyes, and open them again.

"Brent?" I whisper loudly in shock.

He immediately puts his finger to my mouth to shush me. He looks over his shoulder at Jason sleeping. "We need to go, *now*!"

I nod my head, entwining my fingers with his as he pulls me up from the couch and leads me to the door. The floorboard squeaks beneath me.

"Going somewhere, little brother?"

I jump back, startled.

Brent pulls me behind him immediately. "Yes. I'm taking Raina home."

Jason chuckles once. "Home? You mean that insufficient town filled with those useless mortals?" He walks over to the fireplace and stabs the smoky ashes. "Does she even know where her real home is, little brother?"

"Of course I do!" I sneer at him. "And those mortals are my friends and family, Jason. Do you *even* remember the meaning of friends and family?"

Jason laughs out loud. "Yes. I remember clear as day." He looks in my direction. "Friends and lovers are great for a good stab in the back." He turns to Brent. "And family? What can I say other than 'disappointment' and 'betrayal.' I am *well* aware of the meanings," Jason finishes, eyes cold as ice.

"Why are you doing this?" Brent asks. "How are you benefiting from all of this?"

"Take a look at her, brother. Why don't you tell me how I will be benefiting from it? *Or*, as a matter of fact, why don't you tell me how you're already benefiting from her?" Jason directs his attention to my aura. "Did you think you could keep her hidden forever?"

"I already told you what my aura is from!" I growl, Brent still holding me behind him.

"Okay, she has a glow, an aura. Now what? What did you plan to do with it?" Brent questions.

Jason walks from the fireplace and stops a couple feet in front of us. "You know as well as I do that there is something different about her this time around. I can see it in your eyes. You're scared, which means whatever is going on with her, whatever changes have taken place, are some big ones, and I intend on finding out what those are."

I squeeze Brent tighter. I see a dangerous underlying threat to his words, and I'm nervous. There is no way he is going to let this go. And if my family and I stay in our home, we are going to be like sitting ducks, so where does that leave us now?

"Jason, you have to let this go. Please, let us leave in peace." I beg.

Jason studies me for a moment before responding.

"I'm sorry, but I can't do that," he states.

"Have you told the others?" Brent asks.

My eyebrows draw together in confusion. The others? Could he be talking about the other immortals? My heart flutters in what seems to be the beginnings of a panic attack. God, please no. From Brent's mouth to my ears, "Raina, they will come for you."

Jason glares back at Brent, knowing just where he is going with this line of questioning. "Let's just say they were warned that I would be coming home. You know if I do not show, they will come looking for me."

Brent understands his words very clearly, but he also understands that his brother is an exceptionally good bluffer.

"I'm not here to fight. I just want to take Raina home safely. You still haven't answered my question. Just be straight with me for once in your life, Edmund."

Jason looks as though he is pondering Brent's question, and then a light seems to click on. "Interesting choice of words. Maybe you should follow your own advice, little brother." He looks towards me and asks, "Raina, why don't you ask Brent here about your first life as an immortal?"

I can feel Brent's muscles stiffen. It's painfully obvious that he has hit a nerve, and it's clear Jason has amused himself with Brent's reaction: his jaw clenched and fists balled tightly. Jason is betting on my curiosity getting the best of me, and I can't lie, temptation is a bitch.

"Now is not the time! She is not ready for that yet," Brent snaps.

I've never seen him with so much anger. Not even when it came to his fight with Jaime. Brent's body is shaking uncontrollably. He looks like a teakettle about to explode under pressure, and it's scaring me. Jason is getting the exact response he was hoping for, and being brothers, he knows just the right buttons to push.

"Brent, please, it's okay," I whisper, stroking his back. "You're right, now is not the time to shed any sort of light on my past. Not in this way. Do you *hear me, Jason*?" I snarl. "Not like this!"

I feel Brent's muscles begin to relax as he listens to my voice. His breathing becomes steady, and I tangle my fingers with his for strength and support.

Jason snickers while watching our scene of love unfold in front of him. He claps slow and loud. "Well done. Well done."

He steps back, takes a seat in the chair near the kitchen table, and crosses one leg loosely over the other. "It doesn't matter how many years or how many deaths have gone by, one thing never changes: you will always stay whooped by the idea of love. Your greatest downfall."

"No, *brother*, that is where you are wrong," Brent

clarifies with a mocking tone. "Love is our greatest gift, our reason for life, and that's where you went wrong. You gave up on it," Brent tries to reason.

Jason rushes up to his feet. "You stole my love from me and left me empty! You not only took my heart, but you crushed my soul to pieces!" I can actually see pain rippling through him. Jason *actually* feels, and I can see he is still hurting from whatever happened in the past. A tiny part of me aches for him, but I don't know why.

"Now I see what this is all about," Brent says. "You're still in love with her, so you are punishing me because of it. She was never yours to begin with, Edmund. You have to let her go. Our paths were already chosen for us before we were born," he softens his voice in hopes of connecting with him.

She? Who is she? This can't possibly be because of me.

Jason's lips turns up with an evil, vindictive thought. "And *this* is why you have failed decade after decade. That is where you are wrong. I *have* let go. I let go a long time ago. And now, thanks to Raina, I have a new mission on my hands."

"What now, Jason? Killing me is no longer top priority on your list?" I question sarcastically.

Brent turns to look at me. "What are you talking about, Raina?"

I shift my gaze to Jason. "Would you like to tell him or shall I?"

Brent turns his attention to Jason who looks unsure of himself. By now, Jason has to know that his past choices will be his undoing.

"What did you do, Edmund?"

"Lets just say I used every open opportunity to my advantage."

I move to the side of Brent. "What he means, baby, is that he waited until you were too consumed with our love to kill me."

Brent looks mystified. "Impossible," he says under his breath, wheels turning.

I lay my hand on his forearm. "No baby, it's true. All this time, you believed that we have been cursed with my deaths because of the mixture, but it was Jason the whole time. He changed the ingredient to the mixture without anyone knowing. He killed me off time after time so you would join him in his quest for power. He thought if I was out of the picture, you would no longer be blinded. And when that didn't work, he had to take drastic measures.

"He found a witch that craved immortality just as much as he craved power. They traded off, and he was given the ability to suck energy from the living as an energy vampire." Brent doesn't shift or move. I can barely see movement in his chest, and his eyes are penetrating Jason with immense revulsion. The fact that he is not reacting at all is what is making me nervous, and it's clear that Jason is feeling the same way.

Jason meets Brent eye to eye. "Now you know. But don't worry, I have no desire to continue on with my charade, little brother." I can hear the taunting and sarcasm flooding his voice.

With no warning and no preparation, Brent lunges towards Jason like a lion ready for the kill. My hand flies to my mouth in disbelief. Jason doesn't even see it coming until Brent smashes his fist, like a bowling ball, straight into the side of his brother's face. Jason's head snaps back, and his body crashes onto the kitchen table, crushing it to pieces. Wood splinters and fragments fly through the air.

"Brent! Watch out!" I scream as I watch Jason spring up from the floor and set in his defensive stance.

Brent doesn't miss a beat, though. "You son of a bitch! I am going to kill you!" Brent threatens, stalking him move for move.

Eternal Mixture

Jason watches Brent very carefully and seems to be enjoying every minute of it. "Is that all you got? Come on, I killed your girl!" Jason baits him.

"You only killed her for your own selfish reasons. I know you better than you know yourself, *brother.* You can fool her, but you can't fool me!"

I watch them going tit for tat, but Brent's last words sting me. "Are you guys arguing over me, Brent?"

"Yes!" They both shout simultaneously without breaking eye contact.

I jump back. But more than anything, I get cut with the reality of the whole situation. Jason told me there are many sides to him and that I don't always see things as they really are. He's more or less like an illusion. Brent might be able to see him for what he really is, but if he loves me or loved me at one point, wouldn't that mean that some small part of him has to be good?

"Haven't you put me through enough? You took my parents from me! You killed *our* parents, Edmund! And now this? The love of my fucking life!" Brent raises his voice with extreme hostility and hurt.

I see one single tear drip down his cheek and plummet to the floor. It feels like a trigger has just been released at the sound of the teardrop hitting the ground.

Jason swiftly grabs the broken tabletop and throws it full force, hitting Brent like a block of cement. He then jumps through the kitchen window, leaving only shattered glass behind.

"Brent! Wait!" I scream, but before I can beg him to let Jason go, he is already gone.

I can't let him go off by himself. Right now it's each for his own, and I won't allow him to do anything he may regret. Regardless of the past, Jason is still his brother. I pull on my big girl panties and follow their trail.

I remember Brent telling me I have powers I haven't even come close to using, and my heightened

Shevaun DeLucia

senses are one of them. I stop in my tracks, not moving an inch, and listen quietly. I close my eyes, empty my thoughts, and allow my hearing to drift off. I shift through the branches rattling, the music of the wind whistling, and the owl hooting above me. I take another deep breath and allow myself to drift even farther through the trees and the bushes until I can finally pick up the sound of arguing in the distance.

The light from the moon shines down upon us, leaving a small shadow of light highlighted against the trees, but it's still not bright enough to allow me to see ahead. I move forward in a hurry, allowing the sounds of their voices to guide me. The brush is thick and overgrown, making it almost impossible to move fast.

Each grunt I hear is followed by an ear-splitting crack of a tree falling to the ground, leaving a quake that rumbles beneath my feet. This is getting extremely dangerous. They're obviously trying to kill each other, and if I don't get a move on it, I may be too late.

Something inside of me begins to burn with power. I feel awake. I can feel the strength of my aura humming through me, and the faster I run, the more my body escalates with immense heat. The darkness surrounding me lights up, my vision becomes impeccable, and my strides become effortless. My immortality soaks every inch of my being, and I feel untouchable.

Another loud crash shakes the ground as I come up behind them. They are engulfed in a circle of broken destruction, cracked limbs and snapped trees sprawled out around them. Jason seems to be consumed by a dark force. His face is emotionless and his body trembles with the need for energy. His left hand wraps around Brent's neck, strangling the life from him. Brent looks helpless beneath him.

There is no way I am living a life without him. My world would be meaningless and forever damned. Brent is the good in me, and I am the good in him. I don't know if he would come back to me in another life, and I am not about to find out now.

The seconds seem to go by in slow motion as Jason lowers his head. I know what lies next, and I won't allow him to suck the energy from my beloved. "Jason, stop!" I scream from behind him.

He looks up, momentarily distracted by my blazing, brilliant light. He's in awe of the beauty that cascades off my skin. I smirk with the satisfaction of knowing this gives Brent the chance to regain the upper hand.

Jason recognizes the glimmer in my eyes, but before he can respond, Brent has already positioned over him. Jason is aware of the pain that is about to be evoked upon him, and instead of looking frightened, he closes his eyes and smiles, almost welcoming it.

I turn my head as Brent's foot meets Jason's face. I hear the loud thud as his body hits the ground with a pain-filled moan. "Is that all you've got, little brother?" Jason's pain interrupts his laugh.

"I told you I was going to kill you!" Brent spits on him. "You are no longer my brother." Brent kicks him again, this time in the ribs. Jason groans, and rolls to his side on the ground.

"Brent, *please* stop!" I beg. I can't watch this go on any longer. I may despise Jason, but a tiny part of me hurts watching this scene unfold in front of me. I have caused this rift between these two, and the worst part is, I can't remember what I've done to cause it.

"Jason, just leave. Go home, and we'll forget this ever happened," I promise him. I reach my hand out to Brent, and we lock fingers. He turns his back on his brother and allows me to guide him away with my light. He would follow me to hell and back if I asked. I look back with a warm, grateful smile, feeling as though we may end up all right. But I see Jason's hand slung back only inches away

Shevaun DeLucia

from stabbing Brent in the back with a wooden stake.

"*NO!*" I scream.

There is no second thought or doubt as to what my next move must be. Putting someone I love before myself is something that comes natural to me, and dying a million deaths is something I will gladly do in the name of love.

Before Brent can even call my name, I have already begun the fall to the ground. "No, Raina! *Nooo!*" Brent yells as he catches me mid-air and lays me down softly on the dirt floor.

My ears begin a high-pitched ring as the pain climbs through my body. Darkness invades my vision as my adrenaline tries to kick in overload to keep me awake. I don't know how long I can hang on as tiny white spots blur my vision. I try to reach down towards my stomach where the central pain lies, but Brent grabs my hand and pulls it away.

"Brent," I whisper, looking into his worried eyes. I'm scared, and I am beginning to feel flashes of coldness. Is this what happens when death is near? I must have felt this many times before in each of my lives. If only I could remember, would I be scarred from the memories or could they help me overcome a situation like this?

"No, mon amour. Don't move, the wood is stuck in your stomach. I'm *so* sorry, Raina." The tears roll down his cheeks as he speaks to me. "I was supposed to protect you, and I failed," he whimpers. I can tell he is trying to remain strong for me, but he is ready to crumble into a million pieces. I need this foreign object out of my body so I can heal.

I look him dead in the eyes. "Brent, you need to pull it out now." I will him with my strength and certainty that this is what I want.

He shakes his head with disapproval. "I can't. You will bleed to death!"

I grab his face with my last bit of energy. "Brent,

Eternal Mixture

look at me," I demand sternly. "Pull it out!"

He immediately grabs the wood piece with all his might and yanks it upwards, letting out a deep grunt. I can't help but scream as though I am being torn in half as it's ripped from my body. The pain is so excruciating that I can feel myself slipping into the darkness. Beads of sweat roll down my hairline. I am weak and I am shaking uncontrollably, barely holding on. I look up to Brent, and he is kneeling above me, trembling with the dagger still in his hand.

I never knew agony like this existed, and if my blood didn't naturally heal me, I would have died from the pain alone. As the minutes go by, my wound begins to stitch itself together.

Jason slouches against the tree, watching the whole scene unfold in front of him. I close my eyes for the rest my body is searching for, and Brent takes this as a sign that I am being taken from him yet again. He must think my body cannot come back from a wound like this, and honestly, I would have thought so as well if I didn't feel my tissue mending itself back together.

"Do you see what you have done to her?" Brent shouts to Jason. "Look at her! I was wrong to think you may still have any love for her. You're cold and heartless. Mom and Dad did the right thing by letting you go. They were right—you aren't capable of feeling."

Jason stands up straight. "That wooden dagger was meant for you, not her."

Brent throws the blood-covered piece of wood at Jason's feet. "There. Now finish what you have started," he challenges.

Jason picks it up and begins to stalk towards his brother. Brent stands his ground without moving. As I lie on the ground, I can hear the crunch against the dirt floor with each step he takes closer to Brent. I know I need to stop this before someone else gets hurt.

Shevaun DeLucia

Brent isn't thinking clearly, especially now that he is upset with himself. He feels he has let me down, and he thinks it is his fault I am lying here right now. I *know* him, and I know he is blinded by anger and guilt at the moment, which means reason is nowhere near. I need to stand up. I need to stop him before he or his brother does anything that can't be undone. Brent's not as cold as Jason. Killing someone he cares for will eat at him for the rest of eternity. I won't have that blackness hanging over us.

I gather all my strength. Even though my body is still mending, I push the pain away, roll to my knees, and force myself to my feet. Brent can't see me because I am behind him, but Jason can. I watch the blood drain from his face as I grace him with a smirk. Ending my life is no longer a luxury that is available to him. I watch him stop dead in his tracks, dropping the blood-covered piece of wood beside him.

"How the hell—" he can't even finish his words before Brent bulldozes over him, knocking him to the ground.

"Brent, *no!*" I scream.

Immediately, his head jolts up and he freezes. He releases Jason and looks at me with the same disbelief that Jason just had. Brent stands up and runs to my side, lifting my shirt up to view my wound.

"It's gone!" he says, astounded.

Jason walks forward to get a better look. "What the—" is all he can seem to say.

I grab Brent's face with my hands to make sure he is looking straight into my eyes. "Brent, I am going to be okay." He wraps his arms around me without a second thought.

"I thought I was going to lose you, mon amour. I just couldn't *bare* it. Not again, and certainly not by my brother's hands." He looks me over again and rubs his thumb across the spot where my wound had been.

Eternal Mixture

"Amazing."

"Yes. It is *very* amazing," Jason speaks loudly in delight. "Now I see why the need for such secrecy."

Brent immediately turns to Jason, eyes fueled with the need to destroy. "Back the fuck away, Edmund! If you leave us now, I will spare your life," Brent says so matter-of-factly.

"Sorry, little brother, but this is not something I can just walk away from and forget. If she has the ability to heal herself without the mixture, *imagine* what this means for us?" he says, spreading his arms out.

I am now officially marked. I see Jason's wheels turning in his head as he begins to think about all the benefits of having my gift. The idea of complete domination has always been a dream just beyond his reach and my gift just might do the trick for him. He throws off the energy of an excited child but has the eyes of the devil.

I watch Brent's hands ball into tight fists, and I know he is going to snap again at any moment if Jason doesn't shut his mouth.

"Walk away, Edmund, and forget you ever saw any of this," Brent warns.

Jason laughs.

Brent slowly walks up to Jason, stalking, entering his personal circle of space. If looks could kill, they would both be lying dead on the ground. Their eyes are locked together, and I can't help but wonder who will make the first move. It's debilitating waiting in suspense like this.

My heart is pounding against my chest. "Brent?" I call in a somber voice. "Brent, please? Let it go."

Jason cracks a smart-ass grin. "Yes, little brother. Listen to *our* girl," he taunts.

In one swift, unexpected movement, Brent picks up the wooden dagger and jabs it straight into Jason's gut. My mouth drops as I watch Jason grab his stomach, shock and betrayal registering, while he succumbs to the pain and falls to the dirt floor.

I am so caught off-guard that my mind is still trying to register what just happened. I'm unsure of whom I'm exactly supposed to go to first: the one who loves me or the one who has killed me? One would think this would be an easy decision, but seeing someone in a vulnerable, life-threatening position outweighs anything by far.

Brent turns, his face cold as ice and unaffected by what he's just done. I gasp, taken aback by his lack of remorse. I've never seen him this void before. It's like Brent isn't here right now, because if he were, he would be completely disturbed by what he's just done.

I can't stand here any longer. I run past Brent, but before I can reach Jason, Brent grabs my upper arm with a strong hold to stop me.

"Brent! Let me go!" I heave. "I have to see if he is okay." I try to rip my arms from his grip, but it's no use. His hold is too tight. "You can't just leave him there. He's your brother, for God's sake!"

The look he gives me is lethal, and for the first time, I am almost afraid for myself in his presence. I make no more attempts to move, and as soon as he turns, I follow. I look back at Jason lying on the ground alone and helpless. I don't know why, but I feel the need to be by his side. Guilt overpowers me, and a tear slides down my cheek as the distance between us grows.

I can't help but wonder if maybe this is his karma for what he did to Jenna. It's funny how these things seem to work—the world creating it's own balance.

Brent refuses to slow, his hand is now tangled with mine, no longer forcing me but leading me. I know his reasons for what he has done, and I know I am in all of them. Jason's done enough harm to us in the past, and since Brent was unable to protect me then, he is making up for it now.

I completely get this, but it doesn't mean I have to

272

like it.

Thanks to my aura, we finally reach Brent's car, parked just beyond the cabin, in record time. He unlocks the car and helps me in. The smell of leather from the seats and Brent's manly fragrance rush my nose, making me feel at home and safe. Brent is my sanctuary.

I study him carefully as he sits in the driver's seat and shuts the door. He closes his eyes, leans his head back on the headrest, and takes a long, deep breath. For the first time, I can see his barrier wall about to crumble. His hands are shaking as he grips the wheel, and his face is smeared with devastation and regret. The results of his actions are finally sinking in as the reality of his brother's loss hits him full force.

I thrust my body against his in hopes of being his rock. It's ultimately because of me that this has occurred. If I would have just listened and stayed put, none of this would have happened.

"I'm so sorry, Brent," I say. "This is all my fault."

Brent pulls back to look me in the face. "No, Raina. This was his undoing. Not yours. Don't ever think that," Brent demands. "Edmund released me as his brother the moment he took your life."

I can't hold myself back from him. His loyalty and his devotion are rare and divine gifts you barely see from young men these days, and I feel like the luckiest girl in the world at this moment.

"I love you."

His eyes twinkle. "I love you too, Raina."

I place my hands on the sides of his face and pull him into me. His lips, so soft and sweet, fit perfectly against mine. I melt like butter under his touch, but before we get carried away, I pull back with ease.

"I'm worried about you."

"I'll be okay, mon amour."

I continue to study him. "I'm worried about your

Shevaun DeLucia

brother."

He sighs. "Don't be. He wasn't worried about you or I when he ended your lives, did he?"

I remain still, contemplating his response.

"I know. You're right. I still feel like you are going to regret leaving him, though."

Brent brushes his finger down my cheek. "Raina, the only regret I have is that I didn't stop him centuries ago."

I smile and allow my eyes to shut while I let his mesmerizing aroma fill my lungs. I feel his eyes still on me, and when I open mine he grins with his wicked charisma.

"Do you need me to drive?" I ask.

He shakes his head with certainty, squeezes my hand, and starts the ignition. We pull off, leaving his brother behind. A small twinge of guilt flutters through me as I think about the bottle of mixture that I threw on the dirt floor before I walked into the gauntlet.

# Chapter 21

Weeks have passed since Jason almost destroyed our lives. Things are beginning to settle back into routine. Thanksgiving and Christmas were quiet and cozy with it being just the three of us: Brent, my father, and I. My mother and Lillian are still looking for Eve, but no luck so far. Thankfully for me, they got a tip as to what Jason was up to while they were on their search. Some of the others were already notified by Jason that he would be on his way with very important merchandise, and that's how Brent figured out how to find us—one of his safe houses. Of course, Jason never made it back, which is going to eventually raise some questions. Covering our tracks will be crucial.

Jenna seems back to her normal self, except for the sadness she feels from Jason abandoning her, but each passing day brings her more strength and confidence that the future will be okay. It's nice to finally have our friendship back to how it used to be. I missed her.

Unfortunately for me, I have been officially taken out of school due to a serious "illness" until after the New

Year. This has given Brent and I a lot of hours during the days to get to know each other again. I'm head over heels in love, and this feeling only grows stronger by the day.

Brent has made sure to keep me on my toes the last couple of weeks so I wouldn't go stir-crazy. We've been on a numerous amount of day trips, only to the places that remain vacant and free of roaming eyes. Brent has become my protector, my savior, and my best friend, and I now take his direction very seriously.

Bailey, Maddie, *and* Jenna spend many of their days after school with us at our house. Of course, I had to give them the old "I have mono" line to keep them from wondering anything further. They just make sure to stay clear from direct contact with me, because staying away from me all together is not an option they choose to take. They've grown to adore Brent just as much as I have, and Brent in turn feels the same.

My aura has not dimmed or died down. It remains a constant brilliant light that Brent has grown to love, and I have grown to cherish. There's still so much I have to learn from it, and I still feel as though I have only just scraped the surface. I have capabilities that hold immeasurable powers. I just know it. I can *feel* it. Now I have to figure out how to release it.

Today is New Year's Eve and Brent and I plan on spending it alone. My father, like always, is at the lab still trying to come up with a way to dilute my light. He's extremely worn down with exhaustion and defeat, but this makes him even more determined than ever. Giving up is not an option for him, especially when it comes to me.

My eyes flutter open, squinting to adjust to the light.

Brent meets me with a warm smile. "Good morning, mon amour," he says with a deep, raspy voice, left hand propping his head up while he lies on his side, facing me.

Eternal Mixture

"Hey."

He kisses my forehead. "You look so peaceful when you're asleep, just like an angel."

"Have you been up for long?"

He grabs my hand to play with my fingers. "Just a little while. I was just thinking about our plans for tonight while watching you sleep."

I'm intrigued. I feel like an excited child eager to uncover the surprise. "What are we doing?"

He chuckles, amused by my enthusiasm. "It's a surprise, silly."

Butterflies flutter in my stomach. I get to bring in the New Year with my love, what more could I ask for? It has been a crazy couple of months, but I wouldn't change it for the world. Everything that has happened has brought me closer to Brent.

Eternity is not something I cringe from any longer. It's something that I now embrace. I look forward to going back to the beginning where it all began: Alberta, Canada. Brent promised me that we would venture back to Lake Louise this summer, and he would introduce me to some of the other immortals. I'm hoping that going back to the first moments of my immortality may trigger my memory.

I have a need to feel complete and to step into my future with my eyes wide open. The only thing I have on my side is time. Forever no longer seems so bad with Brent near.

"Hmm, surprise, huh?"

He taps my nose with his finger and slides out of bed.

"Yes, surprise," he smirks while pulling his white T-shirt over his head. I can't help but let my eyes devour the sexy ripples that flow down to his faded trail. "Are you hungry for some breakfast?"

My stomach immediately responds with a grumble. "Starving."

"I'll go down and get breakfast started. You get up and meet me down there," Brent directs and turns to head downstairs. I can't help but watch his amazing rear end leave the scene.

I roll onto my back and stare at the speckled ceiling. I grin in complete bliss. I can't help but think how lucky I am. Brent's so sweet and thoughtful, and the thought of him having enough self-control to wait for the perfect moment to consummate our love while I am constantly throwing myself at him makes me appreciate him that much more. He holds the control and the reasoning for the both of us.

I sit up, grab my hoodie off the end of the bed, and pull it over my head with a shiver. The cotton has a chill against my skin. I slide my legs off the side of the bed and slip into my cozy slippers.

Brent already has the bacon sizzling, eggs beaten, and the bread in the toaster, leaving nothing for me to do. I take a seat at the barstool to observe him, and I can't help but enjoy the view in front of me. A man in the kitchen is such a turn-on.

"*So*, what's on the agenda for this afternoon?" I ask. Brent slides the bacon and scrambled eggs onto two plates. He turns to butter the bread. "Um, I was thinking we should just lounge around and store up our energy for tonight," he says, placing the steaming food on the counter in front of us.

I take a long, deep whiff. "Mmm. This looks so good," I appraise him happily. I take a bite of the crispy bacon. Just the way I like it. "Lounging around sounds good. What's the dress attire for tonight?" I ask, shoveling some eggs into my mouth.

"Warm and comfy," Brent instructs.

I get up to grab some orange juice from the fridge. "You want some?"

He finishes chewing. "Please."

Eternal Mixture

I grab two cups from the cupboard and pour us both some. "So you're not even going to give me a little hint about where you're taking me?" I bat my eyes, using my womanly advantage to get the info out of him.

He leans into me. "Nope." He gives me a sweet peck on the lips.

I can't help but sulk. "Fine."

We both turn, hearing the front door open.

My father comes bolting into the kitchen with a look I do not recognize. His expression is glowing with excitement, his exuberance is uncanny, and his eyes gleam with satisfaction and accomplishment.

"Hey guys!" he greets us. He gives me a kiss on the cheek with a tight embrace and turns to Brent, giving him a quick squeeze on the shoulders. Brent and I exchange glances quickly.

"Hi, Dad." I study him carefully, trying to decipher what could possibly be going on in his head. Why is he so chipper? "What's going on? Is Mom coming home today?"

I see sadness flash across him, and then its gone like a jolt of lightening. "No, baby, she's not. *But*, I have an announcement to make!"

"What is it, Daddy?"

He walks over to me from behind the island and grabs my hand so lovingly. He's making me nervous and uneasy, but the undeniable vivacity that radiates off of him is something I haven't witnessed in a very long time. It makes me weary and giddy all at once.

"I cracked the code!"

Brent and I look at each other.

"Wait, you mean the project you were working on?" I ask.

Brent jumps in. "Alonzo, are you saying that you found the missing piece to dilute her aura?"

"Yes."

I can't even begin to comprehend what he has just

said. I remain in shock until I see Brent's ecstatic face. He squeezes my shoulders from behind. My daze clears as this information begins to sink in.

"Dad, are you saying that this will dilute just my light or my powers all together?" With the understanding now comes fear. I can't allow anything to remove what I still have yet to uncover. I won't do anything to jeopardize my God-given gift. I don't care if I have to stay hidden for the rest of my life, I'll do it.

"No baby, what I have discovered is amazing. All these years, decades, and centuries of losing you and you coming back to us have been a gift. But I've always wondered—and I've never admitted this before—if the reason has *truly* been the bond that ties us all together or if what you and Brent hold is actually an eternal bond."

My mind is completely blown away by his pure honesty. Brent begins to fidget on his feet. There's just something so uplifting about his confession. All this time, I have felt that I was the only one thinking this, but to find out my father has been wondering the same thing makes me feel at ease. I just wish he would have been open with me when I asked him weeks ago.

"I know I have never admitted this out loud, and I'm sorry for coming clean now in this situation, but I have the answer. I *finally* have the answer!"

"I don't understand, Dad."

"Alonzo, what exactly are you trying to say?" Brent asks, worry smeared across his face.

My father runs his hand through his hair. "It's your blood, Brent."

"Wait, what?" My heart pumps fiercely.

"My blood? You're not making any sense." Brent looks mystified and just as confused as I.

"Yes, your blood. That was the missing piece to the formula," my dad informs us. "Brent, when you came to the lab to help out, I took your blood. Do you remember?"

Eternal Mixture

Brent nods. "I was trying to figure out the difference between her blood and a non-relatives, and it was the most beautiful thing I have ever seen under a microscope. Your blood infused with hers immediately! I can't believe I never thought to attempt this before. It's the perfect eternal mixture," he explains in delight.

I stand up from the barstool and begin pacing. I'm on overload. "Okay, so what you're telling us is that if Brent's blood is in my system, it will counter the aura and I will no longer have any worries of the others seeing it?"

"That's exactly what I am saying," my father confirms.

"How long does it last for?" Brent chimes in. "How long will my blood stay in her system, I mean?"

My father finally takes a seat at the kitchen counter to wind down. "That's what I am unsure of. I haven't gotten that far yet." He sounds slightly defeated.

"But for now, we know that with a daily dose of my blood, she will be incognito?" My father nods his head. Brent turns to me, gleaming. "Raina, do you understand what this all means?"

I look at him with the knowledge that everything we have fought for has finally paid off. *His* belief in our love has finally paid off. I can see clear as day where I am supposed to be for all eternity, and that is with him.

Brent's blood is the key to my survival. He is my protector and the guardian of my secret. We are bound to each other in every sense. I no longer need the mixture to keep me immortal, and I no longer question the reasoning behind our love. He is my soul mate and my true other half. If he dies, I am forever cursed.

"Yes. It means we belong to each other. It means we are one. I am your true other half, as you are mine."

I see the pride in Brent's smile as the words glide off my tongue. He has been waiting to hear these words for more than a century now. It's sweet music to his ears. His eyes close with a mixture of triumph, ownership, and complete bliss. I am his, and he is mine.

Brent closes the gap between us, his eyes glued to mine. He reaches up to my temple and strokes his fingers down to my jawline, so gentle and loving, leaving a trail of burning fire behind. "I love you, Raina," he declares. I move closer to mold my body to his. "And I love you." I only see him. The rest of the world doesn't exist and drifts into the background in a blurred haze. That is, until I am forced back to reality.

My father clears his throat loudly and I jump. I look at him apologetically as my face heats with embarrassment. I straighten myself out. "Sorry, Daddy. I just got carried away."

My father laughs. I mean *really* laughs. I haven't seen him this happy in a very long time. I see the bold satisfaction settled across his features. The pain of him unable to protect me has fled from his face. Every single day of my life, he has worn the tattoo of his deep-rooted defeat, and I have never known the true extent of it until now. Fathers are supposed to provide and protect for their children. My father felt as though he failed life after life, not being able to protect me. He felt helpless, and in turn, it ate him alive.

I always wondered what it was that haunted him so, and now I know.

I can't help but laugh along with him. Seeing him full of proud triumph and pure happiness is the best gift he could give me. I run up to him, jump up into his arms, and give him a long, tight hug. He takes me off my feet and twirls me like he did when I was a little girl. "I love you, baby."

Tears spill out of my eyes with joy. "I love you too, Daddy," I whisper back.

He sets me down and looks between Brent and I. "Brent, I hand my most precious gift into your care. I trust that you will keep her safe and protected for the rest of eternity?"

Brent walks up to my father, and my father embraces him like a son. "You have my word, Alonzo." My eyes swell up, tears threatening to fall again as I watch the respect and adoration pour out from the two men in my life. This is a moment that will be stamped in my heart for all eternity.

They both look my way with love. "Well, I'm going to leave you kids to yourselves. I need to go make a phone call to Mom and tell her the good news," he says as he heads to the front door.

"Tell Mom I love her!" I yell behind him.

He turns. "I will, baby girl."

He shuts the door behind him.

Twilight has now passed and midnight is upon us. A New Year with all new possibilities lies ahead of us. It's exciting and thrilling to have the thoughts of forever twirling in my mind, and as I sit beside Brent, blindfolded in the passenger's seat of his car, I feel flooded with his warm surge of love.

"Brent, are we almost there yet?" I ask impatiently.

I hear him chuckle. "Almost."

I can't help but pout like a spoiled child. Being held in the dark is driving me bonkers. All my other senses are heightened as I concentrate on each tiny movement. I refuse to allow him to turn on the music. My vision is disabled by this blindfold, but I won't allow my other senses to be—they're all I have left.

I feel a sharp turn to the right as my body rolls heavily towards the door. Instead of pavement, I now hear the crunch of gravel beneath the tires, and I know we are coming close to our destination.

My stomach is in knots, but in a good way. This type of surprise is like the anticipation on Christmas morning. The car comes to a halt, and he clicks the gear into park.

I smile ear to ear. "Are we here?" I ask, jumping up and down in my seat.

I hear Brent chuckle at my excitement. His laugh melts my heart. "Yes, baby, we're here."

The ignition turns off, and I can hear the door open and close. I wait with intense anticipation, ready to explode. A gust of freezing air forces it way through the car as Brent opens the door. I shiver and mentally prepare myself for the coldness before I step out.

I close my jacket tight. "Brent, it's freezing!"

He reaches for my hand, I relax with his touch, and he guides me out. "I know. It will pass once we're cuddled in some blankets." I immediately hear the waves crash against the shore. The smell of rotten driftwood and crisp, fresh air hits my nostrils at full force. It's not hard to guess where we might be.

"We're near the water?"

He places his hand on my lower back and steps forward, supporting me and directing me every step of the way. I'm anxious. I feel lost and vulnerable without my sight, but he makes me feel safe as he leads the way. He stops and unties the cloth that blinds me. It falls down my face.

I am wide-eyed and ready to take in my surroundings. There are light poles lining the dock ahead, glittering in the reflection of the rippled water below to help brighten the path to the boat. I look to Brent, eyebrows lifting with wonder.

"Is that boat for us?"

He leans down to kiss my lips. Every time is like the first. He takes my breath away. "Yes, baby. I chartered a boat so we could be under the stars as we listen to the ball drop."

I can't help but jump into his arms, wrap my legs around him, and cover him with kisses all over his face. He laughs with my movement and anchors his hands on my ass cheeks to support me.

"You're amazing, Brent." He smiles and carries me to the dock. He releases me once we're in front of the boat, and I slide down to my feet. The waves are fierce and loud as they rumble beneath the dock.

Brent jumps down to the swaying boat and holds his hand to me for support. I gladly slip my hand into his and hop down. He immediately unties the boat from the dock and goes behind the wheel to start the engine. The boat roars to life.

I decide to investigate the cabin below while he pulls off from the dock. I step down the small, narrow staircase and land into a small but cozy kitchen. It holds a teeny breakfast nook to the right with built-in benches. To the left, marble counter tops and cedar cabinets line the back wall of the kitchen.

The hum of the engine grows louder as the pressure of the increased speed pushes me back. I grab ahold of the counter so I won't fall backwards and wait for the speed to level out. After a couple of minutes, I am able to walk ahead.

The living area holds two love seats on opposite walls, and only three steps farther lies the door to the bedroom. I now stand in the doorframe in front of the large queen-size bed. Suddenly, it hits me. We are alone. In the middle of a lake. With no one in miles of us on New Year's Eve. My mind drifts to thoughts of *finally* becoming a woman. A chill of excitement flows down my spine, and in between my thighs, I feel a warm wetness. I shiver with the unknown lying in front of me and suddenly become overcome with nervousness.

"Raina! Come see this!" Brent yells from up top.

I rush up from the stairs and stick my head out of the cabin. "Turn off the lights down there." I turn off the lights and head towards Brent at the bow of the boat, grabbing a blanket on the way.

"Look up," he says.

My gaze follows his. I instantly suck in my breath with the beauty that is spread out above us. The sky is clear, a blanket of a million stars twinkle brightly above us, and the moon, in its almost-full phase, glows with a great intensity against the black sky. *Amazing*. Beautiful.

I look back to Brent, and he no longer stares at the beauty in the sky; he stares at me. His eyes say it all. He is in love. If there was any doubt hiding in my shadows, it has now been shattered.

He sits down on the bench and pats the seat beside him for me to sit. I comply.

"Brent, this is just perfect," I tell him, gazing back to the sky.

"No, you being here with me makes it perfect," he clarifies. "My world is only perfect when I have you in it. You are my everything, Raina."

He reaches his hand to me and cups my face. "It's time."

"Is the ball about to drop?" I wonder, eyes wide, tapping my feet against the boat with exuberance.

"No, baby. It's time for you to take my blood."

I blink. Reality setting in. This is it. This is the moment we have been waiting for for weeks, but why do I feel so uneasy? Shouldn't I be ecstatic? I can finally go back to living a normal life, but for some reason, this all feels so *wrong*. And then it hits me.

The only way I am taking his blood is if he takes mine as well. He has given me *everything*: his love, his patience, his undying loyalty and commitment. I am standing here today because of him. Our souls are bonded, and now the only thing left to bond is our blood—and then our bodies.

I shake my head. "No, Brent. I want to give you mine first."

Shock paints his face. He drops his hands and is washed over with sadness. He looks away from me with an emotion I do not recognize. I don't understand what just happened. My gut sinks with worry.

"What's wrong?" I ask.

He looks back at me, pained. "Raina, I would never ask you to give me something so precious just because I am giving you a part of me. I'm not doing this to take advantage of you or for you to feel obligated to give me a part of you. I am doing this because I love you."

I grab his face forcefully so he can't break my gaze and wait until I have his full attention. "And I love you. I want you to listen to me and listen to me carefully. I *want* to give you this. This isn't about you; it's about me. I may be a little selfish in my offering, but that's just because I want you as immortal as me. I never want you to leave my side. I want you with me *forever*. I don't ever want to be afraid of losing you, and this is my way of ensuring that. So, you see, I am the one with a motive here. This is *my* gift to give, and I want to give it to you. So will you accept my offering of pure immortality?"

Brent smashes his lips against mine with urgency. My answer is confirmed. Our breath runs ragged with need and complete desire. I nip at his bottom lip, and his tongue dives into my mouth. We sink into a slow dance. I can't get enough of him.

He retreats with quick kisses to my lips, cheeks, and nose. I smile at his cuteness.

"Are you ready?" he asks.

I gulp and nod my head. He grabs the knife that lies beside him and holds it to his palm. My heart begins to race. Red oozes as he glides it across his skin. I grab the knife and quickly do the same, opening myself up to him.

He holds his hand above mine and squeezes. Droplets fall into my cut, mixing with my blood. The reaction is immediate—his blood infusing and coating my veins. My aura slowly begins to fade with each drop of his blood melded with mine.

I feel as though I am having an out-of-body experience. "Brent, do you *see* it?" He nods, unable to form any words as he watches me.

My aura is now non-existent as he squeezes his hand one last time. My blood feels like liquid power as his cells bond to mine.

I grab my blanket and apply pressure to his palm. Mine, of course, has already healed.

"Are you ready for me?" I ask him this time.

"I am." His eyes twinkle.

I keep my eyes on his as I again slide the knife across my palm. I know with all my heart that I have made the right choice by loving this man, and my heart flutters with the anticipation of knowing a part of me will soon be inside him as well.

I hold my hand slightly above his and squeeze, directing the warm eternal liquid to drip into his open wound. To my surprise, it doesn't take much before he is healing before us. I've never watched anything so beautiful.

"Incredible," I whisper.

Neither of us can seem to look away.

"Yes, it is," Brent whispers back.

I wipe the stained blood from his palm and mine. He brings my hand up to his lips, kissing my skin softly. I can't help but lean into him.

"Thank you, Raina." He kisses the top of my head and pulls me in closer to him. "This is the beginning of forever for us."

A huge *boom* echoes through the air and colored fire lights up the sky.

My lips curve and I look up to him. "Eternal love."

Eternal Mixture

He is like a drug to me, and I am forever addicted.

Shevaun DeLucia

# Acknowledgments

Writing *Eternal Mixture* has been a wild and amazing experience. Who would have known that starting with one single idea, a novel could blossom. It took a year. A lot of late nights and many hours away from my everyday life, but I've completed it, and I am a proud mama.

For this I have many to thank.

To my editor, Jinelle Shengulette, whom I've worked with for a couple of years now and whom was with me from the start when I first dipped my feet into the world of writing, I'd like to thank you. Thank you for your patience and your amazing ability to turn my words into the perfect combination. We both know my grammar is "rusty," so to speak, but you were able to edit my writing into the perfect masterpiece I knew it could be. For this, I am eternally grateful.

To the photographer and designer of my book cover, George Parulski, what can I say? You are a brilliant, extraordinary, and creative genius! No words can express what you have done for me. You've not only gone far and beyond what I had hoped for, but you smashed my ideas out of the park! I want to thank you for guiding me through the self-publishing process. Without your assistance, I may have gone insane. You're not only an amazing photographer, but you are my mentor and my friend. I look forward to working with you on my next adventure.

I may have never taken the leap of self-publishing if it weren't for my favorite author, Jaime McGuire. I want to give a special thanks to you for taking a moment out of your busy life to respond to my email in literally lightning-speed time (one hour to be exact). You gave me the encouragement to believe in myself, and in that moment, I realized my destiny was in my own hands. So, thank you. Your story alone is an inspiration.

Friends come and go, but a true friend is hard to find. So, in this case, I'd like to thank my best friend of eighteen years, Kristen Swenson, for always listening to my crazy ideas. Because of our friendship and our ups and downs, I was able to allow the bonds between my characters to shine from firsthand experience. And to my childhood partner in crime whose soul is lost: I will always fight for you, just as Raina fought for Jenna. I have hope for you.

I'd like to thank my personal cheerleaders: my sisters. Luna has been nothing but excited for me every step of the way. Your belief in me has meant more than you will ever know. Leila tells me the sky is the limit, as a mother should, and to go for it, as a sister would. It was nice having you in my back pocket. You have never once doubted or faltered in having my back every step of the way, and I am grateful. Thank you sis.

Next, I want to thank Jonathan Nick, my cousin. Because of your willingness to allow me to use your expertise, I was able to create my website with your help. Though we have only met a handful of times, you helped me when I most needed it, and that's what family is about. So, thank you.

Shevaun DeLucia

To my four crazy, nutzo kids: Mar, Lexi, Dom, and Ang. Thank you all for being you! Even though you interrupted me each and every time I sat down to write, somehow it all worked out. To my boys: always fight for what you believe in, no matter what. And to my daughter, who is finding her way in the first stages of teenagedom may you one day find the kind of love that Raina and Brent share. Remember, your love is a gift, so cherish it with all you've got.

Last but not least, my husband, my lover, and my friend. Our love has been tested in more ways than normally possible, but we've made it. Thank you for not giving up and always fighting for us as Brent fought for Raina over those hundreds of years. I know you would do the same. As far as this book goes, you remained very patient and understanding of the time it took away from us to write this. You encouraged me to go for my dream, and for that, I want to thank you. You are my eternal love.

Made in the USA
Charleston, SC
24 May 2014